PRIVATE INVESTIGATIONS

LARA ARDEN
BOOK 2

ROB GITTINS

This edition produced in Great Britain in 2024

by Hobeck Books Limited, Unit 14, Sugnall Business Centre, Sugnall, Stafford, Staffordshire, ST21 6NF

www.hobeck.net

Copyright © Rob Gittins 2024

This book is entirely a work of fiction. The names, characters and incidents portrayed in this novel are the work of the author's imagination. Any resemblance to actual persons (living or dead), events or localities is entirely coincidental.

Rob Gittins has asserted his right under the Copyright, Design and Patents Act 1988 to be identified as the author of this work.

All rights reserved. No parts of this book may be used or reproduced by any means, graphic, electronic, or mechanical, including photocopying, recording, taping or by any information storage retrieval system without the written permission of the copyright holder.

A CIP catalogue for this book is available from the British Library.

ISBN 978-1-915-817-60-0 (pbk)

ISBN 978-1-915-817-59-4 (ebook)

Cover design by Jayne Mapp Design

Printed and bound in Great Britain

How can the dead be truly dead when they still live in the souls of those who are left behind?
Carson McCullers

PRAISE FOR I'M NOT THERE

'Everything is cleverly brought together in a thrilling climax.'
   Sarah Leck

'It had the feel of one of those books that gets a plug and then suddenly takes off to be a top ten best seller.'
   Pete Fleming

'Dark, gritty, well crafted characters and some gut punching shocks, first rate crime writing.'
   Alex Jones

ARE YOU A THRILLER SEEKER?

Hobeck Books is an independent publisher of crime, thrillers and suspense fiction and we have one aim – to bring you the books you want to read.

For more details about our books, our authors and our plans, plus the chance to download free novellas, sign up for our newsletter at **www.hobeck.net**.

You can also find us on Twitter **@hobeckbooks** or on Facebook **www.facebook.com/hobeckbooks10**.

For Alfred Bradley, John Tydeman, Richard Imison, Alec Reid and Michael Bartlett

PROLOGUE

MY NAME IS LARA ARDEN. I'm twenty-eight years old. Twenty-two years ago, my mother vanished on a crowded train.

I grew up reconciled to never solving the mystery of what happened to her. A year ago, I did, but that isn't what this is about.

When I thought she'd walked out on us, simply abandoning me and my elder sister, Georgia, I wasn't interested in finding out anything about her. Now that I know that's not true, I want to know everything. I want to reconstruct her life, from the age at which she herself was abandoned to the moment she disappeared on that train. I want to meet, in a sense, the woman and mother I never knew.

As a cop, my life is all about investigations, but this is different.

This is a private investigation.

PROLOGUE

PART ONE

PART ONE

CHAPTER ONE

WHAT THE HELL this lot were doing coming to a hole like this, he had no idea. He wouldn't put his dog up in any of the rooms in this place, and he'd always hated that flea-bitten mangy old mutt.

No wonder the managers here turned over like clockwork. He'd never have taken the job himself if he hadn't been desperate. Yet here they were again, the same minted suits who turned up once a month, regular as clockwork. He didn't know their names, but he knew the cars.

This time, the Bentley arrived first, followed by the Merc. A Range Rover was next, followed closely by a Jag. Then, without saying a single word either to him or to each other so far as he could see, the drivers headed into the large meeting room at the rear of the building.

He'd never been inside. No one had. For as long as the room had been leased – which was as long as anyone who worked there could remember – no managers had ever been allowed in, and no cleaners had ever visited. It had been a condition of the original booking, and as the amount they paid each year probably kept the rest of the crumbling old ruin going, it was a condition that had always been strictly observed.

Sometimes he did wonder though. He couldn't help it. It was like an itch he just had to scratch. What happened after the doors closed on the drivers of all those upmarket motors? He'd hovered on the edge of trying to find out many times, but his nerve had always failed him. But one day he knew he was going to have to do it. He was going to have to find out.

The manager of the seaside boarding house eyed a second Bentley as it arrived and parked next to all those other upmarket cars, and he felt a familiar excitement begin to build inside.

Maybe today was going to be the day.

They'd arrived ten minutes ago – two weekend sailors, city boys probably, on a jaunt across from the mainland. Andrea, the trainer and owner of the gym, was seeing more and more of them these days. If white collar boxing hadn't quite become the new golf, it was getting there.

Some of the newer practitioners took it seriously of course. They'd do the obligatory cardiovascular steps, as well as the upper body press and abdominal sit-ups, before a session with the punchbags and the weights. Then there were the others. Shadow boxing, for them, would be an excuse for them to flex their pecs. Weights would be a prop to do the same. The pair that had just walked in were all about appearance, top show, the exact opposite of the small, slight, female figure who'd just emerged from the changing rooms and was about to start her own extended session on the punchbag.

She was serious, Andrea knew that; their paths had crossed many times before. The problem was that she really didn't look like any sort of real deal to a casual observer, and Andrea could already see the city boys exchanging smirks as they moved across to watch her work out. These two sensed sport here, and not the kind Andrea usually permitted in her gym. She'd worked hard for her trainer's licence and only tolerated people who took her chosen profession as seriously as she did.

But Andrea was also an entertainer. All boxers are to a lesser or greater extent. And the entertainer in her was making her hesitate, because Andrea knew exactly what that small, slight female currently strapping on her 10oz Lonsdale gloves was capable of. Detective Inspector Lara Arden of the Isle of Wight police had proved that to her, and to others, on many occasions.

Andrea moved closer. The two weekend sailor city boys didn't know that. It might be interesting to watch them find out.

The beam in the ceiling of the room at the rear of that old ramshackle seaside boarding house had been specially supported. The rope that hung from it was high-quality Kevlar. The pulley on the end of the rope had been constructed using hardened tensile steel.

Previously, something much more makeshift would have been more than adequate for the task in hand. Children in the past who'd been singled out for this sort of punishment, had been light, if not positively scrawny. None came from what you might call advantaged backgrounds, and most of them were little more than skin and bone. But that was then, and this was now.

He'd been brought in a few minutes before, trussed as he had been for the last few hours, his arms and legs strapped together with duct tape, with more tape clamping his mouth tight shut. A heavy-duty bag made of sackcloth covered his head, secured by sailing twine around his neck. He'd been delivered to the meeting room via a small side door that had been let into the old wooden building for just that purpose. The Range Rover that had reversed up to it also covered it from view, making the transfer totally secure. It had been another necessary precaution, much like the specially supported beam, the high tensile rope, and the hardened steel pulley, precautions they'd hoped would never be needed. The events of the last week had proved them wrong.

Peter Allen stared around as the sackcloth bag was removed from his head, blinking in the sudden, yet still, dim light, before focusing on each of the figures standing in a semi-circle, eyeing him in turn.

In the hand of the lead accuser directly in front of him was a note. He could see the same note in the hands of the other figures flanking him, too. He recognised it immediately, of course: a copy of that note had been hand delivered to him as well. No one had seen who'd delivered it; no one knew who'd written it, but speculation had been intense ever since, and they all had powerful reasons to find out, and quickly. And the different sets of eyes currently trained on him told Peter more eloquently than words alone could have managed that they believed they'd done that. This kangaroo court was ample evidence.

'You've got this wrong.'

He could scarcely gasp out the words. His lungs felt as if they were being constricted inside some sort of giant press. His heart was pounding so much that he felt as if it might burst out of his ribcage. All he could see was the pulley and the rope and, for a moment, he experienced an involuntary flashback as, from years before, he saw, again, the children who would also stare up at it, blank at first, unaware of its purpose, unsure why it was there – the first time, anyway. After that, they had much the same expression on their faces as he had on his right now: pure and simple terror.

'This is nothing to do with me.'

It was one of them though, he knew that; they all did. The level of detail in those notes meant they had to have been written by someone who was there at the time, who'd witnessed at first hand all that had happened. The conclusion was inescapable. One of their own had broken cover, had poured decades of shame out onto the page in what had turned into an increasingly hysterical confession.

Momentarily, it had pierced his defences, he had to admit. Indeed, he had admitted it. Briefly, and sickened by the images that note had conjured back before his eyes, he'd confessed those feelings of guilt and shame to at least one of the figures there that night. He'd given way, albeit briefly, but it was a single, isolated moment of weakness and he'd swiftly reasserted the self-control they'd all exercised all those years.

But the genie had been released from the bottle, and it had clearly been enough to damn him.

The lead accuser stepped forward, as two of the figures to Peter's side grabbed his still-trussed legs, fixing the hook of the pulley inside the binding, yanking him skywards, his world suddenly inverting as he was suspended, head pointing down towards the ground. In the old days they'd now take turns to use sticks to beat the badness out of all those wicked, dirty, itinerant boys and girls.

The knife in the hand of his lead accuser was yet more ample evidence that a very different punishment was now in store.

No more words would now be heard. There was nothing he could have said to stop what was about to happen and he knew it. But as he looked around that room, for one last time now, he knew he wasn't alone. Maybe it was the advancing years; the ever-present sense they all must share that soon they were about to meet their maker. As he locked eyes with each of those men, he knew they'd all felt that same devastating shame, had all experienced, even if only for an instant, that same gut-churning loss of self-control.

Then there was a sudden flash of silver in front of his eyes, He felt his neck muscles tense, an instinctive reaction as the blade slashed across his windpipe. Blood gushed before his eyes, spilling directly into the purpose-built drain that had been cut into the floor directly beneath him. Around the room, Peter's accusers watched as the life ebbed out of the one man who'd done the unthinkable, who'd given way, broken ranks. All the while, total silence reigned as a problem was consigned to oblivion.

And because that silence was total, they all heard it. It was coming from the rear of that ramshackle, but secure old building.

It might have been faint, but they all still heard it.

Lara wasn't aware of her two spectators. She was locked in her own private world and had been from long before she'd arrived. There was only herself and the punchbag in front of her.

Lara warmed up with a few practice punches, feeling her upper arm muscles flex, the lactic acid beginning to build, at least in one of her arms. The other was still very much playing second fiddle and had been since a train attempted to sever it from her body just over a year or so before. A team of crack surgeons had managed to save it and now it was a case of slowly building the limb back to full strength. Partly, that was what today was all about. But it was about a lot more than that.

Dimly, she was aware of a voice from somewhere to her side, an aside sounding, a braying laugh answering in turn, but only one thing mattered right now, and that was total absorption in the moment. Lara knew that only then – when her body was completely concentrated on something else – could she permit her mind to wander over everything that had just happened.

Suddenly, there it was once more: a second aside, another braying snort of laughter, and now she saw them, the two men eyeing her, assessing her indeed, their eyes following each dart of her body. For another moment she struggled to concentrate, but the spell had been broken and one of her punches missed its mark.

Lara suddenly let rip. Her right hand turned into a blur as a dozen, then two dozen blows, suddenly landed. Her left couldn't keep pace but the jabs she managed still echoed around the gym in a series of loud and devastating cracks. All other sounds stopped as, one after the other, all the other boxers training in there that day paused to watch.

———

Andrea watched the two weekend sailors, the smirks wiping from their faces as they stared at the fists of that small, slight figure before them, and she could see it in their eyes. All they were seeing now were their own faces being attacked like that, their bones cracking, eye sockets rupturing into jagged shards, teeth splintering into tiny slivers.

Then Andrea focused back on Lara. She'd seen her like this many times before. Locked away, closed down, working out whatever demons were currently assailing her, be they work-related or otherwise, pushing her body to the limit and beyond. However, today was different. This was extreme, even for her. And as her fists, finally, began to slow and as the now-whey-faced weekend sailors turned towards the door, probably in search of a much-needed restorative Pimm's, Andrea couldn't help wondering what was behind a workout that more resembled some sort of assault.

But – and as ever – Andrea knew better than to ask.

———

Half an hour later, the room had been comprehensively cleaned, all traces of the execution that had taken place cleared away. Now there was just one last task left to perform.

The remaining men gathered in another small semi-circle. The lead accuser ignited a lighter, played the naked flame on the bottom of the hand-delivered note that had started all this, then watched as the flame spread across the single sheet of paper before dropping it down into the drain where it atomised, as the body of their former companion would also soon atomise, to dust.

One by one, the remaining members of what was now a dwindling clique did the same. And as they watched their copies of those notes burn in turn, one thought gnawed away inside all their minds, and it was the driver of the Range Rover who finally gave it voice.

What if there were more of those notes out there? What if Peter had sent it to someone else as well? Meaning this might not just be a sad and weak old man's end-of-life confession, but a time bomb, too.

The lead accuser as ever took charge, calmly pointing out that they had no way of knowing one way or another, so any speculation of that sort was futile. But it was also redundant because they all knew what would happen. That would be a new problem and it would be dealt with in exactly the same way as this problem, which was now a problem no more.

A few minutes later, the cars departed, a Bentley first. In the boot was a body. That much was planned. Peter would now be driven to his final, and perhaps appropriate, resting place.

Then the Range Rover followed, and there was a body in that boot as well. That hadn't been planned, but it wasn't totally unexpected either. One by one, almost all the short-term managers of that old and ramshackle seaside boarding house gave way to temptation, tried to find out what happened inside that room at the rear of that building.

Those occasional, short-term managers would only do it once, but once was enough. They made sure of it.

The gym's dressing room comprised a large, open plan reception-type area, around which were grouped individual cubicles for those who wished to change in private.

Normally, Lara didn't bother with the cubicles. Most days and nights, she came in, changed, and was out in front of those punchbags and on those weights in something close to seconds.

This time, Lara retreated inside the furthest cubicle from the door and locked it behind her. Hesitating for a moment, she reached into her sports bag and took out the single sheet of paper that had been hand-delivered that morning.

Lara read and re-read the words she'd already read and re-read many times since. Then she stared, unseeing, at the locked door in front of her.

This could all be the work of a crank, of course. Some internet troll who'd picked up something of her mother's story from her time in her old, and now closed, home. Lara, working with other officers, had kept a lid on it for the most part but some of the fall-out had still been played out in public. Someone could easily have done some digging and found out more.

Lara looked back at the note. Only this really didn't read like the work of a crank or troll. This was raw, visceral. It had all the hallmarks of a lived experience, but if the author of that note had indeed lived all this, then why write it down, and why now?

And why send it to her?

In her bag, Lara's mobile pulsed with an incoming call alert. Looking at the display, she snapped back into work mode as she saw the name of her DS, Jordan Banks, flashing back at her.

'We've got a shout.'

Jordan plunged straight in, no preamble, no small talk. It was the way things were done in Lara's home unit. There were also no ma'am's or guvs. It had been one of her very first stipulations when taking up her new post as DI.

'Accident involving a van and a pedestrian on the road between Shanklin and Sandown.'

Lara paused, puzzled. This sort of call was usually sent out to traffic cops, not officers from their newly christened Major Crime Unit.

'We're going to attend an RTC?'

Jordan's tone as he replied was cool, even.

'It may not have been an accident.'

CHAPTER TWO

ONE HOUR EARLIER, all Amy Waite was seeing were shadows, which made no sense. The sun was high in the sky. Night wouldn't be falling for hours. Yet they were still there, lurking on the very edge of her vision. Every step she took – and she'd taken a lot of steps along a lot of major and minor roads since she'd set off those couple of hours ago – those same ghost-like presences kept pace with her, intent on one thing only: doing her harm.

These were demons of her own imaginings though, they had to be, and Amy stood still for a moment, as cars, vans and motorbikes roared past on the busy road, desperately trying to banish them. There wasn't really anything or anyone out there. No one knew where she was right now, still less what she had in mind, so how could there be? Amy suddenly wheeled round as a horn sounded close by, but it was just another passing van. Turning back, she tried to reassert control, told herself she had to concentrate, keep calm.

Get to the ferry terminal, get off the island.

Get safe.

Another few hours previously, it had been an all too familiar story. And it hadn't. That made no sense either, and Amy's mum, Carey Waite, knew it. Rows between mothers and teenage daughters were part and parcel of their lives, they didn't seem to be able to get through a single hour these days without Amy flying off the handle, usually over absolutely nothing.

Like today. All she'd done was ask – totally innocently – what time she expected Amy to be back from her friend Donna's in the morning and would she want breakfast, or would she eat at Donna's house before she left? But Amy had suddenly flown into that now all too familiar rage. *Why was she asking? Why did she want to know? Was Mum checking up on her? Did she think that she wasn't staying over at Donna's tonight, that it was just some story she'd invented? Call Donna herself if she was that bothered, check!*

Carey remembered she'd actually put her hands up in a surrender gesture. She could still see herself effectively apologising for nothing, as Amy had pushed past her and stormed out of the house. Matt, her husband, had heard the tail end of it and he'd walked past her towards the kitchen, shaking his head in bewildered amusement at yet another mother-and-daughter spat.

Carey had stayed rooted to the spot for a moment because the strangest feeling had just crept over her. She couldn't explain why, but she knew that something about this was different.

Back on the road, Amy pushed on. The sun was slightly lower now, but she knew she still had plenty of time to make the ferry. She just had to keep putting one foot in front of the other, keep taking one step at a time, just focus, and then everything that was threatening to overwhelm her right now would disappear.

An exchange from her childhood floated in front of her eyes, her mum telling her that all she had to do when faced with a whole sea of what seemed to be impossible problems, was to separate them out, isolate them, deal with them one at a time. And if she dealt with them, one by one in that way, then one by one they'd vanish. Briefly, tears stung her eyes as she felt a sudden lurch in her heart. All she now wanted to do was turn round, go back, go home, see her mum again, listen to her once more. But that door was closed, and she knew it. She just had to keep taking that next step forward.

Amy reached into her pocket for her phone to check on the updated sailing times. The weather was good, but sometimes there were incidents out in the Solent which meant there were delays. Then she stopped as her fingers closed on empty space.

And suddenly, her metronome-like steps faltered as she remembered, all over again, just why she was doing this and what was at stake.

Amy's brother, Aaron, was also feeling uneasy, without being able to explain why. He had been ever since Amy had first appeared in his bedroom doorway.

Aaron had been trawling the usual sites up to then. He'd done a session on Fortnite and Minecraft already, but he'd set up a group session on Call of Duty: Warzone, although one of his friends had said he might be able to get a pirated copy of Black Ops Cold War. Then, suddenly, the door opened and there was Amy, her iPad in hand. For a moment he thought she was going to ask to join in, which would have been a definite no-no because she was useless, but she just held out her iPad instead, and asked him to hide it.

Aaron had stared, stupidly, back at her. What was she talking about? Why did she want him to hide her iPad? Hide it from who? And why? She'd cut him off before he could even start to ask, everything suddenly pouring in what seemed like a great torrent, telling him that she'd broken it, but she didn't want mum or dad to know because they'd go ballistic. She was going to get it sorted but in the meantime all he had to do was hide it, keep it safe and don't try and mend it, in fact don't even look at it, he couldn't, he mustn't. It was important, really important, and did he understand that?

A beep sounded on his laptop, an alert from one of his friends. Aaron was still just staring at his sister. And he kept staring after her long after his bedroom door closed behind her and he heard her heading down the stairs, leaving him with her iPad.

Someone was behind her. Amy was sure of it.

There'd been other people on the road of course, some approaching, then walking past, some passing her from behind. But they'd been on their way to or from somewhere and had hardly given her a second glance. Whoever she could now sense wasn't approaching and walking past, or passing from behind. She didn't know where they were, not exactly, but they were keeping step with her, she knew it. She'd tried speeding up, then slowing down, but she could sense them matching her, maintaining the same distance between them all the while.

Briefly, she contemplated turning round, confronting them. As she hesitated, she stumbled slightly, swaying to her left momentarily, towards the road itself, provoking a passing van or car to sound a warning blast on their horn. Amy watched the vehicle – a large van – as it sped on its way, a yellow flash on its side.

Then she stilled as she saw its brake lights suddenly illuminate.

A few miles away, and at the same time as her best friend was staring at the illuminated brake lights of that van, Donna Collins locked her bedroom door. Her parents didn't barge in anymore, like they used to, uncaring what she was doing or who she might be talking to. Those days were long gone, but she still took precautions. Then she took out her mobile and seated herself on her bed.

Her old cat, Tammy, stretched out a lazy claw as he felt the bed bow beneath him, then settled back to sleep. Donna listened for a moment just in case her mum or dad had registered the click of the key – she'd tried to make it as silent as she could, but she didn't rule out one or the other of them pausing outside her door as they passed, wondering why she might be taking those sorts of pains to not be disturbed, and trying to listen in.

Donna pressed the speed dial button on her mobile, muting the ringing tone, all ready to unmute the handset when her call was answered. The phone kept ringing, and ringing, and, as no answerphone service cut in, Donna felt all the uneasy doubts that she'd been trying to keep at bay claim her again.

Amy always answered Donna's calls. Donna always answered Amy's, too. It was their most solemn promise to each other. It didn't matter what might be happening, where they might be, whenever they saw each other's names on their displays, they took the call. They were there for each other, they covered for each other, stepped up for the other, no matter what. It was why she'd agreed in an instant when Amy had asked her to say she was staying with her that night, and why she'd told her parents, as casually as she could manage, that Amy was dropping by later.

Only she wasn't, but they wouldn't investigate. But as she remained seated on her bed, Tammy now purring gently beside her in his sleep, Donna suddenly wanted them to investigate, because something was wrong here.

It wasn't just that Amy wasn't answering her phone, it was the fact she wouldn't even tell Donna where she was going that night. It had to be something to do with a boy, and she had a shrewd idea which one, too, even though Amy hadn't really talked about him much lately.

But why she was meeting him, and where, and what this was all about, Donna didn't know because Amy had just told her it was best that she kept that to herself, which made no sense either because they always told each other everything.

Back on the busy coast road, Amy remained where she was for a moment, uncaring now who might be keeping step with her, because suddenly she saw it again.

The van that had passed her just those few moments before, the one that had blasted its horn at her as she stumbled on the pavement, was heading back her way. It was the same van, she was sure it was, it had the same markings on the side, that same yellow flash.

Amy stared at it as it drew closer, seeming to be gaining speed all the time. Dimly, she sensed a figure approaching again from behind, but all she could see right now was the van. Its windscreen seemed darkened, the driver obscured, and suddenly it seemed to be heading straight for her.

A moment later, Amy shuddered as a great crash sounded, as she heard brakes squealing as tyres scrabbled for grip, and then she sensed rather than saw a body flying high up into the air. Then she kept watching as that same body fell back onto the unforgiving tarmac.

She just had time to realise it was her own body lying there.

Then, suddenly, there was silence.

CHAPTER
THREE

LARA AND JORDAN took the cross-country route from the capital across to the east coast of the island, passing the island's airport on their way, emerging between Sandown and Shanklin.

Not that there was much in the way of differentiation between the two places, geographically at least. These days they seemed to merge, one into the other, even though they couldn't be more different. Sandown was old-school, bucket and spade and fish and chips. Shanklin was chocolate box, ornate thatched cottages, and well-tended gardens. The road that linked the two was usually packed with holiday traffic but, right now, it was eerily quiet, only the distant hum of diverted cars sounding in the near distance.

'She was walking alone, heading north.'

Jordan had updated Lara on the drive down there, consulting notes on his laptop as Lara manoeuvred her own car – a Mini Cooper, vintage 1968 – along the winding country roads. With all surrounding roads backed up, she had no idea when they might come across one of the island's legendary traffic jams and have to seek out farm roads or even tracks across fields. A throwback to a time when cars were smaller and leaner could prove useful.

'A few eyewitnesses have come forward to say they saw her

just before the impact. They all say she seemed disorientated, she seemed to be walking, then stopping, then setting off again, as if she was lost or something. And she was looking round all the time, too, as if she was looking for someone.'

Lara cut across.

'Or worried that someone was looking for her?'

Jordan nodded. It was the first thing that had occurred to him as well. One of the initial reasons he'd decided this report was worth a look.

Lara pressed on.

'So, the van, the one that hit her?'

'The driver didn't stop. Maybe he didn't know he had hit someone, according to the same eyewitnesses she was only struck a glancing blow, so it's possible he didn't feel the impact. Or maybe he was drunk, and just panicked.'

Lara cut across again.

'Or something else.'

Once more, Jordan didn't reply. He didn't need to. That latter possibility was another reason a DI and a DS from the island's Major Crime Unit were speeding to the scene right now.

Lara glanced sideways at her companion; his six foot-five-inch frame crammed inside her small car. They'd worked together for almost four years now and knew each other's ways well. Lara rated him highly. He had his demons – no one was immune to those – and he was still working through some pressing personal issues with a teenage daughter who'd been more than usually troublesome lately. Not to mention an ex-wife who could rival anything their daughter had ever got up to on even her most extreme walks on the wild side. Then Lara looked ahead again. Right now, she was fast coming to the same conclusion as her junior officer. This didn't have the feel of a usual road traffic accident to her either.

Lara heard the whistle of a train in the distance. As always, when she heard that sound these days, her stomach clenched, but it was a momentary, instinctive, reaction and one she quickly dismissed. Old horrors had no place here. A new one was the priority now.

The lead paramedic had stabilised the unconscious young girl and was supervising her transfer into the waiting ambulance and onto the island's St Mary's hospital. Accident investigation officers were already taking measurements and lifting tyre samples from the tarmac. Lara elicited a swift update from the paramedic, but it didn't amount to much. The accident victim had suffered multiple injuries, including a possible fractured spine, but they'd know more once they got her into A&E. Jordan had been liaising with the ambulance driver and he'd been able to add a little more colour into the mix. Ironically, it was making all this murkier by the moment.

'No ID.'

Lara looked at him.

'The ambulance driver checked while the other paramedic was treating her. No phone, or if she did have one, maybe she was holding it in her hand when she was hit, and it was flung somewhere in the impact, I've asked uniform to check, but there's nothing else on her either. She had money, and quite a lot of it, too, a few hundred quid in cash, but that's it.'

'Did any of the eyewitnesses report seeing her on her phone?'

'No.'

Lara worried away at it.

'What teenage girl goes out without her phone or any ID? What if she wants to get into a bar, buy some cigarettes?'

Lara knew Jordan was thinking the same thing. A girl who maybe didn't want to leave any trace. She looked out at the completely straight stretch of road in front of them. There were no bends and no blind spots here, so no apparent reason why a van should suddenly collide with anyone.

Unless the van driver decided otherwise of course.

CHAPTER
FOUR

TWENTY MINUTES LATER, Lara was walking back into the main open plan office of the Major Crime Unit, another member of the team, DC Mairead Devonald, meeting her with an update.

'From the last six months.'

Mairead handed Lara a list of names and faces.

'Missing female teens from the island, and from the nearest counties on the mainland.'

Lara stared at it. She was well aware that upwards of a quarter of million people went missing in the UK each year. Seeing that comprehensive compendium of all those names and faces still rocked her though.

'We don't know if she is missing yet. Maybe Jordan will be able to tell us more when he talks to the medics at the hospital, but I thought you should see this in case any of the faces ring any bells.'

Lara sifted through them, but none, at first glance anyway, resembled the unconscious girl she'd seen being stretchered into the back of an ambulance. She'd go through it all in more detail of course, but, for now, the mystery of who she was remained.

Turning away, a grateful Lara took a coffee proffered by the unit's resident tea lady and comforter of all detectives in distress,

Peggy O'Riordan, then tensed as a bark sounded from the open doorway leading to the corridor outside.

'DI Arden.'

Lara turned to see their new DCI, Paul Conran, staring back at her. Conran had been drafted in while their old DCI, Paula Monroe, took a period of what was turning out to be extended leave. Peggy shot her a glance filled with her usual warm fellow feeling. But not even her legendary efforts with detectives in distress could work its magic now. Conran had only been in his new job two days, which was already proving forty-eight hours too long for everyone in the unit, judging by the openly hostile stares that were greeting him right now. Not that it seemed to bother him that much.

Still framed in the doorway, Conran nodded at her.

'A word.'

One minute later, Lara was standing opposite Conran in his office along the corridor, the door closed behind them.

'An RTC?'

Conran didn't elaborate; his stare said it all. Budgets were tight, resources limited. Why would an RTC merit the immediate attention of a DI and a DS? It had been, as Lara would have to grudgingly admit, her first reaction, too, but she'd given Jordan his head and was growing increasingly convinced she'd been right to do so. Conran's expression said it all. He was far from feeling the same way.

'Several eyewitnesses testify to the accident victim being in an agitated state leading up to the impact. The van that hit her didn't stop. The road where she was hit isn't one of our usual accident blackspots. There's clear lines of vision for a good couple of hundred metres in each direction.'

Conran interrupted.

'Don't tell me.'

He eyed her.

'Something about it smells wrong.'

It had been one of Conran's first instructions on his arrival, delivered in his trademark staccato fashion. He believed in evidence, in facts. He did not believe, and would never act, on the basis of a copper's nose.

'If there was any intent involved on the part of the van driver, and this young girl doesn't recover, that makes this a potential murder inquiry.'

'She could equally be a stupid young girl, off her head on God knows what, stumbling along with no idea where she is, even who she is or where she's going, an accident waiting to happen in fact.'

Conran stopped as a knock sounded on the door, and Mairead appeared a moment later, a print-out in hand. Ignoring Conran without making it too obvious she was doing so, Mairead nodded at Lara.

'I've accessed all CCTV images from around the crash site. Cameras cover the hundred metres or so to the south of the impact and a hundred or so metres to the north, but there's nothing covering the site of the actual impact itself.'

Lara looked back at Conran. Those cameras would have been clearly visible to anyone travelling along that stretch of road. So, if anyone had wanted to target a pedestrian at any point, that would have been one of the very few places, they could have done so, confident that they wouldn't be caught by any prying electronic eyes.

Just then her mobile pulsed with another incoming call. Once again, it was Jordan, who was now in the hospital. Lara took it immediately.

'No news yet on the condition of the girl, she's still in theatre, we should get an update in the next few hours, but we do know one thing.'

Jordan paused.

'We've got more than just the one victim.'

Aaron had almost done it. He'd almost reached the magic number. It had been thirty-two yesterday, now it was sixty. He didn't know why it changed each day; it just did. Then, just as his fingers were flashing across the keyboard and the count was racing up into the high fifties, and just as he could feel all the tension beginning to bleed from his shoulders, there was a knock on his bedroom door, and his mum appeared.

'Another hour, OK?'

Carey nodded in at him, softening the stern-sounding instruction with a smile.

'You know how you get if you stay on too long.'

Aaron hadn't been on Fortnite, Minecraft or Call of Duty, even though one of his friends had managed to source that pirated copy of Black Ops Cold War and everyone else had been absorbed by it for hours. But his screen was inclined away from his mum, and she couldn't see that. Besides, from the way she was now hesitating, she seemed to have other things on her mind.

'Have you heard from Amy since she left?'

Now she sounded troubled, too. Aaron felt the same, but he just gave a small, slight shake of his head instead, concentrating on the screen in front of him. Most of their conversations were conducted that way right now, so Carey didn't notice anything particularly amiss.

'I don't suppose any of us will till tomorrow at least, the mood she was in.'

She hesitated again.

'And if I phoned Donna to see if she's OK, then she really would bite my head off, wouldn't she?'

Carey struggled a brave smile back at her seemingly absorbed son.

'Don't know what's wrong with her these days.'

She turned, closing the bedroom door behind her. As she did so, Aaron looked away from the screen to the cupboard where he'd hidden his sister's iPad. Then he turned back to his laptop, started tapping the keyboard once more even though the machine was turned off. Now he had to tap sixty-eight times.

Tap that keyboard on that same spot sixty-eight times without stopping, and then whatever was happening with Amy that evening, everything would be all right.

CHAPTER FIVE

MILTON DAVALLE, the hospital consultant in charge of the accident victim's admission and treatment, was a type that Lara had come across many times before. She'd worked, briefly and all too regrettably, for a few of them and had enjoyed the experience about as much as the young female nurse standing opposite him seemed to be enjoying her similar experience right now.

Lara studied him. Davalle was wearing a Savile Row suit with a faint cream chalk stripe running through the weave. The slim briefcase on the desk behind him was made of the finest calf leather. His open mouth revealed an arsenal of what looked like expensively capped teeth. Lara was only catching around one word in every two that was coming out of that mouth right now, but she had a shrewd suspicion he didn't really care who was listening anyway. Only one thing mattered right now and that was the sound of his own booming voice.

'We have rules, guidelines, procedures designed to protect our patients, protocols put in place for their wellbeing and the wellbeing of their families.'

Lara switched off again. Apparently, the young nurse shouldn't have told Jordan that the RTC victim was pregnant. It was a breach of confidentiality, punishable by all sorts of savage sanctions, but, most particularly, having to listen to the braying cadences of a patrician consultant.

But not for much longer. Lara wasn't sure if he'd finished. She wasn't sure if he'd ever finish. She'd already heard more than enough though.

Lara cut across: 'All patients have a right to a confidential medical service.'

Davalle paused. He didn't appreciate the interruption, but at least this police officer, whose name he'd been told and had then promptly forgotten, seemed to have something resembling half a brain. He nodded, briefly at her, before turning back to the hapless young nurse.

'Confidentiality is the cornerstone of any doctor–patient relationship and patients have to be able to trust us with their lives.'

Lara cut in again. 'It's standard GMC guidance.'

Davalle translated the acronym in case the nurse didn't understand it.

'The General Medical Council.'

Before he could continue, Lara rolled on once more.

'Guidance that came into effect on the 15 October 2007 and which was updated on the 25 May 2018 to reflect the requirements of the General Data Regulation and Protection Act.'

Davalle stared at Lara as she continued.

'But exceptions arise of course. You're required to disclose or volunteer information to the police under the Road Traffic Act of 1988, for example.'

Davalle's lips began to ascribe a perfect sneer. 'Oh for Goodness' sake—'

'Not to mention the Terrorism Act of 2000.'

Davalle's perfect sneer began to wobble a little.

'As well as any discovery of the act of Female Genital Mutilation in a girl under the age of 18.'

Davalle cut across in turn. 'None of which applies in this case.'

Lara nodded back as the bewildered nurse looked from one to the other.

'Exceptions are also made in circumstances where a patient lacks clear mental capacity. In that case the Mental Capacity Act of 2005 applies, and disclosure would be justified if it reveals information which could be demonstrated to be in the clear best interests of the patient.'

Lara moved closer to the now-staring consultant, her tone hardening all the time.

'We don't know anything about this young girl as of yet. We don't know who she is, where she came from, where she was going. What we do know is that she's suffered serious injuries in an accident that may not have been an accident at all and, until we can say whether it was or it wasn't, we need all the information we can get, and information like this could be absolutely vital in establishing why she was on that road in what seemed to be a potentially distressed state and why a person or persons as yet unknown might have targeted her.'

Davalle's mouth opened, but no words were now coming out.

'So, had your colleague not reported this to us, and had you failed to report it, too, I'd now be reporting you for obstructing police officers in their execution of their duties. But as your colleague did report it, I want to put on record the Major Crime Unit's grateful thanks.'

Lara nodded at him, leaving the perfect interval to the single word that followed.

'Sir.'

Across the room, the young nurse stared. She'd never heard that usually respectful address invested with such invective, almost bordering on contempt.

By Lara's side, Jordan stifled a smile.

Davalle's mouth was still doing its impersonation of a guppy, but he did manage to force some words out now at least.

'Do you know who I am?'

Jordan looked at Lara who returned his gaze. It was a well-worn routine and one they'd played out many times before, but they still enjoyed it. Jordan hit a speed dial button on his mobile as Lara looked at the consultant almost pityingly for a moment, before nodding to the young nurse to follow her towards ICU.

As they left the room, Lara just heard Jordan asking the head of hospital security to step along and help them out here as they'd found a middle-aged male who didn't seem to know who he was. The nurse, who obviously hadn't heard that one before, spluttered as they exited and even Lara permitted herself a grin.

Yes, it was an old one, but sometimes, as the time-honoured saying had it, the old ones really were the best.

Five minutes later, Lara was with the young, but now considerably more emboldened, nurse, sifting through the clothes and the very few personal possessions they'd stripped from the accident victim before her transfer to theatre.

The ambulance driver's initial report had proved correct. Those personal possessions comprised money, but no bank cards, and a piece of paper with some scribbled times that seemed to be of ferry sailings. There was nothing that might identify her, which had to be deliberate. And there was no phone either and still none found at the accident scene, which was the one detail that seemed to really exercise Natalie, the young nurse, whose name Lara had now established. She doubted Davalle would have even been aware she had one.

'What girl these days goes out without her phone?'

Lara shrugged, the rest of the scant evidence they'd amassed so far painting the same picture, and it was one she'd already rehearsed with Jordan.

'A girl who didn't want anyone to know who she was.'

Natalie's mind was running on different lines.

'Or a girl who didn't want anyone to see what was on it.'

Lara paused and looked at her. Then her mobile pulsed; Mairead's name on the display. And, like Jordan before her, Mairead didn't waste time with small talk.

'We've got something.'

CHAPTER SIX

IN LARA'S OPINION, George Orwell had always been remarkably prescient when it came to matters of personal surveillance. His belief that there was no way of knowing whether you were being watched at any given moment, except perhaps in pitch darkness, was as true now as it was then. How, or, on what system, Orwell's Thought Police kept watch wasn't known, but these days there were any number of networks that could be used, including 3D-matching, geometric and statistical systems or even thermal recognition.

And at least one of the systems recently developed by law enforcement agencies around the world, including Lara's own unit, could now monitor a target even in pitch darkness.

It was late the same evening. Lara and Mairead were in a small, private, dining space at the rear of a building they'd used as a meeting place many times in the past: a family run garlic farm, some four or so miles from the capital. The last of the late guests were already drifting away so Mairead, once again, didn't waste time.

'I worked back from the spot she was hit and first picked her up outside Godshill.'

Lara studied the face captured by the camera again: a pretty, but otherwise unremarkable, teenage girl who looked to be in her mid to late teens. Behind, the village's cute trademark cottages could clearly be seen.

'Uniform are already doing house-to-house calls in case she lives there, and all the secondary schools on the island are being contacted in case she's local, too.'

Lara cut in.

'Did she meet anyone along the way, stop to talk to anyone?'

'Not that I've found so far.'

Mairead spread out another series of images on the table in front of them as, behind, a family of ducks passed by the window setting up a raucous chorus accompanied all the while by the farm's resident dog, called – from what Lara could dimly recall – Ruthie.

'I fed those images into all the usual social media sites to see if we can come up with a match. Nothing so far – or nothing definitive anyway – to be honest she could be one of thousands of matches we've found so it's going to take some time to whittle them down.'

Mairead paused.

'But I also spread the net a bit wider, going back over the last couple of weeks as well, just to see if she crops up anywhere else on the island.'

Lara sifted through yet more images. This was a longer shot, but as they had precious few shots at all in their locker at present, anything was worth a try. She'd done exactly the same herself a few months previously when she was trying to track the activities of their previous DCI, Paula Monroe, and that had led to a breakthrough of sorts. It had also led to the discovery of the body of Paula's dead lover, one of the reasons, Lara strongly suspected, she was enjoying, or perhaps enduring, her current period of enforced leave.

Mairead hesitated, then continued.

'Again, there's little that's conclusive, although I have found one image that's clearer than the rest, even though it's taken late at night. If it is her – and it does look like her – she's out in the country at the entrance to what seems to be the driveway of an old house. She's alone again, but she seems to be waiting for someone by the way she's looking up and down the road and checking her phone.'

It took a moment for Lara to place exactly where the young girl was. But when she did, it was like a huge bucket of the coldest water had just been thrown over her.

Mairead stayed silent for a moment. She knew exactly what demons this particular image must be summoning up for her senior officer. But that was personal, this was police business so, and after that moment, Mairead pressed on.

'Then she disappears from view, so presumably she's walked inside.'

Lara still didn't respond. She couldn't. She'd felt chilled a moment before. Now that chill had just turned Arctic.

CHAPTER SEVEN

'Updates.'

The barked instruction early the next morning was brusque and a million miles from the invitation to pool thoughts and responses that would have been extended to the rest of the unit by Lara.

But, as DCI Conran had pointed out on more than one occasion in the last ten minutes alone, DI Arden wasn't there.

Why Lara hadn't turned up that morning, no one seemed to know. As Jordan was on leave that morning, too, it was left to Mairead to swiftly run again through the various sightings she'd uncovered, and the leads provided by social media. They all added up to the same thing: they were still no closer to an identification than they were when the accident victim's broken body had been found on that road.

A new member of the team, a rookie DC called Hendriksen, took it up, reporting a similar lack of progress so far with the local secondary schools on the island, before Mairead provided the next update, on the vehicle involved. CCTV had picked up a large white van a few hundred metres from the crash site a few moments after the impact, but there was only CCTV at the scene, no ANPR, automatic number plate recognition. It wouldn't have proved much help anyway as the registration number of the van was obscured by dirt, deliberately or otherwise. A partial registration had been picked up, just two letters – EL – but that was all that could be made out. And the van itself must have turned off the main road onto one of the many side roads on offer soon after, because it wasn't picked up by the next camera along.

There was also little in the way of an update from the hospital. At present, the accident victim was in an induced coma, to protect both herself and her unborn baby. A second update from the hospital had placed her at just under five months into her term.

There had been another update from the hospital though, as Conran himself now made clear. An eminent hospital consultant had contacted him to complain about his treatment at the hands of a female police officer. And now Conran wanted to know what light Mairead could shed on all this, seeing as how the female DI in question was still absent from the unit and still not answering her fucking mobile!

Mairead did what she always did when a member of her unit – particularly Lara – was under any sort of attack. She retreated behind her usual stonewall, which wasn't difficult as she hadn't actually been there. Then she watched as a frustrated Conran tried again, and failed, to reach Lara herself.

Briefly, she felt a stab of sympathy for the new boy in a very tightly knit unit that was fast closing ranks against him, but it was only brief. Conran hadn't displayed any interest in the various updates on the accident victim. The only animation he'd displayed had come in the wake of a complaint from a consultant who, from all Jordan had told her, was a smug, supercilious, self-important prick. And as complaints of that type were a million miles away from anything that would have counted as a priority for Lara, Mairead maintained her trademark stonewall.

Unlike Lara's absence from work that morning, Jordan's had been logged in advance.

His wife was due home from hospital in the next couple of weeks, after becoming caught up in the fall-out from Jordan's last major case. Strictly speaking, Edie was his ex-wife these days, and they hadn't lived together for more than two years following the break-up of their marriage, but she was still the mother of Coco, their teenage daughter.

Coco had been on a more or less even keel lately, and Jordan was desperate to keep her on that newly discovered straight and narrow, after a period when she'd journeyed many more dangerous paths. So, a destabilised Edie was the last thing she – or he – needed right now. It was the last thing Edie herself needed, too, and that's what today's meeting with the hospital's after-care support team was all about. Edie was coming to them for a few days before she returned to her own home, and the after-care officer wanted to make sure the flat was fit enough for even this limited period of convalescence.

As Jordan let himself in, he could already hear Coco talking to someone. He checked his watch. Had the after-care officer arrived already? Then he realised it was only Coco he could hear, so she must be on her mobile. Jordan was about to head into the kitchen to make a pot of coffee, but then he paused, although it wasn't what Coco was saying that made him still in the doorway like that, it was the tone.

'No, don't say anything.'

Coco's one-sided conversation floated through the closed door in front of him. She sounded tense, panicked even.

'I don't care, we can't.'

Jordan couldn't help himself. He moved closer to the door and so heard Coco's next exchange loud and clear.

'No, especially not to my dad.'

Jordan stood, rooted, in the hallway, then turned towards the door as the bell rang. Back in the sitting room, Coco instantly cut her call. Moving almost mechanically, Jordan let the after-care officer in, took her coat and offered her the coffee he'd been just been about to make. All the time, his mind was racing.

What couldn't Coco say?

And especially not to her dad?

CHAPTER
EIGHT

LARA HADN'T BEEN BACK THERE in over twelve months. Up till last night, she couldn't imagine ever being there again. Till she saw that CCTV image of their accident victim standing at the entrance to a driveway she knew only too well. A driveway she'd walked down herself all those months before.

Lara stared at the same old ruined house she'd seen then, too. To her, it still looked exactly the same. The crumbling walls and decayed, rotting windows seemed to positively reek of evil, but there was a good reason for that. Time had moved on, most of the principal culprits were now long dead, hopefully anyway, but the memory of all they'd done, and all that had happened there, still hung in the air like a cloud of invisible, malevolent ghosts.

Lara pushed her way through a rusting iron gate, wincing at the lament of metal on the creaking hinge. Then she wheeled round as a shout sounded behind her.

'Mr Ferguson?'

Lara stared at a young woman, early twenties, an executive-style briefcase in one hand, a set of car keys in the other, who stopped, flustered.

'Well, not actually Mr Ferguson of course, sorry.'

She stopped again as Lara kept staring at her.

'I've been trying him for the last two days, has he sent you instead?'

Lara took out her warrant card. In her experience it tended to concentrate minds, and sure enough, within another minute or so, and with the two of them now sitting on a nearby wall, Susie, the young and flustered estate agent and owner of the executive-style briefcase, was suddenly making a lot more sense.

'He called last week. To be honest it was a bit of a bolt out of the blue, we hadn't had any interest in the place for years, which isn't surprising I suppose. Well, just look at it.'

Susie swept an explanatory hand around the ruin behind them, but then rolled on again quickly, suddenly remembering she was there on business.

'But it definitely has potential, some of the detailing in the architraves, particularly on the upper floors really is quite exquisite.'

Lara interrupted. She'd been upstairs. And the last things she'd been looking at back then were architraves.

'So, you met him, yes?'

Susie nodded.

'He called into the office. There was just me manning the place at the time, everyone else was off on a team-building afternoon in Blackgang.'

A wistful note crept into her voice.

'I was so jealous. I love that place, especially the Cliffhanger.'

Lara cut across again. The second to very last thing she was interested in right now was theme park rides.

'And he wanted to arrange a viewing?'

Susie nodded again, then hesitated, bringing out a thin sales brochure.

'It was a bit odd, looking back. But whenever I suggested coming over here to look at the place in person, he started to backtrack. Every date and time I suggested seemed to be a problem. To be honest, I thought he might have taken one look at some of the photos and was too embarrassed to say he'd had second thoughts.'

Susie shrugged.

'But then he called again, and he wanted more details – and more photos, too – as many as we had. Then he asked for a land search. I sent everything he asked for, which is when we fixed on an actual viewing for today.'

Susie looked down the driveway as if she was still expecting him to appear.

'I called him a couple of days ago to re-confirm, but his phone seemed to be out of service. I tried yesterday, too, and this morning, but it was the same story. But just in case he'd changed his number or something and had forgotten to let me know, I thought I'd better come anyway.'

Susie faltered, a new thought suddenly striking her. Maybe there was a reason why the high-flyers in her agency office had been taken away for team building that afternoon, and the willing, but clearly rather dim, Susie had been left behind. Maybe one of them might have asked her next question rather sooner.

'Sorry, but...'

Susie glanced down towards Lara's warrant card, still visible in her pocket.

'What, exactly, has all this to do with the police?'

———

A short time later, Lara walked through a small clearing to a patch of waste ground. As it had twelve months previously, that patch of ground played host to a strange, half-size windmill, perhaps a child's former playroom. No one seemed to know.

Lara's mother, Esther, had once played in that strange windmill. She used to sneak out of her children's home a hundred or so metres away with another childhood friend, a boy called Finn.

Esther managed to assimilate and rise above the atrocities that had been perpetrated on her by the staff of that old home. Finn did not. Years later, he caught up with Esther on a train, which was the last time the young Lara had seen her mother. Unable to take revenge on those responsible, he'd transferred all that rage and torment onto her instead, and Lara had become an orphan.

She suddenly felt her body go into a small, involuntary spasm, almost as if her mind was willing her to move on, move forward, focus on what she may be actually able to change rather than all that could now never be changed – to go back to the investigation in hand, in fact, rather than rake up an old one.

But what if this new investigation had something to do with that old one? Why had their still unidentified accident victim been seen here, hovering at the entrance to the driveway, just a couple of hundred metres away, seemingly wavering over whether to step foot inside?

Who, exactly, was this Mr Ferguson and what was the real nature of his interest in a place that, even though it now had a different name, she'd always know by its former name of Kenwood?

And did this have anything to do with the note that had been hand-delivered to Lara's flat? The note that contained chapter-and-verse details on the abuse that had been meted out on this very spot?

Then Lara paused as something else struck her. That note had arrived two nights ago, which was around the same time, according to Susie, that her enigmatic Mr Ferguson seemed to have disappeared.

Lara opened her mobile to re-read the electronic scan she'd made of the note, but as her phone fired into life, she saw she'd had six missed calls from Conran. Those she discounted. They'd keep. Then she saw a missed call from Mairead.

Lara hit a speed dial button and Mairead's now tense-sounding voice came back down the line.

'We've found her. The female RTC. She's local, from the island.'

Mairead paused.

'I'm going to see the parents now.'

CHAPTER
NINE

AARON COULD ALWAYS SENSE his sister, even if he couldn't see her. And he always knew she was there, even if she wasn't.

They'd always had it – the ability to know just what the other was thinking without either of them saying a word. But it was more than that, too. If he closed his eyes, it was like he was inside her mind somehow. He'd be seeing all she was seeing, sometimes feeling the same emotions at the exact moment she was experiencing them, which made all that was happening now even more frustrating.

He wanted to ask Amy so much. He wanted to ask her why she'd been in such a strange mood yesterday. Why she could hardly even look at him as she'd slipped into his room. Why she'd made him promise, solemnly promise, that he would hide her iPad, that he wouldn't let anyone else know he had it and that he would never – as in ever – try to open it up himself and why she'd come up with that ridiculous excuse about breaking it and not wanting mum or dad to find out.

He'd agreed, of course he had. He had no choice. Amy had always had that ability to sweep everyone before her, to bend other people to what was her, often implacable, will. He also didn't press her because he knew he didn't need to. Within a short time, she'd have calmed down and then they'd communicate as they always had, if not face to face, then through one mind locking onto the other. It was all back to that connection again.

But now something had happened. It was as if Amy had disappeared behind a veil, which was why he was pacing the floor, taking sixteen steps to move from one wall to the other, then sixteen steps back again. If he could complete ten complete circuits that would be three hundred and twenty steps in total, and that would then unlock all this, he knew it would.

Dimly, he was aware of the doorbell ringing downstairs, but he blotted it out. He still had forty-two steps to go. Voices intruded as his mum or his dad opened the front door, but he blotted them out, too, and pressed on. Then another voice cut across, sounding urgent, panicked even, and it was his dad's voice, telling him to come downstairs but there were still twenty-one steps to go so obviously he couldn't.

Briefly, the voices muted, presumably as their visitor or visitors had gone into the sitting room. Just eight now to go.

Then Aaron stopped as he heard it: an almost animalistic howl reverberating around their small house. He stared towards the door, not even knowing what it was at first, but then he realised it was his mother screaming. A moment later, he heard a pounding on the stairs, and he stared at his dad as he flung open the bedroom door and told Aaron to get downstairs, now.

The police were here.

His now wild-eyed dad didn't understand what they were saying, none of it.

But there was some terrible news about Amy.

CHAPTER
TEN

PATIENTS ARE ADMITTED to ICU for all sorts of reasons. Sometimes they've had a major operation and need specialist treatment to recover. Sometimes they've been involved in an accident and need round-the-clock care to repair the, often devastating, effects. Sometimes they're simply in the throes of an illness, usually, although not exclusively, of the most serious kind. Whatever the specific cause, all patients who end up there have one thing in common: their bodies have ceased to function properly, and they need urgent, and often constant, help.

Lara looked at Carey and Matt Waite, holding each other as they looked down at their daughter, Amy, with their son, Amy's brother, Aaron, standing to one side. And right now, it wasn't just Amy who looked in need of that urgent and constant help.

No one was speaking. No one, indeed, had said a word since they'd all been ushered inside. Lara had questions she needed to ask, but for now she just let the silence stretch, looking down instead at the specialist leaflets they'd all been given.

From them, she learnt that the patient being visited may well be connected to several machines and drips and will often look very different to how a family member or friend would remember them. The fluids that may have been administered to keep the patient hydrated, for example, could cause them to look bloated. Bruising may also be caused by the different machines to which they're connected. All that is completely normal, the same leaflet reassured her.

Lara looked up. The expressions on the faces of the devastated family grouped around the girl in the bed said it all. Nothing about this seemed remotely normal to them.

Then Lara stole a glance across the room to Mairead. She was always her first choice of companion on occasions like these. Jordan was good in the sympathy stakes, but she was more than usually empathic. But in the last few moments, Lara had been wondering whether that had been something of a misstep as another passage from the same leaflet floated in front of Lara's eyes. Sometimes, the leaflet counselled, the patient may be on a breathing machine, also known as a ventilator, and nurses must regularly clear the chest of mucus by putting a thinner tube into the breathing tube to suck up the fluid. It was a procedure that could seem intrusive and may cause the patient to cough or retch.

Lara kept looking at Mairead. She knew all this, and only too well – her own father had been on a similar machine for weeks until, as his only surviving relative, Mairead had made the decision to turn it off. And from the look on her face right now, Lara could see that she was re-living that decision only too acutely.

Then Lara gave herself a slight shake. There was no time to pursue that, and they also had no more time to give the shocked family the space they needed to even try and absorb all this. There was an investigation to pursue, and every minute that went by was a minute they'd never get back. Lara permitted herself one final glance down at Amy. They may just have an attempted murder on their hands.

'This happened on the coast road, between Shanklin and Sandown.'

The parents barely seemed to hear her at first. The brother,

Aaron, looked towards Lara as she spoke, softly but insistently, but he also seemed to be on a different planet right now.

'Have you any idea why she might have been there? Could she have been going to meet someone?'

Carey, the mother cut across, sounding every bit as agitated as she looked right now.

'She was supposed to be going to her friend's. She was staying the night with her. Donna doesn't live anywhere near there.'

Then Carey stopped, abruptly.

'I don't understand.'

Lara stayed silent. Jordan had already called Amy's equally shocked friend, who'd quickly come clean. That was a cover story, and one they'd both used many times before to reassure respective parents they were having a sleepover with the other. Lara spoke again, cautious once more, but no less insistent.

'And the baby?'

This time it was Matt, the father, who cut in.

'We didn't know anything about a baby.'

Then, suddenly, he stopped, looked across at his son as a thought struck him.

'Aaron?'

Aaron, still looking as if he was on that other planet, just shook his head as Carey reached out, stroked her daughter's unresponsive arm.

'We didn't even know she had a boyfriend.'

Across the room, the dedicated ICU nurse watched her, wary, and Mairead knew why. It wasn't unknown for a distraught relative to start pulling out the drips and tubes that were keeping their loved one alive, trying to return the alien-looking figure before them to the person they'd known before. Mairead had felt like doing it herself in the dark days leading up to the death of the father she missed ever more keenly as each day rolled by.

Lara wasn't watching Carey or Matt or Aaron. She was making connections, joining dots. Because it was possible that

Amy didn't have a boyfriend of course. She was fifteen years old. She was away from home and away from the friend she was supposed to be with, on her way somewhere. Wherever that was, she never arrived. Something or someone had intervened, and this pregnancy could well be the key.

Was Amy an abuse victim and was this baby the result? If so, that made it virtually certain that this was no accident.

Also, if this was an abuse case – and Lara once again couldn't help the thought floating once again into her mind – could this be anything to do with Kenwood? Any connection seemed barely credible after all this time, but what was this young girl doing walking down the driveway to a children's home that had closed years before she was even born?

Lara looked back at the parents and the brother. All they wanted were answers right now. She knew exactly how they felt.

Across the room, Aaron didn't need answers, because he already knew exactly what had happened here, and as he looked across at his dad, he felt one of the most powerful surges of rage he'd ever experienced in his life. Why hadn't he just let him finish that circuit of his bedroom and complete his count? Why had he stopped him getting to those all-important three hundred and twenty steps? If he'd done that then none of this would have happened. Those police officers wouldn't have called, and Amy wouldn't be lying there. The fate – the Gods – the spirits – whatever they were, he didn't know and didn't care – they would have intervened like they'd intervened so many times before.

He hadn't been allowed to complete that count, and now look what had happened.

Then everything else was wiped from Aaron's mind as, from across the room, it began: a low, almost unearthly, keening.

The ever-present and ever more wary nurse had already begun to move towards Carey Waite, doubtless haunted by images of all those past patients pulling out tubes and drips, and, initially at least, she seemed to have good cause. The distraught mother seemed to be all but disintegrating before her eyes, but it was Mairead who reached her first, lowering her gently down onto a nearby chair as she did so.

Carey looked up at her.

'This is all my fault.'

Mairead stared at her, as did Lara.

'I should have known.'

Carey shook her head, wracked, grinding her hands together, her nails scoring deep weals into her palms.

'What mother wouldn't?'

Across the room, Matt Waite made no move towards his wife. He barely even seemed to register what she was saying. The brother, Aaron, was maintaining what seemed to be his trademark, almost catatonic, silence, too. Mairead looked back at Carey and all she could see in the mother's anguished eyes was something she recognised only too well. She saw indeed the same lacerating emotion on her own face as she stared in the bathroom mirror each night.

Carey Waite was drowning in guilt. Not guilt at what she'd done, what she'd just said wasn't any sort of confession. But it still led to the same dark place.

The circumstances were totally different. The cause was different, too. But at heart they were two sides of the same coin. Because Mairead was drowning in guilt right now, too.

CHAPTER
ELEVEN

IT WAS ABOUT to become a red-letter day for Staff Nurse Carmen Morrison, and in more ways than one.

She loved her work in the hospice, even though most people she knew – even some of the colleagues she worked with – found the place unutterably depressing. Hospitals could be grim places at times. But at least most patients in there recovered, re-joined their families, and many went on to live long and happy lives. No such prospect was promised for these admissions. There was only one way out for them, once those front gates closed shut behind them, and that was via the local undertaker.

She actually found that knowledge often concentrated the mind though. With limited time left, a lot of her patients seemed to live more in a few days and weeks than others managed in months and years. A lot of them, bodies and minds permitting, plunged into all sorts of activities and endeavours, sometimes spending hours committing to paper, or to the one of the hospice laptops, life stories that would live on long after them, alternately delighting and shocking family members left behind. Each day, in its own way, became a celebration of the human spirit, a testament to all life could offer even as its end was near.

It made John Weston even more of a sad little case. He was

washed and fed along with all the other patients, but there was no interaction. John just lay there, unaware, not comatose exactly, but as good as. Locked in, was the only way Carmen could describe it. Totally withdrawn from his surroundings and from all around him, awaiting only death.

It didn't help that, in contrast to almost all the other patients she cared for, he had no visitors: no family or friends had ever called to see him, and no old colleagues had dropped in, either. He'd previously worked in some administrative capacity in some company or other, so his notes said, but no one from his old workplace had ever even enquired about him. Maybe he'd retired too long ago. John Weston seemed to be a man who'd simply slipped through the cracks, his imminent death destined to be unmarked, and probably unlamented.

Then, a few minutes ago, there'd been a knock on her door. The porter had just let in a new visitor, a young woman and – wonder of wonders – the visitor was for John. A delighted Carmen recorded her name and address, all the while providing an update on his current condition, cautioning his visitor that he was very seriously ill of course, but sounding an encouraging note, too. She'd seen even the most serious cases respond when a familiar face and voice suddenly appears at their bedside, as it proved a few moments later, making this a double red-letter day.

As she ushered in John's visitor, and as that visitor seated herself beside him, telling him that her name was Lara Arden, there was a faint, but definite, reaction. The old man's breathing caught momentarily and, for the first time, too, some sort of light seemed to have ignited behind his eyes.

Weston was the only permanent member of staff Lara had ever managed to trace. Every other old Kenwood employee had remained resolutely under the radar in the years since the home had closed, re-inventing themselves probably as respectable members of the new communities in which they'd settled, excising all trace of their former lives.

Weston had broken ranks, albeit unwittingly. Since Kenwood, he'd lived the life of a virtual hermit, but tracking back through his medical records after his various hospital admissions had provided the small, but vital, link, courtesy of a regular prescription that had been delivered to the home for him for just over three months. If Lara had hoped that would lead to her tracing more of the home's past staff members, she was to be disappointed, because that was when the trail had gone cold. There'd been no further links and, with Weston now fast approaching death, no realistic prospect of finding any either. Till now, perhaps.

Lara looked down at the letter in her hand, the letter that had been hand-delivered those couple of days before. Weston hadn't written it, his current state of health well and truly precluded that. But Weston had witnessed the events detailed therein. So maybe something in there may force some connection to be made. His brain was still alive, even if the rest of his body was ravaged by illness, so something may just penetrate the fog. Maybe, by the simple fact of Lara speaking some of those words out loud, he'd see, once again, the pictures that seemed to be tormenting another of his former partners in what they all now knew was a litany of crime.

Lara already knew the passage she was going to read out to him. It involved a small child, not her mother, but a boy. Perhaps it had even been Finn, her mother's childhood friend, who'd turned into her captor and persecutor later in life. Maybe the passage she was about to read out to him was one of the contributory factors.

Lara leant close to the uncomprehending body in the bed in front of her and started.

She told him about the small, shaking boy that had been picked out in that classroom that day.

She rehearsed, again, the way his tormenter would linger

over the choice of sticks in front of them, which only made that small boy shake the more. But it wasn't a stick he picked up, but a rope that clamped the boy's wrists together before a large metal hook attached to a pulley was inserted, and the now mewling child was propelled up into the air.

And then the first of those sticks was selected, and now Lara winced, involuntarily, as she continued, almost as if she could now actually see and hear the blows as the questioning began.

Where are you from?

Where do you live?

Questions that were accompanied all the time by harder, and ever more vicious blows.

Where is your home?

That was a nonsense, of course, and every child in that room knew it, because he was like them all, he was a river child, he lived anywhere and everywhere, and he tried gasping that out, but it was the wrong answer, as his tormenter made only too clear as he struck him again and again, each blow spinning him round, affording fresh territory to attack, which was when the small child soiled himself.

All the time, the rest of the children kept smiling, a few of them even miming smiles at the others by way of desperate encouragement, because they all knew what would happen if they didn't.

Lara looked down at Weston again. Still, just steady breathing was sounding from the old man in the bed.

Did that small child survive the beating? Did he succumb to his injuries? Or would Weston not even know? Did the faces of all those children now merge?

Now Lara couldn't go on, but that wasn't just due to the cumulative emotional toll of reading aloud all this past abuse. This was an ongoing litany, too, reaching down through the generations. Somewhere out there was another twisted soul, Lara's stepsister, the product of Finn's rape following his abduction of Lara's mother from that train that day. A girl named after her mother, Esther. A soul twisted out of shape by events that had taken place decades before she was born, more to be pitied than censured in a sense, but a deeply evil soul in her own right, nonetheless. The campaign of linked murders she'd embarked on just twelve months before, a series of murders for which she continued to evade justice, was ample evidence of that. And an ample demonstration, too, of how corrosively the past can infest the present.

Lara looked at Weston again but, that tiny rally as she'd walked in aside, nothing she said seemed to have penetrated, and she was becoming convinced that nothing would. So, Lara stood and exited, not even saying goodbye to the kindly-looking nurse who'd ushered her in for her visit. She knew the hospice staff would often ask for a few words from a visitor they could repeat to a patient after they left, something that might give them some moments of comfort. All Lara could have said was rot in hell, which wouldn't have proffered too much in the way of comfort but was definitely no less than Weston deserved.

———

The driver of the Bentley had taken the call five minutes previously. Briefly, as he'd listened, he'd felt a sudden, unaccustomed, fear claim him, but he quickly banished it. Replacing the phone, he made a call of his own and then another. And then one more.

The porter at the hospice had done what he'd been paid his modest retainer this past year or so to do. He'd reported back to them news of a visitor for Weston, his first. He'd also earned himself what he hoped would be a sweet little bonus by reporting not only the name and address of that visitor, culled from the staff nurse's log, but also snippets of their one-sided conversation which had seemed to consist, according to the largely puzzled porter listening from the other side of the door, of extracts from some kind of letter.

Little did the porter know, but that last little nugget of information wasn't going to earn him any sort of bonus, sweet or otherwise. Just in case he ever repeated anything he'd just overheard he'd now join the recently deceased manager of that ramshackle boarding house at the bottom of the Solent where he'd, too, feed the fishes. But that wasn't even remotely the matter of the moment, because clearly their previous fond hope had been just that little too fond. That incendiary letter had ended up in more than just their hands. In fact, it had ended up in just about the worst hands it could, those of a cop.

All that was left now, was to decide what to do about it.

CHAPTER
TWELVE

LARA CROSSED to the floor-to-ceiling window and looked down onto the seemingly endless stretch of water below.

The rent was still ridiculous. The neighbours still might as well not exist for all she saw of them. The on-site concierge was still the same one who'd been there to greet her on the day she first moved in, and he remained pleasant enough, but on some days, particularly at weekends, his was still the only face she saw. But each time she stood by that window, she felt just as she'd felt on the first day she'd walked in.

At any time of the day and night she could watch pleasure boats, working barges and sleek yachts all passing outside her window, along with swimmers, kayakers, and jet-skiers. Life experienced vicariously, some might say, but it was still the reason why, even if she could sometimes go the whole of a rare work-free weekend without speaking to a single living soul, she never actually felt alone.

Then Lara turned and looked across the room at a small collection of papers stacked on a low table. It was where she'd assembled the material she'd been able to collate so far on her dead mother. The case notes and journal entries from various social workers that documented her passage from a traumatised young child, recently released from the bonds of Kenwood, to a young woman on the verge of adulthood. These were the case notes that Lara had collected to reconstruct the mother she now barely remembered; to begin, in fact, the first of her private investigations.

Lara was well aware what would happen the minute she started reading. She'd no idea what process was in place here and couldn't even remember how it had first started. But somehow, when she started reading those notes, it was as if some strange empathic re-creation took place. From just a few stray details – in this latest case involving a visit to a set of prospective foster parents and the record of a disciplinary offence recorded in a different and later home from Kenwood – it was as if Lara began to live the life she was living back then.

As if she was inhabiting the mind of her lost mother.

CHAPTER THIRTEEN
ESTHER – LARA'S MOTHER

JADE COULDN'T HELP HERSELF. *The more the staff shouted at her – and one member of staff, Miss Cline, shouted at her in particular – the less able she was to control herself. Every morning, Jade would wake up on urine-sodden sheets.*

Which was when Jade would be snatched up out of the bed and dumped in an iron bath, as the protector on the bed was hurled into the laundry by two of Miss Cline's disciples. A few moments later, Jade was snatched from the freezing cold bath, handed a large cleaning rag, and told to scrub the protector clean, dry it and put it back on her bed. Until then, she wasn't allowed to dress or eat breakfast.

That was bad enough. But last night the protector had slipped from the mattress. Jade's fumbling fingers hadn't secured it in place properly. And Jade was snatched up by Miss Cline the next morning to reveal the mattress underneath, also yellowed with a fast-spreading stain.

Jade wasn't hurled in the iron bath this time. She was beaten, badly, before Miss Cline stormed off to tell the principal what had happened.

Quickly, we stripped the mattress from the bed. Four of us carried it to the next room along the corridor. We carried a new mattress back. By the time Miss Cline, still breathing fire, returned with the principal, every bed in the dormitory was neatly made, Jade's the neatest of all. Miss Cline flung back the sheets to reveal a pristine mattress with no trace of a stain. Swiftly, she flung back the sheets on every other mattress, too. All revealed themselves to be similarly stain-free.

The principal stared at the bemused Miss Cline. And as he walked back out, Miss Cline following, we heard him wondering, in a low voice, whether she shouldn't take some of that holiday leave she was due.

An hour later, I left the home for a rare day out. Two prospective foster parents had arrived to collect me. I'd met them before, they'd told me to call them Uncle Alan and Aunty Lillian, but this was the first time I was to stay with them for the night. They took me down to the beach where we played on the sand before taking me back to a small cottage that might one day become my home. A small dog bounded up to meet me as we drove in through a wooden gate and for the first time in my life, I fell in love.

They made me tea with fruit buns and honey and each mouthful was like an explosion. We played board games I didn't understand, but it didn't matter, because they let me win. When it came time for bed, I got the shock of my life as I slipped inside the sheets to feel something already in there. Aunty Lillian laughed so much she almost cried, and I did, too, when she explained that it was only the large metal bed warmer that Uncle Alan had forgotten to take out. The bed stayed toasty hot for hours, even after he came to retrieve it, and I just lay here revelling in the warmth.

The next morning, I was dropped off back at the home. The rest of the children dashed up to me, desperate to tell me what had happened the previous night when Miss Cline had gone to bed. Apparently, her screams on finding the urine-soaked mattress we'd swopped from Jade's bed onto hers had woken the whole house. We high-fived each other, which is when I saw Miss Cline herself looking out from one of the ground floor windows. I held her stare and to my amazement, she was the first to look away.

Later that afternoon, I was called into the principal's office. I already knew he'd received a formal application from Uncle Alan and Aunty Lillian to take me as their foster daughter. The moment I was told that, I felt as if I'd died and gone to heaven. Yesterday was the final visit before that application was confirmed, and it had to be confirmed, I knew that, because everything had gone so well, so there was no reason why it shouldn't.

But now he slid a different piece of paper across his desk towards me. I picked it up, reading it without understanding it, so he spelt it out.

A few hours before, a member of staff had made an allegation of an unsuitable advance on my part towards her. When she rejected the unwanted advance – which apparently was blatantly sexual in nature – I'd taken my revenge by soiling her bed. Her allegation had been backed up by two more members of staff, who'd also witnessed my advance and its aftermath. The home was duty bound to inform all prospective foster parents of any disciplinary issues and in the light of this one, and its specific nature, Uncle Alan had reluctantly decided that perhaps they should look elsewhere for a foster child instead.

I walked out of his office in a daze. Down the corridor, Miss Cline and her two companions were standing together, and they stared at me. This time, I was the one who looked away.

CHAPTER
FOURTEEN

THE SINGLE EXTRACT from those sparse collection of notes still in hand, Lara stood once again before the floor-to-ceiling window.

How much of all that was fact and how much was her imagination, she didn't know. The incidents were real enough. There was a Miss Cline in the home her mother had been sent to after Kenwood, and there was a record of an improbable-sounding unwanted advance on her part towards her. There had been a set of foster parents who'd shown interest initially in adopting her but had then seemed to quickly cool. There had been a smaller girl called Jade whom her mum seemed to have taken under her wing. That much was recorded. The rest, the details, the colour behind those stark facts, Lara seemed to have conjured up all by herself.

Or had the events of the last year or so unlocked her mother somehow? Up till then, Lara had walled her up inside, her memory tainted by the betrayal of her apparent abandonment, but now it was almost as if the mother she'd lost was painting pictures for her somehow.

Lara kept staring, unseeing, out over the water.

CHAPTER FOURTEEN

PART TWO

PART TWO

CHAPTER
FIFTEEN

FOR THE SECOND time in her life, Mairead watched a man tether a captive to a chair using thick leather straps, before another participant – a female this time, although it was difficult to be certain under the gimp mask – handed him sheets that had been soaked in water for at least the last hour.

The rising temperature in the room and the heat from the captive's body meant the moisture in the sheets started to evaporate the moment they were wrapped around his legs and arms, causing the material to visibly tighten before everyone's eyes. Then the final trademark touch was applied, heavy duty black duct tape wound round both the straps and the sheets.

Mairead stared at the trussed and bound figure just a few metres away from her own masked eyes. He was helpless, totally at the mercy of others and, just like the last time she was here, the expression on his face made his feelings only too clear. He absolutely loved it.

The first time she'd been at a gathering like this, Mairead had been on duty, investigating assaults amongst the local S&M community, attacks that had been difficult to take seriously at first, given assault or at least a form of assault, was pretty much the point of those sorts of meetings in the first place. At least, until the hospitalisation and near death of one of the participants changed attitudes and minds. Mairead had found it all largely repulsive at the time, as she'd been the first to admit. But today, she was here in a private capacity. And now her feelings were much more complicated.

She'd been in a whirl ever since that visit to Amy's parents and the subsequent dash down to St Mary's, which was hardly surprising in a sense. To witness a family receive news of a devastating accident involving their much-loved daughter, and then to discover that daughter was pregnant as well, was a double whammy that would have tested even the least uncaring of officers.

It was more than that though – grief and loss, she understood and only too keenly with her own father. It was everything that had come afterwards that had really lacerated. She'd tried talking about it to the staff at the hospital and they'd tried reassuring her in turn, telling her that everyone in her position felt the same at some point with the same questions assailing them.

Why didn't I act sooner?

Why didn't I seek help for him quicker?

Why didn't I see this coming until it was too late?

It was the same guilt she'd seen on the faces of Amy's parents, Carey and Matt, as they stood beside their daughter's bed those few hours' before, the same questions reflected in their impotent eyes. But in her case, it was even more than that.

A day or so ago she'd been contacted by her local crematorium. They'd recently launched a new initiative called the Tree of Life. Artificial leaf-type structures were to be hung from an imitation tree trunk in one of the visitors' rooms, leaves that would be decorated with the names of loved ones along with a short inscription. Would Mairead like to reserve one? And, if so, what would she like inscribed?

Mairead knew exactly what she wanted inscribed. It was just one single word. *Sorry*. But not for any failure to act sooner, or for not seeking help quicker, or for not seeing her father's illness looming before it was too late. Mairead's guilt stretched back much further than that.

She couldn't remember where they were going that day. She couldn't remember why she was alone in the car with her mum and why Dad wasn't with them, and she'd never asked. She didn't even remember getting into the car in the first place, but she did remember being cut out of it by men in uniform after they'd overturned. Just as she remembered her irritated mum turning round and shouting at her just before it happened, telling her to stop jumping round like that because she was distracting her. Then she remembered the sudden squeal of brakes. And she definitely remembered the crash.

After that, it had just been her and Dad. She had tried talking to him about it a few times, but – and even though he must have been suffering terribly himself – he'd always reassured and comforted her, telling her over and over again that it was just an accident, that it was no one's fault, and definitely not hers.

Over the years she'd almost managed to believe him. Certainly, she'd managed to put it to the back of her mind, probably because it was the only way she could deal with the complicated emotions it summoned up at an age when she was completely incapable of processing them. And, on the occasions when it all inevitably surfaced, provoked by the usual triggers – her mum's birthday, Mother's Day, Christmas – he was always there with his soothing words, and his broad shoulder to lean on once again.

But now he wasn't here anymore. Now there were no reassuring words and no broad shoulder. Now, there was just Mairead and her decades-old demons. A day or so ago, that simple email from the crematorium had reawakened them, and the stricken faces of the Waite family had brought them into ever sharper focus. Looking at Carey, it was as if she'd flashed back in time, as if she was back in that family car again listening to her mum's barked command from the front seat not to distract her, hearing again the squeal of brakes, that sudden scream reverberating as the car turned over, and then the sound of tearing metal and a silence that was more awful somehow than all the noise that had just preceded it.

With unseeing eyes, Mairead stared out again across the fetid room. The captive in the chair had been left for the last few moments for the sheets to tighten some more. The man in the mask checked, but the captive wanted them tighter still, so he turned and asked the rest of the attendees in that overpoweringly claustrophobic space if anyone wanted to be punished while they waited? From out of nowhere, Mairead heard her own voice say yes, and she felt her body move forward.

A moment later, strong hands secured her wrists. Those same strong hands turned her towards the wall from where studded leather straps were hanging. The she felt sharp taps on her ankles, and she moved both legs apart, allowing iron ankle fetters to similarly secure her feet. For a moment, she just stood there, awaiting a punishment that came just a few moments later as a whip cut into her back, one lash followed swiftly by another and then another, a stray lick of the whip catching her arm as well.

Mairead didn't complain. She just stood there and took her punishment. She didn't speak either, although she did whisper, just the once, but so quietly no one in that room heard her.

It was just the one single word she whispered.

Sorry.

CHAPTER
SIXTEEN

BEMBRIDGE AND VENTNOR might have been sited along the same stretch of the island's most easterly coast, but in every other respect they were a million miles apart.

The death knell for Ventnor, as a seaside destination, tolled in the 1960s with competition from cheap foreign package holidays along with the rising popularity of motoring as a mass form of transport. The former saw the town enter the twilight era that characterised so many English seaside towns back then, with its boarded-up shops, faded lodging houses and run-down hotels. The latter saw the town's last railway station close in 1966, but it was the pier that seemed to signal most clearly the town's decline. Damaged by fire and ravaged by the elements, it fell into disuse and was finally demolished in the 1990s. The town might have undergone something of a renaissance in recent years, with the development of the Haven and the re-opening of the Winter Gardens, but it was still that world away from Bembridge just a short distance along the coast.

On returning to the unit, Lara's first call of the day had been to a modest house on a steep hill behind Ventnor's Esplanade, home to Donna Collins, the friend Amy was supposed to be staying with on the night of her accident. As they'd already established, that story had quickly revealed itself to be the subterfuge practised by teenagers the world over who wanted to sneak away from their parents for a night. It was an innocent rite of passage for the most part. This one had ended far from innocently and a shocked Donna, sitting with her equally shocked parents, had no hesitation in offering up the little she knew about Amy's actual movements that night.

'I think she was going to see Rhys.'

'Rhys being?'

'Rhys McGuire.'

Lara prompted her.

'And is he Amy's boyfriend?'

Donna hesitated, but not out of any reluctance to break a confidence. She just seemed genuinely unsure.

'They'd been seeing each other for a while, so, yes, I suppose.'

The young girl, sounding ever more doubtful, struggled.

'I just didn't think it was that serious. To be honest, when she asked me to cover for her …'

Donna hesitated again, glancing nervously this time across at her parents, then pressed on.

'I thought she might be going to break it off.'

Then she paused again.

'But if she's pregnant…'

Donna stopped, looking even more lost now, and this time she didn't continue.

Bembridge often laid claim to being the largest village in the UK with a population of just over four thousand. It boasted an intact pier, a lifeboat station, as well as an abundance of independent shops, cafes, and restaurants, catering not only for the needs of the many holidaymakers who flocked there, but for some of the island's wealthiest inhabitants who'd made their homes there, too.

A short time later, Lara was outside a property on the sought-after Swains Road, described by a local estate agent as a cottage. A quick Land Registry search revealed that the property had been bought recently by Rhys's father, Joseph McGuire. Lara gazed up at the three-storey mansion before her. It resembled a cottage in much the same way the settlement she could see on all sides resembled a village; in other words, in no way at all.

There was no reply as she rang the front doorbell and a quick walk round and a check on all the ground floor windows revealed no sign of life inside either. As Lara moved back to the front of the house, she became aware of a neighbour eyeing her warily from the other side of a well-trimmed hedge, a wariness that disappeared the moment Lara showed him her warrant card.

From the watchful neighbour, Lara learnt that the father was often away on business and that a housekeeper would then look after the son of the house, Rhys. The neighbour hadn't seen Joseph for the last couple of days and, now he thought about it, he hadn't seen Rhys or the housekeeper either. Maybe the young man had gone off with his father this time.

Lara returned to the front of the house for one last look round. Opening the letterbox, she checked for a build-up of mail in case the neighbour had mis-remembered his sightings of the father and son, although something was already telling her that he wasn't the type. His interest in the comings and goings of the McGuire house, along with a concomitant interest in all the other houses on that well-heeled street in all probability, seemed to border on the forensic.

Later, she didn't know how to describe it. Instinct, perhaps, although Conran would very definitely have given her short shrift on that count. She couldn't actually see anything out of place, but then she smelt it. A thin, brittle, almost acrid tang in the air. A smell Lara knew only too well. A moment later she'd smashed one of the frosted glass inserts in the door, causing an alarm to wail and the same neighbour to pop his startled head above his hedge once again.

But by that time, Lara was inside, staring at blood on the floor at the far end of the hall.

CHAPTER
SEVENTEEN

IT WAS a special day for the driver of the Range Rover. A grandchild's birthday was always going to be anyway, but five was very definitely something of a milestone. He was moving on fast from the toddler stage now, his changing frame and personality revealing the young man he would one day become.

So, yes, he'd pushed the boat out and he wasn't ashamed to admit it. Outside caterers had been brought in, a children's entertainer had been hired, the pool had even been heated to a good couple of degrees above its normal operating temperature although that really was an unnecessary expense, as his wife and his daughter had both pointed out. Kids that age wouldn't have cared if the water had icebergs floating on top, they'd just plunge in anyway, and they were right of course. But he didn't care. It was the kind of day when everything had to be perfect, and it was. For the first half hour or so of the party anyway.

They were late arrivals. He didn't even catch their names; they were just more of his daughter and son-in-law's friends bringing their own little boy along to join in the fun. The boy in question may even have been in his grandson's class at the local primary school, he didn't know. He had picked him up from there once or twice, but he'd always waited in the car while his wife navigated the playground madness.

But what the driver of the Range Rover did know was that he suddenly felt as if he'd been hit by an Exocet.

The small child just looked up at him and smiled from under a mop of blond curls. That's all he did. The parents – who were also smiling – had made a point of introducing him to the nice man who was hosting this party, and the young boy had flashed him a warm and grateful smile, even though he was already clearly desperate to go and join his friends splashing around in the pool. But suddenly, after all those years, and completely out of the blue, it was back again: that violent shake in his stomach, the sudden, all-consuming dryness in his throat.

The driver of the Range Rover turned away, ostensibly to check on the food and drinks now being ferried into the large garden by the outside caterers, but really so no one could see the turmoil he knew must be etched on his face. Everything was just the same. Children were playing in the pool. Across the manicured lawn, the children's entertainer was setting up his tricks and games. Parents, including his own daughter and son-in-law, milled around chatting to each other as they kept an indulgent watch on their offspring. The world kept on turning as it had a moment or so before, but his world had just shuddered to a complete halt.

All the old urges he'd thought had long been banished were back. In fact, they now seemed to have returned even more strongly, as if they'd just been lying dormant all those years. Almost involuntarily, the driver of the Range Rover turned back again. His eyes instantly picked out the one boy among all the others he wanted to see right now and didn't want to see at all. And now something else returned, too: the almost-overpowering desire to get that young child alone, for the time he'd need to do the things he wanted to do to him.

The driver of the Range Rover turned again and almost stumbling now, headed towards his private retreat, his shed at the bottom of the garden. He'd genuinely believed that feelings like the ones that were coursing through him now were the preserve of some other man in some other country. He'd been so good in the years since he'd bid goodbye to all that. He'd raised a family, donated to charity, had become a pillar of his local community. He'd become a force for good and surely that had to cancel out some of the bad things he knew he'd done in his former life.

Letting himself inside the shed, he switched on the light, telling himself to calm down. Maybe it was that cursed letter again. He hadn't even wanted to open it and once he had, he'd just wanted to destroy it, but he knew it wasn't ever going to be as simple as that. He glanced down at his wrists. Ample proof, if any more were needed.

And then there was the visit to that estate agents. He still berated himself. Even as he was doing it, he knew it was crazy. Something had just seemed to impel him, and it was the same something he knew would also have impelled him to walk across to that small boy if he'd stayed out there for even a moment longer.

So, he'd just remain in here till it passed, as pass it must. The rest of the guests would just assume he'd gone to fetch something else for the party, a small football net he kept in there perhaps. He'd stay there for a few moments longer, let those old demons retreat, taking the man he once was with them. And then the man he'd now become, the good man he knew he was deep down, would emerge out into the garden again.

Just then he heard the door open behind him. For one brief, dizzying, moment, he actually thought it might be him, that it might be that small boy come to seek him out, more evidence of the madness assailing him right now, because how could it be? Pasting on a smile, he reached out for the nearest thing that came to a hand, a table tennis set, his sudden excuse for being in there. Maybe they could set it up on one of the trestle tables when the outside caterers had cleared away the sticky treats and the cake.

But the driver of the Range Rover didn't pick up the table

tennis set. His hands suddenly flew skyward as the world seemed to explode all around him. For a moment there was the most brilliant white light he'd ever seen, a light so bright it seemed to scar his eyes. Then, and as he just heard the last distant strains of children still playing in the pool outside, darkness descended, a darkness that was total.

CHAPTER
EIGHTEEN

'What have we got?'

Since returning from that cottage in Bembridge, which wasn't like any kind of cottage she'd ever seen, Lara and the rest of the Major Crime Unit had been sourcing all the background they could on Rhys McGuire and his father. Forensics had been working on the blood in the hallway. That would take time, they had to be careful to lift samples in a way that wouldn't compromise a potential crime scene, so no updates were expected before the next day at the earliest. But information on Rhys and his father had been more immediately forthcoming.

'Rhys has just turned eighteen, attends the same school as Amy. The mother's dead, she contracted cancer when Rhys was six and passed shortly after. Since then, it's just been Rhys and his father, along with a succession of housekeepers. We've contacted the latest one – a Maisie Gantz – she's only been with the family a matter of months. She's coming in later, but as she hadn't visited the house for the last few days, I'm not sure how much she can usefully tell us.'

Lara broke into Mairead's briefing to the team.

'How often does she usually go in?'

'At least once every other day.'

'So why wasn't she there yesterday or the day before?'

Mairead responded promptly.

'The father's away on a business trip, he's somewhere in France we believe. The son, Rhys, had told her that he was staying with friends, so there'd be no need.'

It was the same story that Amy Waite had told her parents, Lara silently reflected. She was supposed to be staying with a friend, too. She ended up badly injured on the coast road between Sandown and Shanklin and was still in a coma in St Mary's. Where Rhys was right now, and what state he was in, was still to be discovered.

'Phone records?'

Jordan took it up, checking his notes.

'We've traced Rhys's mobile, but it hasn't been turned on since last night.'

'Before that?'

'A couple of incoming calls from France immediately before the phone was turned off – from his father presumably, we're still checking the number – but they weren't answered.'

'And what time, exactly, did Rhys's mobile go out of service?'

Jordan didn't need to check his notes this time.

'At pretty well exactly the same time as the three nines call came in for Amy.'

Jordan didn't say any more. He didn't need to. The minds of every officer crammed into that open plan office right now were running on much the same lines. Was that phone switched off intentionally by Rhys because he didn't want to be disturbed on his date night with Amy? Or was it more evidence of possible ill-intent on the part of a person or persons still unknown? The same ill-intent that had perhaps seen Amy rushed into hospital.

Across the room, the door to the open plan office opened and the duty sergeant appeared. Lara was about to tell him to come back after the briefing. Visits from the front desk usually meant an update on one of the various minor villains currently banged up in one of the custody cells and could keep.

But not this time. The duty sergeant had a young man at reception who was insisting on speaking to Lara personally. He handed her a note with her new visitor's details on it. Lara stared down at it, thrown for a moment, then headed for the door.

Thirty seconds later, Lara was down in the reception area herself, and was face to face with Rhys McGuire.

CHAPTER
NINETEEN

'I DON'T UNDERSTAND.'

Lara stared at the wracked figure on the other side of the interview desk.

'This doesn't make sense.'

Rhys was just under six feet tall with cascading, dark, curly hair covering his neck and ears. His features were almost doll-like in their symmetry, but right now those features were distorted in bewilderment and grief. Bewilderment at the news his girlfriend was pregnant. Grief at what had happened to her.

Lara cut in, gently, as a floundering Rhys tailed off. She'd already sent a message to the unit to stop the search for Rhys, meaning they'd saved themselves one potential waste of police time. If Rhys kept on with his incoherent rantings, they'd just plunge headlong into another.

'Where were you last night, Rhys? Start with that, then we can work back.'

The young boy took a deep breath, still struggling to control himself. Lara prompted him. They knew this anyway.

'You were in Sandown, yes? You'd booked a room at the Premier Inn?'

Lara knew the hotel. It was a small, unfussy, modern establishment just across the road from the beach. Mairead had already checked the booking with the receptionist who confirmed that a double room had been booked for a single night in his name.

Rhys nodded.

'For you and Amy?'

Rhys hesitated, then nodded again. Previously, that had all been a closely guarded secret, shared only by Rhys and his girlfriend. Not even Amy's best friend, Donna, knew where they were intending to spend the night. Now, all issues of secrecy were well and truly out of the window.

'We'd planned it for days. Dad was going to be away. Donna said she'd cover for Amy. It wasn't the first time we'd...'

Rhys hesitated once more.

'...but it was the first time we'd have spent the whole night somewhere. It was going to be special.'

Then he broke off, shaking his head.

'I nearly called it off. I should have done. Maybe if I had...'

The wracked young boy broke off again. Lara leant closer over the interview desk.

'Why did you nearly call it off? What happened?'

He looked up at her. Behind him, the door opened, and Mairead slipped inside, placing a note in front of Lara, before leaving again. Rhys barely seemed to see her.

Rhys had made a gruesome discovery the previous evening, as he next told Lara. His beloved pet, cat, Bella, had dragged itself back inside the hallway from outside, bleeding profusely, the aftermath of some sort of accident, or maybe an encounter with some other much larger animal out in the garden, Rhys didn't know. All he did know was that the cat had then died in his arms.

Lara made a mental note to contact forensics to downgrade the inquiry into the blood discovered in the McGuire hallway. Another potential waste of police resources averted.

'And where's your cat now, Rhys?'

'I put her in a bag. She's in one of the outhouses. The vets do a pet cremation service and they said they could pick her up if we wanted. I was waiting for Dad to come back to see what he wanted to do.'

Rhys closed his eyes, involuntary images dancing before them.

'I haven't got round to cleaning up the hall yet. I couldn't face it.'

'You had other things on your mind anyway? Your date with Amy?'

Rhys opened his eyes again.

'She didn't show. We'd both agreed to turn off our mobiles so we weren't disturbed, but she could have got a message to me through reception, she had the number, so did I. We'd made sure of it in case there was a last-minute problem, her mum finding out she wasn't at Donna's or whatever.'

He took a deep breath.

'I waited, but then I fell asleep. When I woke up, I went round to Amy's, but a neighbour told me she was in hospital. So, I went there, but the nurse outside her room wouldn't let me in, she just said I had to contact the investigating officer.'

Rhys looked up at Lara.

'Then they gave me your name.'

Rhys stared past her, unseeing, confusion and bewilderment etched into every inch of his face.

CHAPTER
TWENTY

A SHORT TIME LATER, and courtesy of that note delivered from Mairead notifying her of yet another shout, Lara joined Jordan in the garden of an expensively appointed house not far from Rhys's own family home. A family liaison officer was already inside, providing what comfort and support she could to the family of a much-loved, and now murdered, grandfather called Edward Mattiss.

Moving among the debris of his grandchild's now-abandoned birthday party, passing the cake, untouched and destined to stay that way, the trestle tables still decorated with balloons and banners, the pool with its inflatable toys still floating on its still-gently lapping surface, the two officers headed for a shed at the bottom of the garden where the gruesome discovery had been made.

Scenes of crime tape were already stretched around it. The unit's regular pathologist, Maisa Abdulkader, was in attendance, conducting her preliminary investigation of the body found inside. As ever, the no-nonsense pathologist didn't waste any time.

'The cause of death is pretty obvious already. And the murder weapon is still here too.'

Maisa indicated a large garden spade, lying by the body, blood staining the metal blade and running partly up the wooden handle.

'The skull's demonstrating a hairline fracture of the right temporal lobe, corresponding to the impact with the blade.'

Maisa crouched next to the victim.

'There's evidence of a second blow, too, which has generated another depressed cranial fracture. I'll give you a more detailed report after I get him back, but my best guess at the moment is that this blow was administered to the right of his skull while he was lying on the floor with the left side against the wooden floor.'

'But by that time, he was already dead?'

Maisa nodded.

'But his attacker wouldn't necessarily have known that. Maybe they panicked and just lashed out again.'

Lara looked out of the window onto the manicured lawn, the detritus from the birthday party still littering the green baize-like carpet of grass. She'd already noticed that while the shed offered a good view of the house and garden, it was very difficult for anyone in that house or out in that garden to see inside. Whether that was simply due to the sun that was still shining directly overhead, or whether the shed was fitted with some special sort of reflective glass, was something they'd have to check on.

Lara's eyes swept round the shed itself which seemed to be just another typical male retreat. Garden implements were stacked in the corner by the door – presumably the bloodied spade used to be there, too – but the rest of the space was taken up by a couple of deckchairs stacked against the wall, a TV on a stand with papers and magazines piled neatly underneath. A place to relax, read a book, and perhaps sip a glass of wine on a summer evening.

Lara looked out towards the site of the abandoned party again. This could be the work of an opportunist thief of course, a thief who'd been taking shelter in the shed, biding their time till all the guests were assembled at the far end of the garden. Then he or she would be free to make their unobserved way up to what was obviously going to be an unattended house for at least the next hour or so as games were played, as kids were entertained and as a celebrating child basked in the strains of *Happy Birthday*.

Lara watched Maisa, now supervising the transfer of the murder victim's body into an HRP. In police television shows and films, they were called body bags, but the actual and correct term was a Human Remains Pouch. Unlike most of the ones Lara had seen on the small and big screens, which seemed to have been made of heavy, black rubber, these were white plastic with webbing-type handles, decorated with a black plastic zip. And, as with everything she did, Maisa was taking enormous pains with the transfer. Going the extra mile in fact, but that had always been the story of her life.

Maisa had first come to the UK as a refugee from Damascus, although for a time it seemed unlikely that she and her family would get much further than a refugee camp in Kanjiza. At which point, and in a now-notorious media incident, her elder brother had taken matters into his own hands. Spotting a UK news crew making a live broadcast he'd approached them, seemingly keen to add his testimony to that of the other refugees they'd amassed so far. Then, with the cameras rolling, he'd produced a knife and had proceeded to calmly and clinically slit his throat in protest at the inhumane hiatus he felt he and his family were currently being forced to endure.

One day later, and with press and TV interest in this family now at fever pitch, Maisa, her mother and the rest of her siblings landed in Gatwick as the border agency fast-tracked their case. Three years on and Maisa began her studies as a doctor. Five years later she graduated, dedicating her new qualification and new life to the brother whose sacrifice had made it possible, and promising to make every moment in every investigation she encountered count.

It was one of the reasons Lara always offered up a silent prayer that this particular pathologist would attend any crime involving her home unit. It wasn't just her work ethic and dedication. Having both known cruel beginnings, she'd always felt that she and Maisa shared something of a common crusade.

Lara moved to her side to allow the body, now in its HRP, to be taken out of the shed. Then she paused as she spotted a small thin brochure amongst the pile of papers and magazines stacked under the TV. Something about it looked strangely familiar and Lara crossed the floor, retrieved it. Then the world seemed to still slightly, and the wind outside seemed to drop. Even the water in the pool seemed to turn glass-like.

For the second time in as many days, Lara looked at an estate agent's flyer advertising the sale of a now-ruined property called Kenwood.

CHAPTER
TWENTY-ONE

AARON WAS ALONE in his room.

He knew his parents would probably assume he'd just gone to ground, shutting himself off from a world that had suddenly turned alien for them all. Privately, they probably both wished they could do exactly the same.

But this wasn't any kind of retreat. In a sense, it was the opposite. Up there, in his small room at the back of the house, this was the only place he could try and re-connect with his sister, but it still wasn't working. Ever since the accident – and he was acutely aware right now that everything seemed to be divided into before and after Amy's accident – he was still experiencing that strange dislocation. Initially, he'd put it down to the effect of her injuries, but as the hours and days ticked by, he was becoming convinced it was more than that. It was almost as if something, or someone, was keeping him from her.

Then, from downstairs, he heard the ring on the bell and suddenly, and for the first time since the accident, he actually sensed her again. It was brief, and it wasn't the direct sort of contact they'd shared before, but for that moment, she was back again.

Aaron crept to the top of the stairs and listened to the voices sounding down in the kitchen. Visitors weren't unusual right now. Plenty of their parents' friends and neighbours had called in the last couple of days to see if there was any news or if they needed anything. This wasn't a friend or a neighbour though.

His mum had told him their form teacher, Mr Taylor, would be calling and had left it up to him as to whether he wanted to come down. Aaron hadn't responded one way or the other and she hadn't pushed him. Now he was here, Aaron crept to a vantage point just outside his bedroom door and perched on the one step of the stairs he knew wouldn't creak and give him away.

His mum and dad had called Mr Taylor over to see if he could shed any light on what had happened. They already knew from the police that neither Rhys nor Donna had any idea why she might have been out on that road that night, particularly as she was supposed to be meeting up with her boyfriend miles away. Neither Rhys nor Donna had any idea she was pregnant either. Rhys had freely admitted they'd been sleeping together but had insisted that they'd always been careful.

So, his mum and dad were spreading the net wider. Now they were trying the school, most particularly Aaron and Amy's form teacher, Mr Taylor. Had he seen anything, heard anything, picked up anything, had she even said anything to him while she'd been in his class?

Much of what Mr Taylor had to say, Aaron knew already. He was aware himself that there'd been a few unusual absences lately, time that Amy had spent away from school that their parents didn't know about. Where she went, even Aaron had no idea. But it wasn't what Mr Taylor had to say he wanted to listen to anyway.

It was him. His voice. His tone.

Because in the last day or so, Aaron had begun to wonder about something. Since his sister's accident, a line from a story he'd once read in class – in Mr Taylor's class, in fact – had been floating through his mind. The story was by Edgar Allen Poe, and it was about the best place to hide something. Aaron couldn't remember the title of the story. But often, so that same story made clear, the very best place to hide was in plain sight.

Aaron continued to listen to the honeyed tones of Mr Taylor as he assured his distraught mum and dad that he'd ask around, take soundings, see if any of the other pupils in the class could shed any light on the situation, and that of course he'd come straight back to them if he discovered anything. And if there was anything else he could do in the meantime, anything at all, then they knew that all they had to do was ask.

And all the time he listened, Aaron was wondering whether it was possible to do a paternity test on a baby that hadn't yet been born.

CHAPTER
TWENTY-TWO

PARKHURST HAD HOSTED many famous prisoners over the years.

The Krays, Reggie and Ronnie, had been held there at one time, as had their fiercest rivals in the London gangland wars of the 1960s, the Richardsons. The so-called Yorkshire Ripper, Peter Sutcliffe, had also been incarcerated there, as had another venal outlier from the north of England, the Moors murderer, Ian Brady. It was also the site of a spy swop when two Soviet agents, Peter, and Helen Kroger, had been incarcerated there before they'd been exchanged for two British counterparts, and it was where all Jewish prisoners on the island had been held at one time, too, as it boasted a synagogue. It had never witnessed an actual execution – at least, not by the state in the form of a judicial hanging, although many lives had been ended there in fights between prisoners – but corporal punishment was regularly employed by the warders up to the 1950s.

A version of that same brutal punishment had been employed the previous evening when a prisoner due to give evidence about an island pimp had been visited by another inmate carrying a plastic container with no lid. Inside was the fabled concoction of boiling water and sugar. The combination – colloquially known as kettling – guaranteed the victim lacerating and long-lasting injuries from the subsequent burns, as well as years of skin grafts. The victim in question just had the presence of mind to shield his face with his arm which still received second degree burns, but at least spared him anything worse. But as a respite, it was to be short-lived. His attacker then punched the prisoner twice in the face before breaking his eye socket with his knee as he fell to the floor.

Jordan was there on two counts. First, he had to see if the prisoner in question still wanted to give his evidence in the upcoming trial. Second, to check on progress in identifying his attacker.

One look at the prisoner's smashed face and bandaged right arm gave Jordan his first answer. The wall of silence from the rest of the prisoners, the victim included, settled the second equally quickly. Jordan could have told Conran all this before he'd even left the Major Crime Unit that morning, but his senior officer had insisted he make sure, for the sake of protocol if nothing else. Jordan was only too aware that Lara would have told him to fuck the protocol and concentrate on some more immediately fruitful lines of inquiry, perhaps by picking up the pimp in question and making his life hell until he squealed. However, on this occasion, Lara didn't mind, because it gave her the opportunity to talk to Jordan away from the unit.

'Kenwood?'

Jordan stared at her, the name coming from way out of left-field. He hadn't heard it for over a year now. Like Lara, he'd had little wish to hear it again.

Swiftly, Lara updated him on the brochure she'd found in Edward Mattiss's garden shed. Then she opened her phone and showed him a screenshot of their young accident victim as she hovered on the driveway leading down to the same location. She didn't need to say anything else. Jordan was already well ahead of her.

'You think this may have something to do with Esther?'

Lara tensed; she couldn't help herself. It was difficult enough talking about Kenwood. Her stepsister, Esther, was even trickier territory. Both Lara and Jordan had suffered at her hands and in both their cases, that suffering had almost been terminal.

Lara hunched closer.

'Her tactic was simple before, we know that. She wanted to take revenge on me. Why, only she really knows. But we do know she used others to get at me, so if this is anything to do with her, has that revenge kick shifted? Her father suffered just as much as my mother in that place. Does she now have Kenwood in her sights, is she maybe targeting the people who worked there, or have some sort of connection to the place?'

Jordan eyed her, looking dubious.

'So, Edward Mattiss, the birthday party victim? Apart from that sales brochure you found, did he have any connection to the place?'

'If he did, you know how these things work as well as I do, that would have been airbrushed out of his past long ago.'

'And he was an accountant, right? A successful one, too, by the look of that house.'

Jordan rolled on.

'So, he could have just been looking for a new investment and, on paper at least, Kenwood is definitely that, especially if a developer decides to raze the place to the ground and start again.'

Jordan hunched closer.

'And so far as Amy's concerned, maybe that was just where she and Rhys used to meet. We already know they had a habit of sneaking off together to out of the way places where they were unlikely to be seen, that could have been one of them. A ruined old house could come across as quite romantic to two teens who didn't know anything about its history.'

Lara could almost feel the knots in her stomach begin to unwind. It was one of the reasons she prized these sorts of inquests with her junior officer. Time and again, over the years they'd worked together, one of other of them would air what could be theories or possibilities. Until one brought the other back down to earth with a healthy dose of debunking common sense.

Then Jordan stopped as he received a text. Lara broke in, cautious, as a suddenly troubled Jordan checked it out.

'Everything OK?'

He hesitated, then looked up at her, nodded back, quick.

'Fine.'

Then Jordan stood.

'Is that it? Still got the paperwork on that kettling to do for Conran.'

Lara nodded, and Jordan headed away. But she watched him all the way. The two of them working so closely together had indeed been beneficial to many an investigation over the years, but it had also given each of them a keen insight into the other as well. And Lara knew that despite his denial, something was wrong right now.

Then Lara looked back at that estate agent's brochure for Kenwood. Then she looked at the image on her phone of Amy standing at the entrance to the very same spot. And she also still felt that despite Jordan's healthy injection of debunking common sense, something about this was wrong, too.

CHAPTER
TWENTY-THREE

RHYS WAS in turmoil and Amy's parents weren't exactly helping. Her hostile dad had pretty well cut him dead when he'd tried talking to him, although Amy's mum had been a little more forthcoming. She'd updated him to some limited extent at least on Amy's current condition and promised to keep him informed if there were any developments.

Rhys had just stared at her. Those were the actual words she used. *Informed. Developments.* As if they were discussing some object, not her daughter, his girlfriend.

Even in the depth of his own distress, Rhys could hear the heartbreak in her voice though. He knew she was a heartbeat away from giving away completely. And he also knew that she was clinging to – maybe hiding behind – those stock-sounding phrases because the alternative was to just give way and howl. Which was exactly what he felt like doing now, too.

At least Amy's mum and dad had each other, and they had Aaron. His dad was still away and wouldn't be back for another day, at least. Rhys could have called him, and he would have dropped everything and been there like a shot, Rhys knew that. But how did he even begin to explain all that had happened – and in a phone call – when he couldn't even take it in himself?

Amy was pregnant. He was still reeling from that revelation. And it had to be his child because he knew Amy. It simply wasn't credible that she'd cheated on him. And if she'd been attacked or assaulted by someone, she'd have told him that, too. He was equally convinced of that. So why hadn't she said she was carrying their child? And why hadn't she turned up in the hotel that night? And what was she doing miles away on that road?

So, now, Rhys was doing the only thing he could think of doing, despite Amy's mum telling him that there was no point, that Amy wouldn't even know he was there. Rhys travelled to the hospital. Once he'd explained who he was, a sympathetic nurse had told him he could look at Amy from an observation window for a few moments, but she really couldn't recommend an actual bedside visit just yet. Amy's condition was being monitored almost minute by minute – along with the condition of her unborn baby – and the last thing any of them needed was visitors getting in the way.

As he approached the observation window, Rhys steeled himself for the inevitably shocking sight he knew he was going to see. Amy had been a totally irresistible force of nature for as long as he'd known her, vibrant and crazy. But the Amy he'd be seeing now was going to be very different.

Rhys paused as he heard someone talking inside her room. One of Amy's doctors must be in with her right now, maybe with another nurse. But then he moved closer to the window, making sure he wasn't seen by anyone inside. He'd had precious little in the way of concrete information from her mum regarding Amy's actual condition, but he might learn more if he could hear what a doctor was saying.

Rhys inched closer. It was still just the one voice he could hear for now, which was strange, but maybe the doctor was dictating notes or something. And the voice was low, really low, so he had to strain his ears to hear anything at all. Then, as he picked out the odd word here and there, he paused, puzzled, because this didn't sound like any sort of medical update, and it wasn't just what was being said either. Whoever was speaking right now sounded broken.

Rhys leant his head closer to the wall, just down from the window. Whoever was in there seemed to be addressing Amy directly, telling her that they would sort things, that she didn't have to worry about a thing.

Rhys stared towards the window, still keeping himself hidden from view as the low voice continued from inside Amy's room, telling her that she just had to trust them and soon, very soon, everything would be OK.

From out in the corridor, Rhys heard the nurse approaching, calling out to a porter with an instruction about a patient that needed transporting from theatre. And now Rhys forgot all about watching through observation windows and treatments that must not be disturbed. Rhys strode towards Amy's door, opening it just as the nurse appeared, behind. He heard her call out to him as he moved inside the room. Then he stopped dead.

Amy was lying in bed before him, and she was every bit as much of a shocking sight as he'd feared. For a moment indeed, he couldn't actually see her beneath all the drips and tubes. But she was the only person he could see. He looked round as the now clearly panicked nurse appeared behind him. There was another door to the room directly ahead of him, so whoever had been in there with her, and whoever had been talking to her like that, must have exited that way.

Rhys kept looking round as the nurse – who was now looking anything but sympathetic – demanded that he leave and leave now. But he hardly heard her. Rhys had no idea who'd just been in there with Amy, he had no idea what they'd been talking about, and he had no idea where they'd gone.

But he knew one thing: that had been no doctor.

CHAPTER
TWENTY-FOUR

AT THE SAME time as Rhys was visiting Amy in the hospital, Lara was visiting her sister, Georgia.

Lara fully expected that Georgia's day would be following the same pattern as her previous day and countless others before it, and that Lara would shadow her as she moved round the main sitting room, balancing plates of microwaved food, before placing them down in front of largely uncomprehending souls who would stare at the day's offerings, blankly. Cottage pie or roast chicken was the usual daily choice with a vegetarian option of tofu.

Occasionally, some of those eyes betrayed some sort of tenuous grasp on what was happening, but as those same eyes looked around at their more or less comatose companions in their largely cheerless surroundings, they betrayed another uncomfortable truth. Maybe it would have been better had they not.

The care home had only been intended as a bed for the night for Georgia. It had been a stop gap, a strictly short-term arrangement. It hadn't even been envisaged that she would see the other usual inhabitants, let alone mix with the resident octogenarians and nonagenarians, as well as a couple of old ladies – but no men so far – who'd received the traditional good wishes from the King.

Then there'd been a delay processing Georgia's paperwork. The rehab clinic to which she'd been assigned following her latest suicide bid seemed to have no record of her impending admission. Her medical records had temporarily vanished somewhere in the system, too. So, and while everyone waited for officialdom to remedy the various omissions, and unobserved by the harassed social services worker charged with overseeing her admission, Georgia wandered through the home.

When the lunch gong sounded, another nod to the bygone age most of the residents also still inhabited, Georgia picked up a plate and followed one of the carers as they handed out food. No one stopped her; any sort of help was welcome. By the time the paperwork had finally been sorted out it was teatime and Georgia helped with that as well.

Strictly as an experiment, albeit an unofficial one, she was allowed to stay and help the next day, too. The activity was repetitive, and it was mechanical, and it seemed to be exactly what she needed back then. By the time that extra day had turned into a week and a week into a month, her stay in the care home had been made permanent. Strictly speaking she was neither resident nor staff, and it wasn't any sort of conventional rehabilitation either, but she seemed to have found meaning in a simple routine, and for now that was all that mattered.

Lara visited as often as she could. Those visits had increased in frequency after Esther had come into their lives all those months before. Georgia had seemed to connect back with the world to some limited degree as the discovery of their mother's body had at least laid that previous uncertainty to rest. Like Lara, Georgia had seemed to take comfort in the fact that they had not been abandoned.

Then she'd begun to sink again. The long walks she'd started taking with Lara stopped, and soon she was back to handing out plates of microwaved food. Lara didn't know why. Maybe, having looked out, for a brief time at least, on all the world had to offer outside the home, she'd decided she preferred the world inside it instead.

On the way over there, Lara had wrestled with her new suspicions. Should she tell her sister about the possible connection to Kenwood she'd uncovered in those two seemingly disparate recent cases? Should she rehearse her fears, however tenuous they may be, that Esther's hand might be behind them? Would that spur Georgia back to re-connecting once again or would it make her retreat even further? And even if there was no way of knowing how she'd react, didn't she owe it to her sister to warn her there was a possibility, however remote, that their former tormenter was back on the scene?

'Has she told you?'

A face swam before Lara's eyes as she was let inside, one of the white-suited staff. Lara still hadn't quite worked out the intricacies of the care home hierarchy, but she understood enough to know that a white suit denoted someone fairly high up the support chain.

Lara looked at Georgia as she now joined them, a tell-tale flush starting at the base of her sister's neck, the same flush she'd see years ago when a teacher in school commended her for her work.

'They want her down in the Grange tomorrow night, too.'

Lara stared at her, puzzled. The Grange was a sister home a few miles away, Lara knew that much. Why they wanted Georgia – and why tomorrow night – was a blank.

'Who knew? We certainly didn't.'

Georgia, that tell-tale flush now suffusing the whole of her neck, moved away with more plates of food, smiling all the while, as the white-suited care worker took out her mobile and showed Lara a video of Georgia taking part in a recent concert for some of the residents.

'The entertainments officer for the group signed her up on the spot. He's even found a course she can go on if she wants to take it further.'

Lara looked back at Georgia, a definite lightness in her step now as she navigated the desserts of tinned peaches and evaporated milk or ice cream and sorbet.

A few minutes later, Lara left the home, having made her decision. Georgia remained ignorant of all her new suspicions, with Lara not wanting to admit that part of her envied her sister her unaware state.

CHAPTER
TWENTY-FIVE

LARA WAS RIGHT; something was troubling Jordan. And, as ever these days, it was all to do with Coco.

Outwardly, in these last few months, she'd returned to being the daughter Jordan had always known. Warm, bright, a normal teenage girl who liked nothing better than going for long walks on the beach with a variety of dogs she'd adopt for the weekend, after working her usual volunteer shift at a local animal rescue centre. The dogs came in all shapes and sizes, but they all performed the same function which was simple therapy. Coco losing herself in uncomplicated relationships where previously hers had been anything but.

There was a dark side to Coco though, and it was a darkness that had almost totally eclipsed her at one point. Partly, and as Jordan was only too acutely aware, that was down to his and Edie's divorce, although even that cataclysmic event didn't threaten disaster at the start. When Jordan had moved out, Coco had initially moved out, too, the intention being that father and daughter would set up in a flat while Edie retained the old family home. But within six months, Coco had moved back in with her mum.

Later, Jordan would reflect that if he and Edie had split up a year earlier, everything would probably have been fine. A year later and they might have weathered the storm. It was sheer bad luck that it had all coincided with Coco's sudden transition into a nightmare teen, a transformation that seemed to Jordan to have happened virtually overnight.

And there'd been another transformation at work, too. Coco had metamorphosed equally suddenly from a gawky adolescent to a svelte young woman. At sixteen she could easily pass for ten years older and frequently did when she rocked up outside the island's many bars and clubs, particularly in some of the outfits she rocked up in back then, too. If she'd walked out of Jordan's flat like that she'd have been called back immediately. Edie, as Jordan had frequently and volubly complained to anyone who would listen, had probably loaned Coco her make-up.

Edie's relaxed attitude to just about everything was a character trait that he'd found irresistibly attractive at eighteen. It was a bit more difficult to take ten years later, when he'd come in from a shift at six in the morning to find a house party that wasn't even in sight of finishing, with drink, and drugs everywhere – and in the middle of it all a small girl who clearly hadn't been to bed. Even the fact that Coco had been afflicted with asthma from birth, and would have to rely on her ever-present inhaler for life, had never dissuaded Edie or her friends from shrouding the house in smoke from just about every substance Jordan could imagine and some he never would.

So far as Edie was concerned, life was for living and rules were there to be broken. No wonder Coco had left her straitlaced police officer dad and moved back in with her mum to start living a life that must have seemed, to a young teen, to be something close to paradise.

But it had all taken its toll. Since Edie's hospitalisation, Jordan had booked Coco therapy sessions, a chance for the young girl to talk to an independent counsellor about whatever might be concerning or worrying her. The sessions were privately funded and cost a small fortune, but it was a tiny price to pay.

The text and follow-up phone call he'd taken in Parkhurst had been from the counsellor. She'd returned his latest set of fees as Coco hadn't shown for the last five of their sessions, despite her telling Jordan that she had. Jordan had tried calling Coco herself only for his daughter to fly into a rage on the other end of the phone for daring to check up on her. Then she'd cut the call and turned off her phone. The afternoon had passed into the evening and still she hadn't been back in touch.

Jordan remained in his flat opposite the island's meat market, his mind running on that other recent disturbing incident now, too.

What had that overheard phone call been all about? What was so important – and so forbidden – that she was so insistent her dad must not find out about it?

And the more he worried away at it, and the longer he sat there, the closer Jordan was coming to crossing a forbidden Rubicon.

CHAPTER
TWENTY-SIX

LARA WAS BACK in Kenwood again, but not to continue any sort of investigation.

The last time she'd been there, she'd gained access to the house via a rotten window frame which had been leaning away from the brickwork. She'd put her hands behind it and pulled it away, sending up plumes of dust that momentarily choked her. Ignoring the wood beetles scurrying for cover at her feet, Lara had hopped up onto the sill, praying it wasn't as rotten as the frame it had attempted to support, and a moment later was inside. This time, she just walked in through one of the many access points offered to her by walls that had also crumbled to rubble in the last year or so.

She knew a little of what had happened to her mother in her time here, as letters exchanged between her mother and Finn – her childhood protector turned adult abuser – had lifted a lid on some of it at least. Through those shared extracts, Lara had journeyed with her again as she'd first arrived at this spot when it had masqueraded as a children's home taking in orphans and other displaced souls from disadvantaged backgrounds. It had a much darker history than that though, Now Lara looked out over an open piece of waste ground – a burial site for dozens of small bodies that had finally been removed in the previous year or so.

Lara looked round some more. The estate agent flyer had described the place as empty, but it was more accurately unfinished, like all hastily abandoned places. The tendrils of its past still clung to it, eerie and other-worldly, as if it was haunted by spirits yet to find their voice.

The first time Lara had been there, and in some desperate desire to connect to a mother she'd lost at an age when she could barely remember her, she'd torn a piece of wallpaper from a room that had once been a schoolroom, a room her mother must have been in at one time. Maybe she'd looked at that same piece of wallpaper from time to time, had maybe even touched it, too.

On returning home it was as if the evil that had infected the place had seeped somehow into that stray piece of paper as well. Every time Lara walked in, it drew her eye. Sometimes she'd just stand there, staring at it, unable to move. So, one morning she took it down from the shelf where she'd placed it and put it in a drawer, but the same thing still happened. Her eyes were still drawn to it, even though she couldn't see it. Somehow it was as if the twisted energy of that home – the residue, perhaps, of all its dreadful secrets – had attached itself to that one stray scrap of paper, and within another few days Lara had removed it from the drawer, taken it out into the small communal garden at the rear of her waterside apartment, and burnt it.

Ever since, Lara had become convinced that the same thing had to happen to Kenwood itself. It had to be destroyed completely. Its old stories still haunted it so strongly that there was no room for any new ones. The only thing that could be done now was to erase it completely, make new space for something untouched. If it remained as it was, then all any new owner would do, even after any restoration, would be to wake something up that had seeped even into a stray scrap of decades-old wallpaper.

Kenwood wasn't unique of course. Similar institutions had

been identified elsewhere in the UK and indeed all over the world. Some months before Lara had travelled to Scotland to stand before a collection of small, unassuming huts scattered across the countryside outside Pitlochry. Barely habitable now, as they had been when they were first constructed, they'd nevertheless housed a chilling social experiment designed to force members of another distinct community, of travellers this time, to assimilate into mainstream society by effectively killing off their culture. It was nothing less than eugenics and families who refused to give up their traditional way of life would have had their children taken into care.

A month later, Lara had travelled to Canada to stand before the sites of two old schools – St Joseph's Mission and Lejac – institutions dedicated to eradicating yet another ancient community. In this case the Canadian government had paid the Missionary Oblates of Mary Immaculate, a Roman Catholic order, to divorce indigenous native Indian children from their language, heritage and culture. The prevailing, and openly avowed, philosophy was to kill the Indian in the child. Beating and abuse were the tactics most commonly employed, and hundreds of small children died as a result.

Now she was standing on the site of a former home on her native island where a similar racial experiment had been conducted, in this case aimed at the equally ancient community that made the rivers and waterways their home, a community that had been home in turn, to Lara's own mother.

Lara looked out over what were now green fields, but she could still sense the evil that had seeped into the very soil. But she'd decided that this visit was to be the final time she allowed it to infect her. So far, she'd only confided her vague suspicions in Jordan, and they were vague, and they probably said far more about the way the place represented unfinished business for Lara, personally, rather than any sort of starting point for any professional investigation.

Jordan had been right, she'd decided. Edward Mattiss had

probably just seen a business opportunity. Amy Waite had just spotted a conveniently private place for a teenage love tryst. As for that note, that probably was just the work of some anonymous troll. She'd been right not to confide any of this to Georgia. And now it was time to put it away and put this place away, too.

Lara turned back, but then she stopped, as, on the very edge of her vision, she caught sight of something.

CHAPTER
TWENTY-SEVEN

IN PEGGY O'RIORDAN'S thirty years patrolling the unit's offices and corridors with her tea trolley, she'd acted as a much-loved and much-prized confidante and comforter to countless detectives and support staff as well as, on one never to be forgotten occasion, acting as midwife to a female DC, now retired. In that time, she'd looked out for everyone and had everyone's back, which was one of the main reasons she was much loved and much prized. She also had a no-nonsense knack of cutting straight to the heart of any matter of the moment, and she was about to do so again.

Hours earlier, Lara had stood looking out over that patch of ground in Kenwood. She'd been unsure at first whether, as well as inventing connections that may well not exist, she'd just hallucinated something, too. As Lara kept looking down, one small section of earth looked different from the rest.

Was this just a curious case of déjà vu? Over a year ago, Lara had stumbled across a differently coloured patch of earth on this same site that later revealed a buried metal box housing childhood keepsakes and letters, which had led her to the truth behind her mother's disappearance and her abduction by Finn. But this patch of ground was bigger.

This time, Lara played it by the book. Previously, as she'd scrabbled away at the unforgiving earth to uncover those childhood mementoes, she'd disregarded all she'd ever learnt about contaminating the scene of any potential crime. This time, Lara called it in. A short time later, a specialist team of scenes of crime officers, carefully excavated the patch of earth in question. Then Lara watched as they uncovered the recently buried body of an elderly male.

A swift, if careful, examination revealed that, like Amy, he also carried no identification. The cause of death was obvious enough, a large, jagged slash to the neck, severing the windpipe. There was evidence of other injuries, too, but the extent and nature of those injuries would have to wait for Maisa.

Half an hour later, Lara was back in the Major Crime Unit, her mind in a whirl. Mechanically, almost in automaton mode, she updated Conran on the new murder victim found at the site of the old children's home. To her senior officer's clear and obvious displeasure, she didn't say what she'd actually been doing there in the first place. There were other priorities right now, most particularly a total rethink on all she'd been debating just that short time before.

Susie, the estate agent, had been shown a photo of Edward Mattiss, provided by his grieving widow, and he had now been identified as the 'Mr Ferguson' who'd made the original enquiry about Kenwood. Now he'd been murdered.

Amy Waite had been spotted heading onto the old Kenwood site. Now she was fighting for her life in St Mary's.

Now, an elderly male – unidentified as yet – had been found buried in the grounds, having clearly been very recently murdered, too.

The conclusion was inescapable. All Lara's earlier fears were not groundless after all. A vendetta of some sort was being mounted. Who was behind it and why it was happening was still to be established, but, in the meantime, protection measures had to be put in place.

'We've found records for a handful of people who had some sort of connection to the place, although they were never formally employed there.'

Behind Mairead who was updating Lara, Peggy was handing around teas, coffees and pastries.

'We don't have current addresses or any other contact details for any of them, but they had all been interviewed by officers in the past. None of them admitted to anything but the most passing of associations, and all claimed they had no idea of the abuse that went on there. It's also true that none were ever charged, let alone convicted.'

Lara cut in.

'But they did all work there?'

Mairead nodded back.

'In different capacities. One worked the gardens, another did accounts for the place, but, yes.'

Lara took it up.

'So, these people need to be found, and they need to be warned at the very least.'

Then Peggy broke in.

'So, if they did have anything to do with all that happened to those poor children.. .'

Peggy didn't need to finish. Lara and Mairead were already struggling with the exact same thought. But Peggy, being Peggy, finished anyway.

'Then you're protecting abusers.'

Mairead mounted a feeble protest.

'What are we supposed to do? Turn a blind eye while a killer picks them off one by one?'

Mairead had her answer without Peggy saying another word. It was written all over her face. Yes, that was exactly what they should do.

Mairead turned away to chase up any more potential contacts as Peggy moved away, too, which was when Lara paused, puzzled for a moment. It was only a fleeting glimpse, and it only lasted a second or so. But as Mairead filed the names and contacts details of those Kenwood connections back into a folder, her sleeve rode up momentarily. And Lara could see quite clearly a red, and clearly new, angry scar on her arm. Mairead tensed immediately before tugging down her sleeve. The injury disappeared from view. Lara hesitated a moment longer but didn't say anything.

In any event, Jordan now approached, and a minute or so later, they were both standing by the water cooler on the corridor outside, their recent exchange at Parkhurst now very much back on Jordan's mind, a complete rethink on all that having now clearly taken place on his part, too.

'If what you said back there was right, then we already have a name in the frame, don't we?'

Lara hesitated. All avenues would be pursued as they would with all investigations. As always, they had to look beyond the obvious. But they did indeed have a name in the frame here.

Jordan nodded at her. 'I think we should get this out there.'

Lara looked at him.

'To the rest of the team, be upfront about it right from the start.'

For a moment, Lara caught something. Something behind Jordan's firm insistence that they had to be upfront and open. But, and as with Mairead's new and puzzling injury, there was no time to pursue that now.

'If you are right, and if this is down to Esther again, it wasn't just you who suffered at her hands.'

Jordan nodded at her again.

'Was it?'

CHAPTER
TWENTY-EIGHT

THE FIRST DAY hadn't been a problem. No one was taking any notice of him anyway.

His mum hadn't left Amy's side. His dad had returned home for changes of clothes, and for a selection of his sister's books and music so they could read to her and play her some of her favourite bands, hoping that some of that would somehow get through, but he'd gone back within minutes. It meant there'd been no one in the house to interrupt Aaron's rituals which meant, in turn, that Amy had not deteriorated further.

There hadn't been any spectacular recovery either, but she was still alive. So, Aaron continued to count, and to pace, and while he did all that, the world remained in balance. His sister remained stable at least.

The next development proved a trickier hurdle to navigate.

The idea had first taken seed on his last visit. He tried to time them with his dad returning home so there was just his mum by her bedside. She was sleeping there now, in a makeshift bed on the floor of her room as she wouldn't think about being away from her for even a single night. She couldn't bear the thought that her daughter might open her eyes to see strangers looking down at her in what must seem like the strangest of surroundings.

With Aaron by Amy's bedside, his mum could be persuaded to go and grab a coffee though or have a freshen up in one of the hospital bathrooms, or even go for a small walk outside and take in some much-needed fresh air. And, with just himself and Amy there, Aaron might just do it. He might just restore the connection.

But there'd still been nothing. Aaron would retreat into their private space, a space that had always been inhabited by just two souls, only to find one of those souls was absent. Amy still wasn't connecting, and they still weren't communicating.

It didn't help that on his last visit, Rhys had appeared, at virtually the same moment Mum had disappeared. He didn't say anything. Aaron was unsure if he even realised that he was there. He just took the seat that Aaron had mentally allotted himself and took the hand that Aaron was about to take, his sister's hand, and held it just as Aaron had meant to do.

Then Aaron had seen the drip. He watched as the nurses checked and replenished the flow. A cautious enquiry revealed that this was how Amy was being fed. Then he'd gone home and done some research.

He'd learnt that when feeding through the alimentary tract isn't possible – as it was manifestly not possible with Amy – nutrients may be given by intravenous infusion. This could be in addition to oral or enteral tube feeding. Or it could be the sole source of nutrition, total parenteral nutrition in fact, as it was with Amy. His research also revealed that while the nutrition itself would be specific to any particular patient, it would always contain a mixture of amino acids, glucose, lipids, electrolytes, trace elements and vitamins.

Aaron stared at his computer screen. A moment later, and courtesy of a few clicks on his keyboard, he'd begun to assemble everything he needed.

The delivery came swiftly, by special courier. He opened it, then spread it all out on his bed – a bag of sterile IV fluid, a 14-gauge catheter, a non-latex tourniquet, a pack of sterile disposable gloves and a pack of alcohol wipes. A short time later, having followed more on-screen instructions, he'd primed the IV tube. Then, and using the sterile, disposable gloves, he'd picked out one of his veins.

Then he heard the door open downstairs and his returning dad called out to him. Five minutes later he was downstairs and staring in horror at two large takeaway pizzas. In a belated effort to impose some sort of normality on a house that didn't feel as it ever could be normal again, his dad had decided that they should have a meal together.

Aaron stared at the food in front of him, and as his distracted dad urged him to eat, he felt his stomach constrict. One mouthful, just one and he knew the fragile connection he was attempting to re-establish would be gone.

Then the house phone rang. His dad sprung up instantly to take the call, but it hadn't been the hospital as he'd feared, but his brother, Aaron's Uncle, checking for news. His dad had taken the call into their small sitting room, his pizza forgotten and Aaron – all the while keeping his ears open for any sound of him returning – had taken the contents of his plate into the kitchen where he tipped it into the bin.

His dad returned a short time later to see that Aaron at least had managed to eat that evening. Meanwhile, Aaron himself was back in his bedroom staring at the IV tube again.

But the moment had gone. Maybe, when it came to it, this was always going to happen, but he just couldn't do it. He couldn't apply the tourniquet, he couldn't pop out his vein, and he couldn't insert the needle. Aaron felt tears prick his eyes. This was supposed to be the moment that they would connect, that Amy would swim through the ether to him, so he could ask questions, could find out what was happening here, and why.

But he simply couldn't do it. He couldn't plunge that needle into his vein and so the connection remained lost.

CHAPTER
TWENTY-NINE

LARA SCHEDULED the briefing for ten the following morning. Plenty enough time for everyone in the building to get up to speed on the hundred-and-one investigations they all seemed to be dealing with at any one time: negotiating the obligatory liaisons with the CPS, receiving updates from the island's two prisons, sharing outrage at the latest inexplicably lenient sentence – or worse, outright acquittal – handed down from the local courts. The usual day-to-day routine in any Major Crime Unit in fact.

No one knew what this latest briefing was about. No one was aware it was less of a conventional briefing and more of a personal statement, until an uncharacteristically hesitant Lara stood up, and told everyone that she needed to have a few words.

Swiftly, she ran through the different strands of what had become the Amy investigation.

She recapped the accident involving Amy on that coast road that may not have been an accident at all and the sighting of her at the entrance to the old Kenwood.

She shared with the unit the connection to Kenwood that

she'd discovered in the murder of Edward Mattiss at his grandson's birthday party.

Lara also updated the unit on the latest body to be discovered on the Kenwood site. That body still hadn't yet been identified but was currently the subject of a postmortem, after which they hoped to know more.

What they did already know was that all these different events and incidents had some connection to that former home. And, with everyone in the room now staring at her, she took a deep breath.

'We can't rule out the possibility that this is something to do with my stepsister, Esther. As you all know, and as some of you here know very well, her previous target was me.'

Lara looked round the room, taking in Mairead and Jordan in particular.

'But others were caught up in all that, too. And if this is anything to do with Esther, if this is part of some new vendetta on her part then the one thing the last one taught us is that she doesn't discriminate. She doesn't care who else gets caught up in it all. And if she's moved on to targeting anyone with a connection, lingering or otherwise, to Kenwood, then she won't care who gets in the way.'

Across the room, Lara could see that Jordan was reliving his own ordeal at Esther's hands. Memories of his family's incarceration in a disused sluice room that so very nearly became a watery grave still haunted him. And its ongoing physical effects were still being even more acutely felt by the still-hospitalised Edie, of course.

Next to him, Lara could also see Mairead's own demons from that time playing behind her eyes. She hadn't suffered the extended imprisonment endured by Jordan, but she had her own to wrestle with in the shape of a rescue mission that had so nearly turned her from rescuer to victim as she, too, faced her death by drowning. Like Jordan, she knew only too well how uncaring Esther could be when it came to collateral damage.

Lara's eyes swept around the room again.

'So, if anyone wants to be excused from this investigation, then just say. This connection's still only tenuous at this stage, but we nearly lost two officers on this watch before at her hands, and I don't want anyone here going into this unaware of that.'

All around the room, all eyes – including those of Jordan and Mairead – met hers. No one spoke, but no one needed to. Not one pair of eyes looked away which told Lara all she needed to know.

Then a voice did sound, and it came from the door behind her.

'DI Arden.'

Lara turned to see Conran eyeing her from the corridor outside the open plan office once again. He inclined his head in a curt gesture back to his own office, then strode back there.

'How long, exactly, have you known about this?'

Lara stood before Conran in his private office. She hadn't been asked to sit down and she strongly suspected she wasn't going to be either.

'I don't know anything. At this stage this is just a possibility that's all.'

'OK, how long have you been entertaining this possibility? When, exactly, did it float into your head?'

Lara stared at Conran who was staring back at her in turn from the opposite side of his immaculately arranged desk. She'd updated her senior officer on that morning's briefing as a matter of courtesy. He hadn't objected which she'd taken as permission for it to go ahead. Strictly speaking, she didn't need that permission but if he felt there were operational reasons for not sharing it with the rest of the team, then he'd had the chance to air them. He'd stayed silent then, but he wasn't silent now. Conran's interrogation had begun the moment he led her back into her office and was showing no sign of letting up.

Lara hesitated a moment. What could she say? She'd hadn't pinpointed exactly the moment herself.

Was it when she'd first received that anonymous letter, that strange part-confessional note detailing some of the more extreme punishments meted out to children – her own mother among them – in Kenwood?

Was it seeing that CCTV image of their young accident victim, Amy, about to walk down its long drive?

Was it the discovery of the estate agent's sales brochure in Edward Mattiss's garden shed?

Or did it all somehow slot together with the discovery of that recently buried body in Kenwood itself?

Or did she need no stray triggers? Was the simple truth that she was forever holding herself in some state of continual readiness, just waiting for the moment when Esther might strike again?

'I asked you a question, DI Arden.'

Lara hit back, hard.

'When? I don't know. A dozen thoughts float through my head just about every hour of every day, dozens of possibilities at the same time. What are you asking, that I come to you, knock on your door every time?'

'Did you do that with anyone else in this unit?'

'Did I do what?'

'Rehearse possibilities? Share stray thoughts?'

An unsettling suspicion settled on Lara because all she could see now was Jordan and their exchange in Parkhurst. Did Conran know about that? Had Jordan told him? But why?

'Because it wouldn't be the first time, would it?'

Lara stared at him again. What was he talking about?

'And it's caused friction in the past, from what I understand. A DI keeping things from her DCI, going out on a limb, pursuing independent investigations, not updating her senior officers on her whereabouts at key stages of an ongoing inquiry.'

Now Lara knew what this was all about. Conran was referencing her own solo trek out to Kenwood all those months before, for what turned out to be her showdown with a stepsister she didn't even know existed till then.

'And it not only caused friction, it led directly, as you yourself has just said, to at least two members of this unit being placed in positions of considerable personal danger.'

Conran nodded at her.

'I understand DCI Monroe had cause on more than one occasion to remind you of the importance of the correct procedures. Take this as another. And from now on, whatever stray thought you might have connected to any ongoing investigation, whatever possibility you may entertain, however briefly, I want to know about it. And I don't mean in a last-minute update immediately prior to the briefing of my team, I want to know about it upfront, well in advance and then I'll decide, as your senior officer, if there's need for any sort of more general update at all.'

Lara didn't reply. She didn't need to. Conran was perfectly at liberty to remind her of what he saw as her obligations as a member of what was, indeed, his team, with Paula, her previous DCI, still on her period of extended leave.

But Lara was perfectly at liberty, too. She could take on board all Conran was saying and act on it. Mend her ways, as he, no doubt, would put it. But would she? Her ongoing silence told an ever more frustrated-looking Conran all he needed to know right now.

He really shouldn't hold his breath.

CHAPTER
THIRTY

A SHORT TIME LATER, Lara stood, once again, before her floor-to-ceiling window looking down on the water.

A small collection of yachts was now tacking up and down the Solent, some deep-sea fishing boats on the horizon heading for open water, as well as a few water-skiers pirouetting close to shore.

Lara stared down at the water skiers for a moment, something about the constant twists and turns they were taking right now resonating. The Amy Waite investigation might only be a couple of days old, but she was already feeling as if she was being twisted inside out by it, too.

Then Lara turned away from the window and looked across at a small table. She didn't know if this was therapy or torture – a welcome chance to think about something else –or whether it was twisting the knife in what had always been the most painful of wounds.

Then, putting that out of her mind just as she had the last time, she crossed to more of her late mother's notes and let her fingers guide her, picking up one at random from all the entries on offer.

CHAPTER
THIRTY-ONE
ESTHER – LARA'S MOTHER

AT HALF PAST EIGHT, *the window in the next room smashed in. One minute later, the ceiling collapsed.*

We'd reached the ferry terminal an hour before, but it was obvious the moment we arrived that there were going to be no sailings that evening. The waves were mountainous, the spray as they hit the moored ferries and harbour walls blinding. A ferry worker, struggling to tie down a small collection of deck furniture yelled at us to go home where it was safe. We looked at each other as he turned away. Little did he know.

We found the house ten minutes later. It didn't look as if anyone had lived there for months. The room at the front had lost one of its windows where a metal bin had smashed through it, shattering the pane, spraying slivers of glass everywhere. All we had to do was clear the largest, jagged slivers and climb inside.

Five minutes later, another front window blew in, too, as a branch from a fallen tree across the road smashed into it, picked up by a wind that had suddenly roared to gale force. At the same time, now huddled together in one of the rear rooms overlooking a small garden, we watched, fascinated, as another large tree started to bend.

'It's OK, that's what they do, they bend, that's why they don't break.'

Then I stopped. The tree was now low to the ground, the branches scoring deep gashes in the grass. Then something emerged on the other side of the tree, a large snake-like tendril that started waving in the wind.

'It's one of its roots.'

I just had to time to gasp it out when there was a great moan, as if the tree had suddenly found its voice. The next moment, it crashed down onto its side, more exposed roots reaching skyward, almost dancing as the storm swirled around them.

And we couldn't help it.

All of a sudden, we looked at each other and started to laugh.

We stayed there for the rest of the night, only falling asleep in the early hours. The wind had started to die down by then. Just before sleep claimed me, I thought I heard it start up again, but the next thing I knew light was poking in through the window.

We looked outside, awake in an instant. Everything was still again, and we charged out into the garden. All around, through gaps in the fence, we could see cars with smashed windscreens where objects hurled around in the storm had crashed into them as well as roof tiles littering the streets, at least two trampolines blown over, one poking out from the roof of a greenhouse, rubbish from upturned bins everywhere.

But all we wanted to see was the tree.

We clambered over it for the rest of the morning. Then we went back into the house, searched through drawers and found a knife. Then we went back out again and carved our initials into the fallen trunk.

Then a voice broke in on us through one of the gaps in the nearby fence. A woman stood there. She didn't ask what we were doing, she just wanted to know if we were all right. We didn't reply, we didn't need to, one look at our animated faces told her all she needed to know. She shook her head. Weren't we frightened? A storm like that should have been enough to put the fear of God into even the bravest of souls, let alone two young kids.

We looked at each other as she walked back to her house, closing the door behind her. She didn't understand, how could she? We'd lived with it all our lives: the certain knowledge that at any moment everything you'd ever known could be turned upside down.

The woman from next door obviously thought that what had happened last night had been extraordinary, but we knew it was anything but.

CHAPTER
THIRTY-TWO

LESS THAN FIVE minutes after reading the latest set of her mother's old case notes, Lara was in her Cooper driving along the coast road to Ryde.

She'd passed that very house many times, she was sure she had. There was no actual address in the case notes, but Lara could remember seeing a house with a fallen tree in the garden just a stone's throw from the ferry terminal. And the minute that memory returned, she knew she had to get into that garden and touch the tree her mother had touched, maybe even walk on it just as she'd walked on it all those years before.

Lara pulled up outside a small property on the road above the terminal. There were no lights shining from inside, so maybe the place was empty, or the householders were out. As a precaution, she rang the bell, but no one came to greet her. Moving round the side, she walked into a garden from where she could see the final ferry of the evening beginning to inch its way out of the harbour to complete the short hop across to the mainland. But Lara wasn't looking at that. She was looking at a stricken tree, lying in what looked like the very centre of the garden.

Small steps had been cut into the trunk, presumably to allow small children to climb up onto it. The bark was covered in moss which was covered in turn with something else – a whole array of initials, a scrawled record perhaps of all the children who had played there.

Lara searched among them eagerly. Were her mum's initials still there, or had the intervening years weathered them away? Lara moved round the trunk, checking every angle, brushing off leaves, scraping away moss. For a few moments, she didn't think that childhood memento had survived or maybe it had just been obliterated by successive generations, but then, suddenly, she saw it.

Lara reached out, placed her fingers on a single initial.

'E'

As she did so, she felt something begin to course through her. With a jolt she realised it was the first time in more than two decades that she'd had any sort of physical contact with her lost mother, had touched something she knew for a fact that her mother had touched herself.

Then Lara stopped. Because there wasn't just her mother's initial carved there. Side by side with her mother's, and alongside the 'E', she could now see a 'J', too. That initial was weathered to the same degree as her mother's, so it seemed to have been carved at the same time and, on inspecting the two sets of initials closer, she could see that someone had drawn a crude heart-shaped symbol around them, enclosing them both inside.

Lara stared at the two initials for a long moment. Her mum hadn't been alone throughout that storm of course. She'd constantly referred to someone else being there. They seemed to have been close, too, if those two interlocking sets of initials were anything to go by, and Lara was heartened by the possibility that her mum might have found a good friend. She could even have been Jade from the last extract she'd read.

Lara reached out and touched the 'J', too.

Then something else happened.

Then a very different feeling began to creep over her.

PART THREE

PART THREE

CHAPTER
THIRTY-THREE

IT WAS UNFORGIVABLE, and Jordan knew it. But there weren't just a teenage girl's feelings to consider here, and that justified everything he was doing, or so he kept telling himself. This was in his daughter's long-term interests.

He still grew dry-mouthed as he imagined Coco's reaction if she found the spy device Jordan had just secreted in her bag though.

The device itself was tiny. It wasn't completely undetectable to the naked eye, but you really had to be looking hard to find it. Despite its size, it housed a hidden Sony CCD camera with a wide-angle lens, a built-in long-life battery, and boasted three different recording modes, namely motion detection, scheduled or continuous recording – and without a spy hole which puzzled Jordan mightily at the start. How did the thing actually record? The answer was simple, via a standard board lens which worked like the tinted windows on some of the pimped up Beemers patrolling the capital's streets. You can see out, but no one can see in.

It had been in place for just over a day now and the first time Coco had walked out of the house with the hidden bug in her bag, everything had been innocuous enough. Jordan had tracked her as she visited a couple of local shops, before having coffee with a school friend. The conversation had been innocuous enough, too, mainly worried updates on what was happening with Amy.

Then, after leaving her friend, making the excuse that she had to go home to feed her latest rescue pup, Coco had doubled back on herself and caught a bus. Alighting some twenty or so minutes later, Coco walked down onto a secluded cove. She dumped her bag on an outcrop of rock and walked away.

But just before she moved out of range of the bug, Jordan stilled as he saw a figure rise from behind some rocks and approach her.

CHAPTER
THIRTY-FOUR

'WHAT HAVE WE GOT?'

The question died on Lara's lips as a pair of ice green eyes, as opposed to the much warmer blue eyes she was used to, looked up from the inspection table, and studied her.

Maisa's assistant – one familiar face around the body lying on that inspection table at least – stepped in, nervously, making the introductions.

'DI Arden, Doctor Sarah Ryan.'

Lara nodded, instinctively, but the owner of the ice green eyes didn't nod back.

'To answer your question, we have a dead body, DI Arden.'

Lara's heart sank. The last thing she needed after her last exchange with Conran was another buttoned-up, smart-arse.

Lara smiled back, quick, thin.

'None of us got too much in the way of conversation out of him when we lifted him out of that shallow grave, so we guessed he might be. I was wondering more about time of death, what caused it and how long he'd been down there.'

'The cause of death is pretty clear.'

The new pathologist indicated the jagged slash to the neck, framed by dried, crusted blood, that Lara had already seen.

'A single knife wound to the throat. Time of death and how long he'd been down there, I'm still working on.'

'Any idea when you might know.'

'Any idea when you might arrest the murderer?'

Lara stuck to her guns.

'A professional approximation will do.'

The owner of the ice green eyes stuck to hers.

'Same question.'

She didn't elaborate. Dr Sarah Ryan obviously didn't offer approximations. Which didn't dissuade Lara from trying again.

'We'll have a lot more chance of arresting a murderer if we have as much information as quickly as is reasonably possible.'

'And you'll have a lot less chance of arresting the perpetrator if I give you information that later turns out to be wrong.'

Lara was about to hit back, and harder again, but then she paused as she spotted something on the corpse she hadn't seen till then.

'What's that?'

Lara moved closer. Now the cadaver was spread out on the table, still angry-looking dark weals were clearly visible on both wrists. Dr Ryan followed her look, pausing now too. They seemed to have struck her as curious too.

'Those injuries were inflicted before death. If you really are pushing me into guesswork, then I'd say they were caused by the victim being trussed by his wrists with a strong rope, probably to stop him struggling before his throat was cut.'

The pathologist lifted one of the victim's wrists to reveal more dried blood running down towards the fingers.

'He'd still have been able to move his wrists to a limited extent, but all he'd achieve by doing that was open up these raw and painful-looking wounds. The direction of the flow of the blood from the wounds also makes it clear that he was suspended by his legs, much like the carcasses of animals you sometimes see suspended from hooks in abattoirs.'

But Lara wasn't listening. All that was flashing in front of her eyes right now was that letter. That confessional note detailing some of the more barbaric punishments meted out to the children incarcerated in the old Kenwood.

A punishments which now seemed to have been visited on one elderly man too.

———

A few hours later, Lara received the first of two updates, both from Maisa's former assistant.

The first was official, an early update from Sarah Ryan herself – and a probably grudging one, reflected Lara – regarding the time of death. The murder victim had been killed approximately two to three days previously. Contamination of the surrounding soil samples suggested that his body had been placed in that shallow grave a short time later.

The second update was unofficial. Dr Ryan's new and unhappy assistant confided that Maisa had been replaced as the unit's forensic pathologist in just the last day or so. The instruction to do so couldn't have come directly from Conran, but had he influenced it even indirectly in some way? No one doubted Doctor Ryan's credentials or expertise, but she was clearly a very different personality to the eminently approachable Maisa whom Lara could call on – and frequently had – day or night. Doctor Ryan, it was equally clear, was going to be answerable to one person and one only, and that wasn't a lowly DI by the name of Lara Arden.

But it wasn't the first recent replacement in the Major Crime Unit of course. Growing ever more uneasy, albeit without quite knowing why, Lara picked up her mobile and tried Paula, her old DCI. There was still no word on when her extended period of gardening leave might be nearing its end. While they hadn't got off to the best of starts; a mutual respect had developed later, but Lara hit a brick wall there, too. Paula's mobile just rang and rang.

So, Lara made another call to a colleague in the Hampshire

HQ on the mainland. From him, she discovered that Paula's period of leave had been indefinitely extended, after an internal police panel had determined that she still wasn't fit to return. The chair of that panel had been Conran.

CHAPTER
THIRTY-FIVE

AMY OCCUPIED MUCH the same position in the same bed. The same drips and tubes maintained her vital functions. Her unseeing eyes still framed the same silent accusation, or so it seemed to Lara, the same raw reminder that the police were no further on in finding out what had happened to her.

But something had changed.

'She had a scan last night.'

Carey Waite struggled to stick to an update she'd already had to make too many times to close friends and family. Across the room, Matt, Amy's father, was just staring, unseeing, at the wall. He was considerably older than Carey, but she seemed to be the one assuming the more senior role right now. Aaron, the brother, was playing a game on a Nintendo. His fingers were moving across the keyboard but in all other respects he looked as detached from any sort of reality, and as divorced from any sort of human contact right now, as his sister.

'They assessed her according to a Glasgow scale or something.'

Carey broke off.

'I didn't know what they were talking about.'

She looked across the room at her withdrawn husband, her isolated son.

'None of us did.'

Lara knew exactly what she was talking about. The Glasgow coma scale – or the GCS – was used to monitor a patient's responsiveness. It was also an indicator of the likelihood of recovery.

Lara looked back at the unaware Amy. It assessed three principal factors, firstly determining whether a patient could open their eyes, with a score of 1 meaning no eye opening and a score of 4 meaning the eyes opened spontaneously.

Secondly, it assessed whether there was any verbal response to a command. A score of 1 meant there was no response, a score of 5 meant the patient was alert and replying appropriately.

Finally, there was the assessment of the extent of any voluntary movement, also in response to a command. A score of 1 meant no response, once again. A score of 6 meant that the patient was able to hear and understand.

Lara kept looking at the prone figure in the bed in front of them. Most patients in a coma would have a total score of 8 or less. A higher score, towards the upper end of that scale, meant there was a good chance of a permanent recovery with few long-term side effects. A lower score indicated more extensive brain damage.

'They're saying she's a 4.'

Lara's heart sank. The survival rate for a patient with that low a score was notoriously poor. Of those who did survive, only a tiny proportion would make any sort of meaningful recovery.

By Amy's side, Aaron's fingers flashed ever faster across his keyboard.

'It doesn't mean...'

Matt broke in for the first time, then stopped, clearly unable to go on for a moment. Carey kept her eyes cast down to the floor. Aaron didn't look up from his screen, but his flashing fingers tensed momentarily, so he was clearly listening to every word. His dad struggled for a moment longer, then pressed on.

'She could…'

Then he stopped again as Carey suddenly turned, made for the door. Lara followed, catching up with her on the corridor outside. For a moment both women just stood there, Carey's head resting on a window looking down onto a car park leading onto the street.

'He keeps thinking there could be some sort of miracle…'

Carey stared down at the world outside going about its business, her voice almost a whisper.

'…that they've got it wrong, that she's just going to wake up.'

Then Carey stopped. Leaning forward she stared out onto the car park. Then she nodded down towards the ground.

'Who's that?'

Lara looked down to see a young woman in the near distance, looking back up at them. They were too far away to pick out any features, but she definitely seemed to be scanning the windows of their floor.

Carey kept looking down at her.

'She was here earlier on. And she was here yesterday, too.'

CHAPTER
THIRTY-SIX

LARA RACED DOWN THE STAIRS. The lifts in St Mary's could be notoriously slow and, right now, she needed to get down to ground level as quickly as possible. The young woman she'd just seen staring up at those high windows could be there for perfectly innocent reasons, unconnected with Amy. But something about her age and build was ringing all sorts of alarm bells for Lara right now.

As she burst out of a ground floor door, Lara could see that the woman was gone. That could be totally unrelated to her dash down those stairs from that upstairs room as well, but she could also have spotted Lara staring down at her from that window in turn and decided to get the hell out of there.

Lara wheeled round, checking for CCTV cameras. There were none covering the spot taken up by the mystery woman. Much as there were none covering the actual spot where Amy's accident took place, too, which could have been another happy accident. Or, and once again, it could have been something else.

Lara wheeled round some more, one face and only one before her eyes now.

Then, she heard it: an engine revving hard, just around the corner, moving swiftly through its gears. Lara dashed towards it, dimly aware of Carey appearing behind her, wanting to know what was happening, but Lara had already turned the corner and was now in sight of the hospital's main entrance. A car was hurtling towards it having been forced to loop around the rear of the hospital by the three-way traffic system before making its escape.

Lara dashed into the road. She caught a glimpse of the same young woman at the wheel, but it was only a fractional side view. Still running, she managed to get herself slightly in front of the vehicle, hoping to force it to stop.

For a moment Lara was unsure if the driver had even seen her. She was on the vehicle's nearside, and the young woman would have been unsighted. But at the last minute, she either sensed or saw that she was there and swung the wheel to her left. Lara felt a blast of air as it passed within inches of her, mounting the kerb as it did so before taking a right just outside the entrance and disappearing.

Lara looked up, checking once again, and this time she saw a sole CCTV camera monitoring the junction. Then Lara paused, fighting to get her breath back. If that camera was functioning – and given its proximity to a busy hospital she was going to raise hell if it wasn't – then they just might have been handed their first lead in her unit's ongoing inquiry into what had happened to Amy.

Then an incoming call alert sounded on her mobile, Jordan's name flashing up on the display.

'Mairead's list. The people who were interviewed about their time at Kenwood.'

Lara stilled as on the other end of the line Jordan continued.

'We've managed to track one of them down. His story is that he wasn't a teacher or one of the so-called support staff. He claims he only worked there a few months, helping out around the grounds, doing some low-level maintenance.'

In her mind's eye, Lara could still see everything her mother must have seen on her first night there, those mounds of newly dug earth littering what had once been a playground, a playground that had turned out to be a cemetery.

'Where is he? Is he still on the island?'

Jordan paused.

'He's still on the island. But he doesn't have what you might call a permanent address.'

Lara already knew what Jordan was going to say next.

'He lives on the river.'

Lara looked up towards Amy's hospital window again. Carey was still standing by the hospital entrance, waiting for her to finish her call, and now Lara could see Matt looking down at her, too.

Jordan hesitated again.

'There's no connection to Esther that I can find, it was the first thing I checked.'

Blood was roaring in Lara's ears now. But he was river folk. Just like that stepsister. And just like her mum

CHAPTER
THIRTY-SEVEN

ALL EYES RIGHT NOW, as ever, were on Amy, which suited Aaron just fine.

Occasionally, his mum would sit next to him, take his hand, utter a few words of empty-sounding reassurance, but that was probably more out of a sudden sense of recollected duty than anything else. But again, he didn't mind. In fact, he positively welcomed the lack of attention because it gave him the time he needed right now, time to build his wall.

The other ritual was still working, to an extent anyway. He'd managed to complete his regular circuits of his room without interruption, so Amy hadn't deteriorated further. There certainly hadn't been the catastrophic collapse there would have been had he not completed those three hundred and forty circuits yesterday evening and those four hundred circuits that very morning.

He still couldn't even think about that self-administered IV though, so, now, he had to try something else. Everyone probably thought he was just playing another of his games, blotting everything out as usual, but he wasn't. Aaron was creating a new space where himself and his sister could meet.

Plenty of his friends played Minecraft. Amy had played it

herself on occasions. But none of his friends had ever used its building blocks in the way he had, and to the best of his knowledge, Amy never had either. Maybe she could now.

It had all started a few years ago. Like so much else in Aaron and Amy's lives, it had started with their dad, but he didn't want to think about that now and so he didn't. The siblings hadn't ever talked about it either. She just spent more time away from the house, usually with Donna, while Aaron built his wall.

The wall wasn't physical; it was something he constructed inside his head, although sometimes it felt as real as any of the actual walls he could see outside his window, or he'd pass on his way to school. It stretched high and wide. And behind it, he concealed all the things he didn't want to think about or see. Occasionally, some would crowd into his thoughts, unbidden and unwanted, but then he just built that wall higher and wider.

And, in the last few days, he'd begun to wonder. In a sense, Amy was behind a wall right now, locked away in some inaccessible place. So, if he could create a safe space, too, then maybe that's where they could connect. Maybe then she'd reach out to him again.

CHAPTER
THIRTY-EIGHT

THE BOAT WAS A JUNKERS, similar to the one Lara had boarded a year previously, although there the resemblance ended.

The one from a year ago had been a working boat, piled high with scrap metal. An upturned beer crate had doubled as a seat on its exposed and open deck. That boat had belonged to Finn's taciturn mother who had worked the river alone and probably still did. From the windows of other passing boats, Lara had caught flashes of eyes as children looked out at her from cracked and grimy windows.

On the decks of another of them she'd seen a large, cage-like structure used to transport livestock. She strongly suspected a similar cage-like structure had been used to transport her mother after her abduction all those years ago. But Lara swiftly put all that to the back of her mind. Today, she had other matters to pursue.

The owner of this rather more upmarket version of an old working boat was Andrew Russell. Mairead had traced him through a tax investigation, that had been mounted well over thirty years previously, which had revealed payments made to Russell by the trustees of the old Kenwood Children's Home. The amounts were small, which backed up his story of only working there briefly, but they couldn't take that at face value. The payments made to many of the staff at the time had often been hidden behind all kinds of dark and devious accounting procedures.

The fact that the payments to Andrew Russell had come to light at all was due to a new clerk in the former home's office making a direct payment to his bank account rather than paying him in cash, as had been the norm for most of the employees. So, those few stray payments could be a portal into a much bigger involvement on his part. And even if he'd only been there for the limited time he'd claimed – and only to tend the grounds as he'd also claimed – had he really been unaware of everything that had been going on?

Now, two men of around his age who also may have had a connection to Kenwood had recently met a violent end. They still hadn't identified the body in the shallow grave, but did Russell know Edward Mattiss? And if so, had he confessed any fears to him in the last few weeks?

There was something else, too, although Lara had no idea how she might even begin to broach it. In his travels out on the various rivers he still quite obviously navigated, even if sporadically these days, had he ever come across a young woman called Esther?

'Take a seat if you can find one.'

Russell was busy as Lara arrived, fitting a clamp to a jar of biscuits. Lara had seen similar clamps in use in Georgia's nursing home. They were an aid for people with limited use of their hands or arms, designed to keep jars stable so they could be opened with one hand only. Lara looked round the neat kitchen area underneath the deck, taking in a kettle tipper as well as a pair of kitchen scales with a speech feature.

'If this is a bad time, I could always call back.'

Russell's mouth twisted into a rueful, wry smile.

'If we waited for a good one, it might take a while.'

Lara hesitated. Those various mobility and disability aids

confirmed Russell's home circumstances, as already outlined to her by Social Services. The social worker had also attested to Russell's care and concern in looking after his disabled wife, Jeanette, and even on this first acquaintance that concern did seem genuine. The few stray payments made to him thirty years ago could be what he claimed them to be, too, fleeting contact with an institution he knew little or nothing about as he toiled outside in its grounds. The next few moments may not tell Lara too much about the former, but she was hoping it might give her some insight into the latter.

Russell seated himself opposite Lara, putting a large pitcher of water and two glasses down in front of them.

'To be honest, I haven't thought about the place in decades. I worked all over back then, especially in the winter months. Most of us do the same. Spend the spring and the summer on the water, moor up the rest of the time, find whatever work we can.'

'So, nothing about Kenwood struck you as odd at the time?'

Russell studied the glass in his hand, casting his mind back.

'The kids kept pretty well much to themselves, I do remember that. I'd see them now and again, going to classes, heading across to what I assumed was some sort of dormitory at night, but we never had any actual contact. The teachers or the rest of the staff didn't actually keep us apart, but they seemed to keep their distance anyway.'

'So what, exactly, were you doing there?'

'They wanted a small copse clearing – some bushes and small trees. I don't even know what for, maybe some kind of playground or something.'

Then, suddenly, Russell's face lightened.

'I do remember one thing though. I only came across it by accident. There was a kid's playroom in the grounds, shaped like a windmill of all things. It had sails, and they worked, too. There was a storm on one of the mornings I was there, and they spun around like whirling dervishes.'

Lara, once again, didn't respond. That might indeed have

been the innocently happy memory it seemed to be for Russell, but she'd been inside that same strange half-size windmill herself just over a year before. It was a far from innocent or happy memory for her.

Swiftly, Lara ran through her remaining questions, and Russell, who clearly wanted to get back to his wife, currently sleeping in the bedroom next door, answered equally quickly. He hadn't been contacted by anyone from the time he worked in Kenwood, either lately or at any time in the previous thirty years, He didn't know Edward Matiss. He'd also had no communication about the place, be that via email or by letter, but Russell promised to let Lara know if that changed at all, and he took her business card with her personal mobile number inscribed on the back.

Lara stood on the bank a few moments later, looking downriver. She remained there, almost as if she was expecting to see another boat appear, and Esther to be on board. No such apparition appeared of course, but as she turned away another image suddenly flashed in front of her eyes. She hadn't particularly registered it at the time, but as she'd looked out from Edward Mattiss's house, she'd seen a glint of water in the distance. Taking out her phone, she inputted his postcode into a search map, then zoomed in on the image that appeared on screen. Sure enough, running at the bottom of his garden was the same river she was standing by right now.

Then another incoming call alert sounded on her phone.

Doctor Sarah Ryan wanted to see her.

Back on board, Russell waited till he heard Lara's car driving away. Then, and only then, did he open the door to the bedroom, slacken the bonds that had been restraining his wheelchair-bound wife before carefully removing the gag he'd fixed in place with strong elastic strips around her mouth. She'd been known to bite in the past when he'd taken similar precautions as other visitors had called, visitors he similarly did not want her to meet. Her body might be frail, but she could still lash out.

She was more than capable of calling out, too. Calling out to visitors from some of the caring agencies would have been bad enough, particularly when he'd told them, in hushed tones, that she'd had a bad night and was sleeping. Calling out to a cop could have been disastrous.

Like Edward Matiss, whom he had known and only too well, Russell didn't believe he was a monster. Yes, he'd been party to some perhaps monstrous acts in the past, but that was decades ago. He'd been like so many of them back then, young and foolish, drunk on an intoxicating cocktail of power and opportunity. And, yes, too, he had to admit his marriage had been something of a foil, masking his true nature and impulses. How his wife, had found out about all that he still didn't know, but she had, and she'd changed from that moment on.

But she'd been even more hostile and cold lately and he knew why, too. She'd seen that letter. Exactly how, he had no idea, but she could still move around the boat to a limited extent and could easily have come across it when he was up on deck. Or she might have hunted it out when he'd been at that hastily convened meeting in their usual guest house along the coast.

But it didn't matter how she'd found it. The point was that she had, and the danger she now posed was obvious. This latest visit from a cop – and that cop in particular – was proof by itself that action had to be taken. Which only left the one question remaining, as his various phone calls to his former associates had made clear an hour or so before.

The question was: not what to do, but when to do it.

And that question had just been answered, too.

Leaning close – because once again, he truly didn't believe he was a monster – he kissed his companion of the last few decades softly on the cheek. They hadn't had a bad life together, for the most part. Straightening up, he winced as a thin globule of spit assaulted him, as Jeanette delivered her own verdict on their life and time together. Then he picked up the syringe filled with the concoction he'd prepared earlier.

Half an hour later, he walked up to the nearby road. He didn't trust mobiles, landlines, or email, not now. None of them could be sure that the police wouldn't be monitoring calls and messages, for the next few days at least. Heading into a nearby car public park, he unlocked the Mercedes he'd treated himself to the previous year, and which had already more than earned its keep. Then he drove to a large house in the middle of the island where he parked next to two Bentleys and a Jag, and updated companions he'd known a lot longer than his now-dead wife on all that had happened that day.

CHAPTER
THIRTY-NINE

'Antemortem injuries are injuries a body has received before death.'

Lara stared at the pathologist as she stood over the body of Edward Mattiss on the treatment table. She knew that.

'They may be a contributing factor in the death or even its cause. On the other hand, they may have occurred many years before.'

By Lara's side, Mairead knew that, too. Neither officer had any idea why they were suddenly being treated to what sounded like an introductory lecture for first year medical students.

Lara didn't understand something else about this summons to the pathology lab either. The last time she'd seen Mattiss's dead body, Maisa was conducting her usual rigorous postmortem investigation. Why Doctor Ryan had taken up a fresh inspection of a body that had already been examined by one of the best in the business was puzzling, and she wasn't doing a lot, so far, to enlighten them.

'One major difference between an antemortem and a postmortem injury is the presence of signs of blood. When a person's alive, the blood's still circulating and any injuries such as cuts or stabs or abrasions will bleed freely.'

Lara held her tongue. There had to be a point to all this even if she really couldn't see it yet.

'There are exceptions. For instance, when a person drowns, their body usually floats face down resulting in the head becoming congested with blood. Scalp wounds sustained after death in those circumstances, from being buffeted about in water or colliding with boats or propellers, can then leak blood, too.'

The still-silent Lara reflected that she didn't actually know that, in all fairness.

Doctor Ryan bent closer to Edward Mattiss's arms, obscuring them momentarily from both officer's view.

'Careless handling of a cadaver may produce some post-mortem bruising which could sometimes be difficult to distinguish from antemortem bruising, but we get round that by analysing damaged tissue. Tissue from antemortem injuries contain a chemical involved in inflammation called Leukotriene B4, or LTB4. Post-mortem injuries have no LTB4. Antemortem injuries, in other words, show signs of inflammation, while post-mortem injuries do not.'

She straightened up, nodded back at the two officers who were still just staring at her.

'So, I can say without fear of contradiction that these wrist injuries on Mr Mattiss – injuries that replicate almost exactly the antemortem injuries I saw on the unidentified body discovered in that shallow grave at Kenwood – were definitely inflicted before death.'

Lara stared at a succession of thin weals, running all the way around both of Edward Mattiss's wrists.

Doctor Ryan continued.

'After your last visit, I read up on the punishments inflicted on the children there. These injuries almost exactly replicate the injuries found on many of them, too.'

She looked down again at Matiss.

'These are relatively recent and they're not the deepest of abrasions, meaning that they were possibly self-inflicted, and he may not have had the courage to inflict too much in the way of pain.'

Mairead cut in.

'But why would he do that?'

Doctor Ryan looked back at her, her tone as cool and even as ever.

'That's very much more your field than mine. But these sorts of injuries suggest to me a man tormented by past misdeeds and attempting to atone in some way by inflicting similar treatment on himself.'

Lara looked back again at the weals around Mattiss's wrists. They would have played no part in his death, the cause of which had been all too obvious. Maisa would have documented those injuries as she'd have documented everything else. But she hadn't seen the new murder victim buried in that shallow grave in Kenwood, Doctor Ryan had. And she'd made the connection.

Lara looked up at a pair of ice green eyes but there was a different expression in them now, an expression that now unsettled her.

A moment or so later, Lara nodded silent thanks for this new lead, if that's what it proved to be, and then turned and left the pathology lab and the unsettling Doctor Ryan as quickly as she could.

CHAPTER FORTY

ONE HOUR LATER, Lara was forcing out the punches again, feeling the lactic acid building in her arms and burning through her system once more. She knew that these sorts of punches, the ones that were making her heart and lungs work overtime, were the ones that really counted. They were the ones that didn't only convert into new and lasting strength, they cleared her thinking, cleansed her somehow in a way she still didn't understand but had nonetheless come to trust.

Because it wasn't just about being strong, and it wasn't just about being fit. It was something more than that. It was as if here, in this small gym, surrounded by weights, standing in front of a punch bag, she was striving to be the very best version of herself she could be. The very best person. The very best young woman. The very best police officer.

That strange, appraising stare from that most unlikely of sources had burrowed its way under her habitual defences. Lara had no idea if that was intentional on the part of the formerly remote pathologist. But, for a moment, something had been there that had very definitely not been there before. A moment pregnant with promise.

Similar moments had happened before in Lara's life, of course

– and with men as well as women – but they'd never developed into anything. She'd never allowed them to, and it all went back to that train journey that day when she was six. There was an invisible thread running back to that frightened and lost young girl on a station platform, standing next to another equally frightened and lost young girl, two small sisters facing a world that had suddenly turned strange and cold.

Something fused inside Lara that day, closing tight inside her. All she'd taken for granted up to then, trust and belief, evaporated. From that moment on she looked out at the world through eyes that were forever wary. From that moment on she never fully let down her guard.

It wasn't the same for both sisters. Where Lara had gone inwards, Georgia had reached out, to everyone and everything, latching onto one relationship after another in much the same way that in later years she'd grasp at one drug after another. For a time, she clung to the belief that the world might contain within it the salvation the young Lara had simply ceased to believe existed anymore.

But Lara was still only human. Connections with other human souls had been made from time to time. She'd made one a few months previously with Jordan but, and like so many other of her other potential relationships, that hadn't developed. Maybe it never would. Lara was also dimly aware there might be some unfinished business with Andrea, the trainer and owner of this very gym, although nothing had ever developed there either. Nothing had been said in that encounter an hour or so ago, but that fleeting half-glance that contained within it the ghost of an invitation – an invitation Lara had immediately side-stepped, as she had with all the others.

It didn't help that she'd never navigated what might be called the usual rites of passage. While her contemporaries had agonised over relationships in school, had sworn undying love one day, made dark promises of eternally enduring hatred the next, Lara had floated above all such vows and promises, the memory of that one single day ambushing her, the day she'd lost a mother she believed would be a constant in her life and, with it, all notion of anything constant at all.

Then, as Lara continued to force out the punches, she began to slow as suddenly another figure swam before her eyes. It wasn't strictly true that there was no constant in her life, Georgia aside. There was one and, with a jolt, Lara began to wonder if that was what her latest session was really all about, because this had happened before, too. When she surrendered herself to the physical, something would coalesce. Sometimes, decisions would be made without her even realising she even needed to make them. And sometimes it forced to the surface something she didn't even know was there.

Lara stood before the punch bag, gripped with a sudden and sickening fear. She'd arrived in the gym believing she was trying to work out an unexpectedly complicated new work colleague, but maybe that hadn't been it at all.

CHAPTER
FORTY-ONE

THERE WAS a certain etiquette involved at these sorts of gatherings. That might seem surprising, given most of the attendees spent the majority of their time there inflicting the kind of punishment on each other that would have attracted lengthy prison sentences had it been meted out anywhere else.

There were customs and traditions, nevertheless. And they didn't include a relatively new member of the S&M club marching into the room, pushing herself to the front of the queue and demanding that she be punished, as in, right now.

What stayed the hand of the other attendees was simple. She was fresh meat, and that always lent a certain frisson to proceedings. No one ever knew for sure how a new member would take to an extended beating, and everyone in that room always wanted to find out. There was also an element of novelty in another sense, too. Most present that evening had seen each other's bodies many times before.

There was more novelty, too, in the way she didn't look at anyone as she arrived. She just stood before the man currently holding one of the whips, nodded at him and then removed her clothes, although she retained, as did the others, her mask. She let her bra and knickers fall to the floor, not even bothering to kick them away, clearly impatient for one thing and one thing only – this latest session, her session, to start.

But not quite yet, because suddenly her eyes focused on the armoury of implements lined up against the far wall. Then she strode over, ran her hands over the treats on offer, which was another clear breach of protocol. Usually, the submissive didn't get to choose the exact form of punishment they were about to endure. No one stepped forward to stop her though. As strange as it might sound given the setting, she radiated a clear and present sense of menace right now and no one wanted to risk getting hurt.

The new arrival studied the ropes and riding crops in front of her. Then her eyes moved upwards to the small selection of studded whips situated above. A small gasp sounded from a couple of the attendees there that evening as she reached out for the largest one. Traditionally, a newbie worked up to the kind of punishment that particular implement could inflict, which was very much for the more hardcore amongst them.

Across the room, another of the attendees stilled for a different reason, as something in the way she reached up for the largest of those studded whips, as well as the way she ran her fingers along the sharpened edges, began to ring a bell. She was still masked, so he couldn't be sure. And he'd never seen her naked before so that didn't help in the recognition stakes either. But he still felt as if he knew her.

The woman turned back and handed the studded whip over. Without saying a word, she turned to the shackles on the wall and within seconds she'd been duly restrained. She tensed, waiting for the first of the blows to land. When it did, that first blow with the whip was misjudged, tentative, and the studs left almost no mark. She then spoke for only the second time since she'd marched in that night.

'Again.'

The instruction was clear and this time the man with the studded whip obliged. Raising it high above his head he scored a clean strike on her back, the studs puncturing the skin sending a thin spray of blood skywards. Her body arched, which was when she spoke again, and it was the same curt instruction.

'Again.'

That elicited a third and even more vicious blow. Blood was now coursing down her back and she spoke again and once more it was the same command. The punisher hesitated, but the temptation was now irresistible. He brought the studded whip down again and then again.

All eyes in the room followed the blood, save one pair of eyes. The man who'd been watching her ever since she ran her fingers along those sharpened studs was now even more sure that he knew her, but how? It wasn't from here, in the club, so where had they come across each other?

Mairead didn't speak again for the whole of the session. She didn't need to. It was obvious what she wanted, and she got it. All the time, Doctor Ryan's pithy assessment back in the path lab, of a tortured soul tormented by past misdeeds and attempting to atone haunted her.

But the human body can only take so much even if her spirit was still craving more and, finally, she put her hand up, the safe signal for the man with the studded whip, now panting and gasping for breath every bit as much as she was, to stop.

Then she spoke again. And just like the first time she was there, it was the same muttered whisper, barely picked up by anyone else.

'Sorry.'

No one would have taken much notice anyway. None of them would have known what she was apologising for, and none would have much cared, either. Another of the attendees that night, emboldened by all he'd just seen, was already stripping off, eager to sample more of the same.

But across the room, the distracted man had suddenly placed her, and it was the change in tone that had done it. That softer, more cajoling note that had just crept into her voice. He'd heard that tone before. She'd used it on him as he'd poured his heart out to her just over a year ago. Indirectly, she was one of the reasons he was here right now, at a place and among people he thought he'd left behind for good.

He kept looking at the woman as she collected her clothes and made for the door, which was when another rule was broken.

They were all supposed to leave this at the door. All punishments were supposed to stop the moment they left that room.

But he didn't want to leave this at the door. He wanted to keep on punishing the woman he could see now exiting, and he didn't want to stop.

CHAPTER
FORTY-TWO

TEN MINUTES after leaving the gym, Lara was in her Cooper again, speeding across the island to a small, ground floor flat in Shanklin.

The flat was home to June, the guard from the train all those years before, the kindly woman who'd looked after Lara and Georgia while they'd searched for a mother who'd vanished before their bewildered eyes.

June had then kept company with them as they disembarked that train at its first stop, had held their hands as they scanned the faces of the departing passengers, searching for the one face they were desperate to see.

June had also stayed with them until a hard-pressed representative from the local Social Services had arrived and had taken them under her wing in turn.

But she hadn't only done all that. She'd also kept in touch with them in all the subsequent years while they were growing up, probably because what had happened on that train that day had come to haunt her every bit as much as Lara and Georgia. As she'd confessed to Lara herself years later, she'd re-lived the events of that day on every train journey she took after that, and it soon proved too much. She left her job and the rail company almost exactly a year after that strangest of days when a family of three got on a train, but only two alighted. Since then, she'd remained that constant presence in the two girls' lives, never missing a birthday or Christmas, when cards would always appear.

But not last month. Last month had been Georgia's birthday and no card had arrived at the home. Lara hadn't thought too much of it at the time. Memories of their last meeting were still all too poignant. Lara could still see June shuffling along the polished floor of the upmarket hotel where Lara had been treating her to afternoon tea, her back increasingly curved from a combination of age and arthritis, her hair almost pure white, one hand grasping an outsize bag that could have contained most people's worldly possessions, while the other clung onto a stick. During the course of the occasionally trying hour or so that followed, she'd stumbled over Lara's name twice and had seemed to have wiped Georgia's entire existence. She'd even forgotten what Lara did for a living. So, Georgia's missing birthday card could be just more evidence of an old lady's failing faculties.

Or, as Lara had suddenly realised with that sickening jolt a short time before, it could be something else.

Esther's vendetta, a year before, had been simple, if chilling. She'd lashed out at a world she felt had abandoned her, trying to turn others into twisted versions of herself. Lara had privately worried that the close relationship she and Georgia had always enjoyed with June would turn their kindly old former protector into a target. So far it hadn't happened, but that didn't mean it wouldn't.

Lara knocked on June's door a few minutes later. When there was no reply, she rapped harder. Still no response. Lara went round to the back and tried the rear door, but it was locked, and no one came to open it when she knocked. One minute later, and using the spare key she'd surreptitiously copied on one of her previous visits without June's knowledge, Lara let herself in.

A second later, she heard a scream from the other side of the sitting room door.

Lara hared inside. For a moment she stopped, disorientated, as another, more extended scream echoed. Then it cut, abruptly, as an old and familiar TV soap theme started up, its trademark pounding drumbeat flooding the room.

Lara focused on a slumped figure in front of the television. Moving forward, she picked up a cushion that had slipped from behind the sleeping June's head and settled it back in place. Looking round, she picked up an empty glass of water on the table beside her, crossed back to the kitchen and refilled it. Replacing it next to the still-sleeping June, she did a final check on the room before letting herself out, relieved that all her fears had proved to be groundless, and further relieved that June would remain unaware she had copied that key.

The island had always been a place of considerable contrasts, with rich and poor co-existing side by side. Huge mansions looked down from high hills on modest maisonettes. The beaches played host to homeless drug users, often hunched metres away from holidaymaking families.

June's flat was firmly in the heart of one of the poorer local communities, but the presence of an upmarket Jag parked just a few doors down from her front door still didn't strike the exiting Lara as in any way odd. If she had paused to think about it, she'd just have put it down to those everyday contrasts again. But she didn't pause to think about it, and that would turn out to the second mistake she'd made that day.

The driver of the Jag watched as Lara drove away, then he took out his phone and photographed the front door of the flat she'd just visited. He'd already done a Land Registry search while she was in there and had noted down the details of its occupant. The driver attached the photo to the scan of the Land

Registry extract and sent it into the driver of the Bentley and to the driver of the Mercedes.

They had to tread carefully. This was a police officer after all. Taking out managers of rundown guest houses and a grasping porter in a Hospice was one thing, taking out a cop was something else, although none of them would rule it out if the occasion demanded. But maybe that police officer had just handed them some useful leverage in the unlikely shape of an enfeebled old lady whose existence they'd been unaware of till now.

And that was Lara's first mistake.

CHAPTER
FORTY-THREE

A FEW HOURS PREVIOUSLY, Jordan had been stood in front of his laptop, unable to take in what he was seeing.

Or, more accurately, just who he was seeing.

The figure he'd seen rising from behind those rocks on that beach had been Rhys McGuire, Amy's boyfriend and – so everyone was currently assuming – the father of her child. So, why was Coco meeting him in that out-of-the-way location well away from prying eyes?

And hard on the heels of that question, came another. Had they got this all wrong? Was there nothing sinister about Amy's accident after all? Had she simply found out about Rhys seeing Coco, and her accident was perhaps some sort of suicide attempt?

Jordan crossed to the window of his first floor flat, stared out, unseeing, over the meat market plying its trade just a few metres across the street, another wracked question following hard in the last one's wake.

Should he task Coco with all this? Should Jordan, indeed, tell Lara about it, too? That would mean Coco would have to find out about the bug he'd planted, which could well signal disaster so far as father and daughter were concerned. Despite his resolute conviction that he'd been acting in her best interests, Jordan really didn't see them coming back from a revelation like that for a long time.

Jordan had dithered ever since, unsure what to do without coming to any sort of decision. Then, just twenty minutes ago, the bug he'd hidden in Coco's bag had emitted another alert. Jordan crossed to his laptop and turned on the video feed. And he'd watched as his daughter hurried towards Rhys's imposing family home on that upmarket street in Bembridge.

Then, just as she reached the house itself, Coco must have dropped her bag or something, because suddenly the bug failed.

CHAPTER
FORTY-FOUR

'DID YOU SEE?'

For a moment, Coco just stared back, stupidly. It didn't make sense and she knew it, but for that moment she simply didn't recognise him. She'd never seen Rhys like this before.

'They were in the house In the fucking house.'

The neighbour, out in his garden and tending an already immaculately maintained lawn again, looked over the low fence, alerted by Rhy's panicked gasps.

'I thought it was Dad, I thought he'd come back early, or Maisie, the housekeeper, I just walked in, called out, and then...'

Rhys stood in front of Coco, just shaking for a moment. Coco had heard him yell – although it was a yell that more resembled a scream – as she'd approached from along the street a moment or so before. The sound seemed to be coming from the side of the house and instinctively, she'd dashed round there, dropping her bag in panic as she did so.

Coco reached out her hand, couldn't help herself. Then she just stood there, her comforting hand holding his arm as his breathing began to slow, and his eyes beginning to dilate back to something approaching normal. Then, with the neighbour still watching while pretending not to, and like a child surrendering to the care of an elder, Rhys allowed himself to be steered back inside.

A few minutes later, two mugs of strong black coffee were in front of them both. Coco had taken a couple of sips from hers. Rhys hadn't even looked at his.

'I saw someone out on the road, earlier on, I thought maybe they were doing some deliveries or something, there was this white van parked down the street.'

Rhys hunched closer, over the kitchen table.

'I couldn't even tell if it was a man or a woman, they just turned, headed away, maybe they saw me looking at them or something.'

Rhys tailed off again. Coco pushed his coffee towards him. Once again, the young man didn't even see to realise it was there.

'Next thing I knew they were here. In the house.'

'Did he – she – say anything?'

Rhys, starting to shake again, shook his head.

'Is there anything missing, have you checked?'

But Rhys didn't even seem to hear that.

'There was someone in the hospital, too.'

Coco froze, stared at him.

'They were in with Amy, talking to her. I thought it was a doctor at first, but it couldn't have been, not with the things they were saying to her, the way they were talking.'

'What kind of things?'

Rhys took a deep breath, desperately trying to calm himself.

'That she didn't have to worry. That she just had to trust them. That everything was going to be OK.'

Rhys, finally, reached out for his coffee, taking hold of it in both hands, but still not drinking it, just cradling the warm mug as if he was holding onto some sort of comfort blanket.

Then he looked up at Coco, almost as if he was seeing her for the first time.

'Who is this?'
Rhys kept staring at her.
'What the fuck do they want?'

CHAPTER
FORTY-FIVE

'WE MIGHT HAVE FOUND ANOTHER ONE.'

Mairead extracted a single piece of paper from a small sheaf she was holding.

'He wasn't directly employed by Kenwood, either full-time or part-time. So far as we can tell, he never took any payment from them either, which is maybe why he's kept under the radar so long.'

On the other side of her desk in the open plan Major Crime Unit office, Lara looked at Mairead, puzzled. That morning they'd received a result from the CCTV camera outside the hospital. The car being driven away by the female driver had been hired using a false licence. A dead end, in other words. This was already feeling like another one.

'If he wasn't employed by Kenwood and was never paid by them...'

Mairead explained as Lara tailed off.

'He was a lay pastor back then. He still is. He's involved with some sort of evangelical sect or something. They've got a base in Ryde, but he travels all over the island. Outreach work, they call it.'

Mairead checked a date on one of the pieces of paper.

'Over thirty years ago, he did some study classes in the home. Bible readings, that kind of thing. He was there every Sunday for about six months, always on a voluntary basis.'

'Name?'

Mairead checked again.

'Kenneth Simon. Pastor Kenneth Simon.'

'And why has this come to light now?'

'About ten years ago, his church applied to the local council in Ryde for a grant to build a new meeting hall. They'd already received funds for a play area to be built, but the hall was going to be a community site as well as a Church facility, hence the application for help.'

Mairead studied the papers again.

'Pastor Simon wasn't involved directly in the original application. Or at least, his name didn't appear anywhere. A couple of the other church elders handled the paperwork and one of them put down Kenwood as one of the places where Simon had preached. It was among a list of other places on the island.'

Mairead paused.

'The odd thing being that when the application went to the council, all mention of Kenwood had been taken out. It only appears on the original copy of the application. After that, it doesn't feature in any subsequent paperwork and his involvement with the old home is never mentioned again.'

Lara considered for a moment. There could be an innocent explanation for that. Rumours about Kenwood had swirled around the island ever since it closed. Kenneth Simon could have decided that he really didn't want to risk his application being tainted by association and had asked a colleague to delete all reference to an innocent involvement he would nonetheless prefer not to come to light.

Or there could be a very different explanation of course.

Lara nodded at Mairead, a silent acknowledgement of her

junior officer's customary diligence, then reached out her hand for the paper, but she didn't get it. The whole sheaf suddenly fell from Mairead's hand as she held them out or tried to. Suddenly, her back seemed to go into some sort of spasm.

'Sorry, sorry.'

Mairead tried to swoop down to retrieve the papers, but a concerned Lara was there before her.

'Are you OK?'

Mairead nodded, quickly, as Lara stood up, the papers now back in hand.

'Think I've overdone it a bit lately. The swimming club's doing a triathlon next month. Been trying to build up my stamina.'

Lara kept studying her, faint alarm bells ringing once more, as Mairead smiled, quick again, turned away.

Swimming had been Mairead's passion for as long as she'd known her, and Jordan, in particular, had cause to be grateful for it, too. It was Mairead's prowess in the water that had released him and his family from their date with drowning the last time Lara had crossed paths with her stepsister.

Lara kept looking after her, those alarm bells beginning to ring louder. This was the second time she'd registered something amiss. First, there was that stray sighting she'd caught of Mairead's injured arm. Now there was this sudden and equally strange back spasm.

Lara hesitated, then turned back to the papers she'd just retrieved, only to find Conran suddenly materialising by the side of her desk and looking over her shoulder at them, too. For a moment there was silence. Then he nodded back at Lara.

'It's a legitimate line of inquiry.'

Lara nodded back, cautious, as he continued.

'But there's others.'

Lara nodded again. 'And we're pursuing them.'

Conran turned, headed back to his office. Lara watched him

go. In truth, he was only giving voice to a caution about these new leads and links that she'd already rehearsed to herself.

But his urging Lara to spread the net wider than just Kenwood could also be a way of preventing those leads and links being looked at too closely.

CHAPTER
FORTY-SIX

THE WALL WASN'T WORKING.

Aaron had stayed behind it all night. He'd told his mum he needed time to catch up on some schoolwork and had locked himself away in his room. He hadn't responded to any friends' requests on his iPad. He'd just stayed behind that wall of Minecraft bricks, waiting.

The next morning there was a knock on his bedroom door. His dad was standing outside, looking as tired as he always did right now. He apologised for not taking too much of an interest in whatever schoolwork Aaron was doing the previous evening and asked if he wanted any help. When Aaron told him he'd finished it already, he told him he'd run him to school that morning instead. He hadn't taken him for ages. And it'd give them chance to talk.

They hadn't managed much in the way of conversation though. Aaron hadn't told him about the schoolwork he'd been finishing off because he hadn't even looked at it. Dad hadn't asked anyway. When he dropped him off, Aaron had the impression it was a relief to them both. Then Aaron walked into the school, which was when everything suddenly started happening in slow motion.

The figure he'd just seen had just turned the corner ahead and was now walking towards him. Suddenly, all Aaron could hear was the sound of his own breathing as he approached.

'How's Amy, is there any news?'

Just as suddenly, the world snapped back into focus. Now he was standing before Aaron, a concerned expression on his face. Mr Taylor, their form teacher, the teacher his mum and dad had summoned to the house to see if he could offer any insight into his sister's frame of mind immediately prior to what everyone was still calling the accident.

'Aaron?'

But Mr Taylor seemed anxious as well as concerned, and Aaron just kept looking at him, unable to work him out. Was he fearful that Amy might not recover? Or terrified that she would? And suddenly, out it came. The words were out of his mouth before Aaron was even aware they'd begun to form in his head. Something took over, much as it did sometimes when he was playing on Fortnite.

'She's been trying to tell us something.'

Now Mr Taylor looked rocked as well as concerned and anxious.

'Amy's come round?'

Aaron shook his head.

'Before. She's said things. Or tried to say things. Started anyway, then stopped.'

Aaron rode on as Mr Taylor's eyes seemed to grow wider all the while.

'She's written things down, too.'

'What things?'

'I'm not supposed to say.'

'But you've read them?'

Aaron hesitated, then shook his head.

'She told me not to.'

Then he hesitated again. Was it Aaron's imagination? Or was Mr Taylor starting to relax slightly?

Aaron nodded at him, watching closely all the while.

'What do you think I should do?'

And it was the strangest thing. All of a sudden, Mr Taylor seemed younger. More uncertain, less assured. Frightened, even.

Then the bell sounded, summoning everyone back to class. The corridor swiftly became a sea of bodies, and Mr Taylor became swallowed up in the throng.

Then it happened again. Suddenly, all sound seemed to cease, and everyone he could see appeared to be walking at half-speed once more. All he could hear was the sound of his own breathing again, but it was louder now, much louder, and laboured, too.

And then, suddenly, he couldn't seem to draw breath.

CHAPTER
FORTY-SEVEN

Coco had left Rhys half an hour before. He was calmer now, a lot calmer. It helped that his dad had called to tell him he'd be cutting short his latest business trip and would be home that very night. Maisie, the housekeeper, was kind and caring, and Rhys liked her, but she was no substitute.

There was another reason Rhys was calm now though, and that was down to her. As Coco walked home she couldn't help feeling a warm glow begin inside. Just before she'd left, he'd reached out, put his hand on her arm and thanked her for doing what he needed above anything else right now, just being there for him, helping him through.

Coco had looked at his hand, at skin touching skin and she didn't know about Rhys, but hers felt as if it was on fire.

If you'd told her even a few months ago that a simple touch from a boy's hand would provoke a reaction like that she'd have laughed in your face. She ran with a different crowd back then, and chaste gestures of that kind were very much the preserve of kids. It didn't matter that she was still only sixteen herself at the time, she could look a lot older when she put her mind to it which she did almost every day. Indeed, Kris, her much older boyfriend, demanded it. He didn't want to be stopped at the doors of the different clubs they frequented back then by a suspicious bouncer demanding ID. For a few short weeks, she lived a life that would have seemed to most girls her age to be the preserve of dreams. Days and nights sped by in a mesmerising miasma of clubs and cocaine, Coco whisked from one to the other by a bad boy in a Bentley.

Then Kris was killed, and Coco was nearly killed, too. And Coco went back, in a sense, discovering again the girl she actually was behind the fiction she'd invented, which was when she'd decided that she'd always rather preferred that girl all along. Since then, she'd returned to everything she'd previously, and contemptuously, rejected: her dad, her school, her friends.

And that was when she'd first noticed Rhys.

Coco knew he was with Amy. And she'd told herself from the start that she was never going to do anything to come between them. That hadn't stopped the two of them talking, hanging out together, albeit always in a group, never alone. There was something between them, she could feel it in the quick glances he'd shoot her way every now and again, the way he'd tense sometimes, almost without seeming to realise it, whenever she walked into a room. But, still, they remained just friends.

And it was as a friend that she'd called him straight after she heard what had happened to Amy. It was as a friend that she was with him as he paced that beach, agitated and tormented. And she'd called round to his house just now as a friend, too, to see whether he needed anything, if there was anything she could do to help.

She wasn't the only one from the school to call, of course. Donna had, too. Rhys had told her. But Coco was pretty sure he hadn't reached out to Donna like he'd just reached out to her. He hadn't laid his hand on her arm like he'd done with her, either. And she wouldn't have felt that molten charge even if he had. That was just between herself and Rhys.

And as she walked on, Coco couldn't stop the thought that now flashed through her mind, the same thought that had been lurking for a while now, on the very edge of consciousness, almost. It was treacherous and she knew it. Yet unutterably exciting, all at the same time.

God forbid it might happen. But if that same God ordained that Amy should not recover, then she wouldn't come out of that hospital – meaning her baby wouldn't survive either, in all probability – Rhys would be alone. Then he'd be in even more need of someone being there for him, someone to calm him, to lay a comforting hand on his arm.

She hadn't been able to banish the thought and she couldn't now quell the sudden surge of hope that kicked inside her, too, and it all took her back to the person she used to be. The person she still was sometimes. The girl who would do anything to get what she wanted.

Coco, growing agitated, brought out her asthma pump as the tell-tale signs of an attack began to assail her, the pounding in her ears, the breathless panic at the back of her throat: the all-too familiar sensation that every breath she was taking right now might be her last.

CHAPTER
FORTY-EIGHT

A FORMER RETAIL unit in a small row of boarded up shops was a strange place to find God, but according to the flyers plastered on the walls, countless island residents and visitors had done just that in the last year alone.

Ryde had also never struck Lara as a particularly spiritual setting before. Back in Victorian days it had been a popular seaside resort, but it was more of a transport hub these days, connecting to the mainland via the various ferries. But according to those same flyers, many had found spiritual sustenance here, too.

The former retail unit was home to the Island Community Church, an organisation linked, but not formally associated, with similar evangelical outfits on the mainland and even further afield throughout Europe. The emphasis was on community rather than church, hence its base in an outlet previously associated with selling various household items for no more than a pound. Devotees claimed it demonstrated a connection with the everyday lives of worshippers absent in more formal religious settings.

The church had also attracted its fair share of critics. Some had pointed to a previous post on its website, hastily removed, which advocated something called deliverance therapy for young women, aimed at curing anything from eating disorders to inappropriate sexual behaviour, most particularly same-sex relationships. Those same critics argued it lifted a lid on its real and underlying small-town, conservative agenda.

Lara and Jordan walked inside to find themselves in a large room, with a whole array of chairs set out in a half moon semi-circle in front of a state-of-the-art TV suspended on a wall. Various musical instruments, from guitars to saxophones and trumpets, were stacked underneath.

A smiling woman, in her early forties, approached as Lara and Jordan entered, leaving two young teens at a table behind her who were packing sweets into small boxes.

'Can I help you?'

'Is Pastor Kenneth Simon available?'

Lara flashed her warrant card, Jordan doing the same, the forty-something woman's practised smile wobbling a little as they did so.

'We'd like a word.'

The forty-something woman's smile restored itself.

'Pastor Simon is making house calls right now.'

'Could you tell us where? Maybe we could catch up with him in between calls.'

'These are pastoral visits to often damaged and vulnerable souls, and he really wouldn't appreciate being disturbed.

She flipped open a nearby bag, took out an iPad.

'Maybe you could make an appointment.'

The woman flicked through an electronic log.

'I could offer you next week, Monday at eleven.'

Jordan was already moving away. The forty-something woman's eyes followed him briefly, but lost interest as he paused by one of the guitars in front of the outsize TV monitor. Just another man on the cusp of middle age, locked in one life, dreaming of another.

Lara smiled, affecting gratitude. She could have adopted the same tactic she'd employed with Milton Davalle. She could have pointed out that she was conducting a murder investigation and a meeting with a person who may be able to offer information some days hence was not even remotely acceptable. With similar, albeit even more recalcitrant human bollards in the past, she'd been known to employ even more extreme tactics

There were other ways of skinning this particular cat and, sure enough, within just a few more moments, and as the forty-something woman was inputting Lara's name and contact details into her iPad, the fire alarm sounded.

The woman stared round as her young teen helpers froze. Jordan was now nowhere in sight. Lara nodded around the room as she called out.

'If you could all immediately vacate the premises.'

The young teens were already standing.

'Leave all personal possessions and make your way to the nearest fire exit.'

The woman glanced hesitantly across the room towards a desktop computer squatting on another of the unit's trestle tables.

Lara smiled at her again, a smile the forty-something woman was beginning to realise was no smile at all, then Lara nodded at her.

'We'll liaise with the fire service. Let you know when it's safe to return.'

Ten minutes later, Lara and Jordan were heading across the island towards St Mary's. A check on the now unattended desktop computer had revealed Pastor Simon had various appointments scheduled with patients on different wards that day, meaning that he wasn't strictly speaking making house calls, as the forty-something woman had claimed. But it was a fine point of difference and, having gleaned the information she now needed, Lara wasn't going to quibble.

The local fire chief also wasn't going to raise any concerns about an emergency call that turned out to be anything but, particularly as it was cancelled within a matter of moments. It was a favour and a favour he'd call in himself one day when any of his investigators required a tit-for-tat diversion staged by the local boys in blue.

But as they made the twenty-minute journey back to the capital, something other than a recalcitrant helper to a local pastor was rather more on Lara's mind. And it had been sparked by that last exchange with Conran back in the Major Crime Unit.

'The killing of the murder victim we found in Kenwood was clinical. A single incision severing the windpipe.'

Lara hesitated, Conran's reminder not to fixate on just the one angle here beginning to play on her mind, almost despite herself.

'It was almost execution-style.'

Jordan looked back at her.

'But Mattiss – the grandfather in the garden shed – that was anything but.'

Lara struggled some more. Much as she hated to admit it, Conran might have a point.

'That second blow has always bothered me. There was a kid's party taking place just a few metres away. It was risky enough attacking him in the first place with all that going on, but why take even more of a risk hitting him a second time?'

Jordan indicated to turn onto the main feeder road leading to the hospital.

'So, what are you saying? We might have two different killers here?'

Then Lara stilled. Jordan, ever attuned to his senior officer's abrupt shifts in mood, looked at her as Lara stared out of the window.

'What?'

'That white van.'

Jordan stared across at it, too, puzzled. They'd passed at least a half dozen similar white vans in the last half dozen minutes alone.

'The registration number.'

Jordan tensed as he saw the letters 'EL'. The partial match they'd identified on the van that had hit Amy.

Less than a second later, Lara was exiting the passenger door as Jordan hit the brakes, bringing the pool car to a screeching halt.

CHAPTER
FORTY-NINE

THE DRIVER WAS ABOUT fifty metres ahead, having just dropped off a delivery and was now returning to his van.

Lara was making the approach on her own. Jordan remained in the car, keeping the engine running. Two officers approaching a mark on foot was poor practice. If that mark suddenly made a run from it, one could chase on foot while the second pursuer could cut him off by speeding ahead in the car.

'Excuse me.'

Jordan saw the driver of the white van turn as Lara approached, warrant card in hand. And he saw the instant fear that flashed across his face, as he stood, irresolute and staring, for a moment.

Behind him, Lara once again took in the registration plate and the 'EL' two-letter partial match she'd spotted those couple of minutes before. But it wasn't the number plate that was telling her all she now needed to know. It was the hunted look on the driver's face.

'I need a word.'

But she was destined not to get it. The man suddenly turned and hared back to his van. He had about thirty metres start on Lara, and she held back. She could have made up the distance, but most likely she'd have reached the van seconds after he'd dived inside and deadlocked the doors, reducing herself to banging on them in an ineffectual attempt to stop him racing away.

Instead, Lara stood still as Jordan raced up to her. By the time the man in the van had started his engine and fumbled the vehicle into gear, Jordan had pulled up alongside, Lara was in the passenger seat and the chase was on.

'Hold tight.'

Lara did just that as the banshee howl of their police siren split the air. Ahead of them, the white van, gathering speed all the while, screamed round a corner, making for a nearby intersection, Jordan's unmarked car in close pursuit. Other cars approaching the same intersection braked hard, alerted by the siren, allowing pursuer and the pursued free passage. Pedestrians paused on the pavement, keeping a wary eye on the car and the van as they snaked past in case one or both of them lost control.

Inside their car, as Jordan fought to maintain close contact with the van, which was now speeding faster, Lara worked the radio, requesting back up pursuit cars to set up roadblocks ahead. If they could manoeuvre him up towards the coast road, they could even use a stinger.

But they didn't need it. Either the driver was panicking, or he really didn't know the island. Because he now veered off the main road leading up towards Cowes, choosing a series of smaller roads instead, and Lara and Jordan both knew the route well. It was going to take him straight to a dead end overlooking the Medina.

Jordan throttled back. There was no point in risking an accident now. The white van increased the distance between them. In its side mirrors, Lara could see the driver's eyes as he checked for his pursuers. Perhaps encouraged by the police car now holding back, perhaps believing he was winning the chase, the van accelerated hard to ram home his perceived advantage – just as the road ahead ended ahead of him and the river appeared in its place.

For a moment the van's rear lights illuminated as the driver stamped down hard on the brakes. But all that did was send the vehicle into a vicious spin. The driver tried to correct it but overcompensated. Two wheels rose up from the passenger side, the remaining two scrabbling for grip on the tarmac. Then the van catapulted off the shallow bank and into the water, its rear lights still illuminated as the desperate driver kept standing on the brakes, his panicked eyes clearly visible in the vehicle's side mirrors again as he mounted a last panicked attempt to regain control.

A few metres away, a teenage boy on the bank saw it all. He saw the van hit the water. He saw the driver – who couldn't have been wearing his seat belt – hurtle through the windscreen. And he saw that same driver crash into the mudflats on the bank, his neck twisting as he hit the ground.

The teenage boy just stood and stared for a moment. Then he did the only thing he could think of doing.

He took out his phone and hit the video button.

Lara was by the driver's side in moments. Jordan was already on the radio to comms again, changing the previous request for help from police stingers to paramedics. Lara tilted the driver's head back. Placing the heel of her hand at the centre of his chest, she placed her other hand on top of it, interlocking her fingers. Then she pressed down, hard, again and again, counting as she did so. There was no response.

Switching her attention to his head, she pinched his nose shut before placing her lips over his mouth and blowing as steadily as she could. Straightening up, she saw what she thought was a faint light begin to return to his eyes. Lara repeated the emergency procedure, and a few seconds later he gave the first of a short series of guttural moans.

Jordan had re-joined her by now. Lara had bought themselves seconds only and she knew it. The driver could lapse into unconsciousness again at any moment. Or worse.

'Amy – that young girl on the road – did you know her?'

The driver struggled to focus back on her. For a moment, as the light started to fade in his eyes again, Lara feared that they'd already lost him. Then, suddenly, and in heavily accented English he managed to gasp out a few words.

'She just stood there.'

Lara stared at the driver as he fought to battle for breath.

'She just stopped. Right in front of me. Then she just stood there.'

Then he stopped, too, as a deep, rasping, hacking coughing fit suddenly claimed him. Lara leant closer, her voice hissed, urgent. She was already fast discounting any previous suspicion of ill-intent here. This driver was wracked, tormented even.

'Did you see anyone else?'

He struggled to focus back on her again.

'Was there anyone else there, anyone near her?'

The light began to fade in his eyes again.

'Just before she stepped out into the road?'

A frown creased his forehead, something seeming to be stirring and Lara urged him again.

'Try and remember.'

The driver looked up at her again, but all he could still seem to see was Amy.

'The girl.'

Lara interrupted, impatient.

'Not Amy.'

The driver shook his head.

'Not her. Another girl.'

Lara stilled. Then another bout of rasping, hacking coughs

sounded, and his body contorted in spasms. And this time, unconsciousness claimed him.

In the distance, a siren sounded, and then an ambulance was seen approaching, Lara straightened up as a paramedic dashed from the vehicle. And as he started working on the driver, Lara looked downriver at a working boat as it headed towards the straits, a male pilot at the helm.

By her side, Jordan was looking at someone else.

On the opposite bank, the teenage boy checked the footage he'd just shot on his phone, a smile creeping across his face. He knew some people called his home island sleepy, but look at what had just happened before his very eyes – and he had it all, here on his mobile. Visions of admiring friends in school swam before his eyes as he showed it round. He even wondered if a local paper might be interested. They'd had a careers talk lately and the advisor had mentioned journalism as a possible career for those, like himself, who'd always done well in English.

A moment later his animated smile wiped as a powerfully built black man shoved a warrant card in his face, before snatching his phone from him and confiscating it, so he claimed, for evidence.

Across the small inlet, Lara hardly even noticed. She was still staring, unseeing, at the boat, which was now disappearing into the distance, the last two words the driver had spoken to her echoing inside all the while.

Another girl.

Lara kept staring out over the water.

Esther?

CHAPTER
FIFTY

IT REALLY WAS *the animal's fault. All it had to do was keep quiet, but it hadn't. So, there'd been no choice.*

For a moment, everything had been perfect. Rhys's chest was rising softly, then falling equally softly, as he enjoyed what looked to be a dreamless sleep. Then, a sudden burst of envy flared inside. It had been so long since the watching figure had enjoyed the same untroubled-looking rest. The world had changed now, and everything had changed with it.

Sometimes – another symptom of the chaos into which the world had been so suddenly plunged – even the face reflected back in the mirror in the mornings seemed changed too. Sometimes, it was like looking at a stranger.

But maybe that was fitting in one sense. Because Rhys was now a stranger too, a fiction, a pretence. That untroubled face concealed something much, much darker. Standing over him in the half-light, the dawn just beginning to break outside, the bad blood coursing through his veins could almost be seen. Whether Rhys was aware of that himself, didn't matter. It was there, just as it was with the young girl in that bed in the ICU unit too. She'd had multiple transfusions by now, but it made no difference. She was still stained by the same bad blood, and nothing could now eradicate it.

So there really was only one course of action and it had to be done now while the young man was sleeping. Just reach out, clamp two hands around Rhys's throat and send him to oblivion. Maybe – if the killing was quick enough – he wouldn't even wake up.

Then something brushed past, close, with a low, guttural, meow. Rhys begin to stir. A second greeting from the cat that had just pushed its way into his bedroom, saw the young man's eyes flutter.

But by that time, the room was empty, and they were downstairs in the hall, the cat's soft purring replacing the previous meows as the animal imagined it was being taken for the food it had just demanded.

A second later its head had been smashed against the hallway wall as, upstairs, Rhys settled again to sleep.

PART FOUR

CHAPTER
FIFTY-ONE

EARLY THE NEXT morning Jordan was back in the Major Crime Unit handling the never-ending paperwork that always had to be completed after a police chase ended in an injury, as well as trying to forestall any flak that might be coming their way from their DCI for instituting that chase in the first place.

Conran, as a sour Jordan reflected, would have played it by the book, checking that all safety procedures were firmly in place before even beginning to apply pedal to metal, by which time the white van man would probably have been disembarking the ferry in Portsmouth.

Then again, that white van man wouldn't now be facing an extended period of convalescence in St Mary's.

Early checks had confirmed all Lara's initial suspicions. He'd only ever been an unwitting threat to Amy and was certainly no hitman. The driver was an illegal who'd crossed from France sometime during the last year. He'd been making a sporadic living working wherever he could for whoever he could, his dubious immigration status explaining why he hadn't come forward in the aftermath of the accident.

The white van driver also had a daughter of around Amy's age. A photo of her had been found in his jacket along with a record of regular payments being sent home for the family he'd crossed a continent to support. Whether he was correct in believing Amy had just stepped out in front of him of her own accord, or whether she was trying to get away from someone, still had to be established. He was like any parent; all the white van driver could see every time he closed his eyes was the moment of impact and his own precious daughter. All he could think about was the torment Amy's parents must be going through.

Jordan stared down at the paperwork. Usually, he'd be irritated by it. Now he was glad of the mind-numbing tedium. It meant that he also wouldn't have to think about the last thing the white van driver had said about some other girl being at the accident scene.

Lara might have seen one face when he'd said that, but he'd seen another. For the next few minutes at least, he wouldn't have to think about any possible connection here to Coco.

CHAPTER
FIFTY-TWO

MAYBE IT WAS that realisation that the white van driver was a complete innocent in all this, but that encounter on that riverbank had brought two other innocents powerfully back to Lara's mind. The mother and daughter whose graves she was now visiting.

The mother was called Chrissie, and she'd been in her thirties when she was killed. The daughter was called Harper, and she had been six when she'd been murdered a week or so later. Just over a year ago, they'd had the misfortune to get caught up in Esther's vendetta against Lara and had suffered the same fate as a handful of others that her stepsister's ever more crazed eye had happened to settle on back then. And, right now, and before she did anything else, Lara wanted to replenish the flowers she'd brought along on her last visit.

As she approached, she slowed. More fresh flowers, and a large display, too, were already in pride of place on the grave, which puzzled her for a moment. Esther had focused on very specific targets, souls who had no living relatives, as she sought to create victims in her own image.

Lara looked for any cards accompanying the flowers but couldn't see any. She bent down and felt the stems, which were still moist, meaning they'd been freshly watered. Then she looked up as a shadow fell across her, stilling as she saw Kieran Walters, Chrissie's old boyfriend, approaching, a large bottle of water in his hand, recently re-filled from an outside tap some fifty or so metres away.

For a moment, neither said a word. Neither needed to. Memories of Chrissie and Harper danced in the silent space between them, robbing them for a moment of the power of speech.

Kieran definitely looked better this time than the last time she'd seen him, but maybe that wasn't saying all that much. At that time, he'd been on the roof of one of the island's churches, a man driven to tormented distraction by a combination of anger and grief, intent on ending a life that had become unsupportable. He didn't look tormented now. But he was clearly still in grief.

'It's Harper's birthday.'

With a shock, Lara looked down at the date on the headstone. She hadn't registered it before, but Harper would have been seven today. As Kieran reached into his pocket, brought out a toy frog, placed it next to the flowers, another memory washed over her. In the days he'd been with Chrissie, days he'd dreamed of becoming Harper's permanent stepdad, taking the place of her birth father who'd died some years before, Kieran and Harper had spent hours together by the small pond in his garden.

He looked back up at her.

'You've not found her yet then?'

Kieran didn't spell out who he was talking about. He didn't need to. His life was as much lived now in the shadow of all Esther had done as Lara's. She hesitated, shook her head. For a moment she tensed, half-expecting a sudden tirade at the useless local police force

But instead, Kieran looked down at the two graves, angry outbursts far from his mind. He'd given into that for a moment, a few nights before in that club. Briefly, he'd toyed with the fantasy of expiating his grief on another representative of her Majesty's

Constabulary who hadn't yet brought Chrissie and Harper's killers to justice. It had been a short-lived madness. One look at the departing police officer in question had told him she was suffering in her own way, too. Whether that was Esther-related as well, he had no idea, but demons were certainly claiming her. Why else would she have been there that night?

'She's still around, isn't she?'

Lara looked at him.

'She's still on the island.'

Lara kept looking at him, unsure if that was a statement or a question. He rolled on.

'I've not seen her. But I can still sense her.'

Then he paused, struggling again.

'When you do find her. When all this is over.'

He looked back at her, then nodded down at the graves and the flowers.

'Don't stop coming. Don't forget them.'

Lara nodded back. She didn't know if she'd ever find Esther. She didn't know when, or if, this would be over. But she knew one thing. She'd make this return pilgrimage from now to the day she died.

Kieran stood in silent contemplation for a few moments more, then turned, made to head away. Then he paused again, struggling now, although what he said next seemed to make no sense.

'Look after her.'

Lara looked back at him, puzzled. Who was he talking about? Certainly not Chrissie or Harper, not now. And, surely, not Esther?

Kieran struggled once more.

'Some people, they're fine. They try one thing, move on to something else, they're just tourists. But with some of them, it goes deep. Too deep.'

Lara kept looking at him. Kieran was miles away now, seeing pictures she couldn't see. Maybe even pictures he himself didn't want to see.

'It's like a sickness and the longer you spend in a place like that, the worse it gets.'

Suddenly, memories of Kieran's past passion, or at least a passion before he met Chrissie, returned for Lara. The S&M scene to which he'd retreated in grief, the punishment sessions he'd re-embraced, perhaps in his guilt at not keeping his new lover and her daughter safe.

But Kieran didn't say any more. He just looked down at Chrissie and Harper's graves again, staring at a future that would now never exist as he inhabited a present that, so far as he was concerned, shouldn't be allowed to. For a moment, it didn't look like he was going to say anything else, but then he placed the full bottle of tap water next to Lara's own flowers, before nodding at her one last time and repeating his enigmatic instruction.

'Look after her.'

Then Kieran turned and walked away.

CHAPTER
FIFTY-THREE

THE HALL LOOKED JUST the same. The same teen helpers occupied the same trestle table; the same forty-something woman maintained her wary, watching brief.

Only one detail was different from the last time Lara had been here and that was the presence of Pastor Kenneth Simon, now returned from the hospital and looking just as wary as that forty-something female helper. Circumstances had conspired to prevent Lara meeting him in St Mary's. But they were meeting now.

'I really don't see how I can help.'

Pastor Simon's practised smile didn't even attempt to reach his eyes.

'The Church did some outreach work there from what I recall, but that was well over thirty years ago, if not longer.'

'So, what else do you recall?'

Pastor Simon stared at her.

'You remember doing outreach work, you've just said, so do you remember any of the children, did any of them stand out in any way?'

'We conducted group Bible readings, there were no individual sessions.'

'The staff then? The teachers? Did anything strike you as odd about any of them?'

The pastor looked at her again, quizzical. 'Odd?'

'Did you see any evidence of maltreatment on their part?'

'I'd have reported it immediately if I had.'

Then his face cleared, some dim detail floating down the years.

'I do remember one thing. And this was odd. I only caught a glimpse of it, but there was a child's playroom in the grounds, shaped – believe it or not – like a windmill. It had wooden sails, everything.'

He smiled.

'And they worked, too, at the slightest breath of wind they started spinning.'

Then Pastor Simon paused, and Lara let the silence stretch. It was the same stray memory recalled by Andrew Russell, too, which could just be two random men bringing back the same unconnected recollection. That windmill would have been a highly unusual sight, after all.

'Did you ever come across any other visitors while you were there? A man by the name of Edward Mattiss perhaps?'

Pastor Simon shook his head.

'No.'

Lara wasn't going to get anywhere here, and she could see it. Whether that was because there was nowhere to go and nothing to uncover, she had no idea. Then she paused as she looked down and saw a banner headline from one of the flyers lying on another of the trestle tables.

'In the beginning, God started creation.'

The pastor looked at her as Lara kept reading.

'On the first day, light was created, on the second, the sky.'

The wary forty-something helper moved over to them as Lara continued reading.

'On the third day, dry land, the seas, plants and trees were created, on the fourth, as well as the moon, sun and stars.'

The pastor's helper took it up. This was clearly something she knew by heart.

'On the fifth day, the creatures that live in the sea and the creatures that fly.'

Perhaps emboldened by the intervention of a disciple, Pastor Simon took it up, too, although even on this short acquaintance, Lara really didn't think he'd need too much help in the enabling stakes.

'On the sixth day, the animals that live on the land and, finally, humans, made in the image of God.'

Lara looked up from the flyer.

'And then he took a rest?'

The pastor smiled.

'Well earned, wouldn't you say?'

By his side, his faithful disciple cut in again.

'Making the seventh day a holy day.'

'And when was sin created?'

The pastor and his helper looked back at her, that question clearly ambushing them both for a moment. Then the pastor cleared his throat.

'Original sin wasn't created as such, it's part of the human condition, as exemplified by Adam and Eve and Eve's decision to eat the forbidden fruit.'

Lara didn't need to study the flyer for her next question.

'And we can't cure ourselves of original sin?'

'But we can escape its consequences by turning to God, by receiving his grace and accepting his love and forgiveness.'

'And that holds true for all humankind?'

Pastor Simon nodded.

'And that was the doctrine you taught at Kenwood?'

'It underpins all our teaching. It's taught wherever we visit and whoever we're preaching to.'

'And if we don't escape its consequences? If we don't turn to God? If we don't receive his grace and accept his love and forgiveness?'

Lara nodded at him, quoting from memory another well-worn Biblical passage.

'Paul. Romans. Chapter 6 Verse 23.'

Lara's mobile pulsed, an incoming text alert from Jordan, as she continued.

'For the wages of sin is death.'

Lara looked at him.

'Did you teach that, too?'

Pastor Simon didn't respond. Neither did his helper. Lara felt their eyes on her all the way as she crossed to the door.

———

What Lara didn't see was the pastor slump slightly as that door closed behind her, almost as if he'd been holding himself in check. It was only a tiny moment, not noticed by the few stray visitors who'd come in from the street in the last few moments and who were leafing through those same flyers, and it wasn't noticed by the teen helpers, who were now beginning to tune up instruments for a service to be held later that day.

But the female forty-something helper noticed.

CHAPTER
FIFTY-FOUR

JORDAN'S TEXT had been news on Amy Waite, and it was devastating.

Lara had initially assumed she was being summoned over to St Mary's to give Carey and Matt an update on all they'd discovered about the white van driver and his role in Amy's accident. But more recent events had now overtaken even that.

Amy had suffered a cardiac arrest. The hospital had managed to re-start her heart, and she was still alive in the sense that her heart was beating and blood was still being pumped to all her vital organs. But that was now courtesy of a ventilator that was maintaining that heartbeat and blood flow. A subsequent brain scan had also revealed no activity. In every sense understood by almost everyone, the young girl was dead.

But her baby was not. The foetus was still viable, in the words of the doctors currently overseeing her ongoing care. The question now was whether that viability should be maintained.

'We can't.'

Even in what was her clear and obvious deep shock, Carey Waite's position was firm.

'We can't put her through something like that, and we can't decide for her either.'

Even in his own clear and obvious deep shock, Matt Waite's position was just as firm.

'We've no choice, not now, she can't exactly decide for herself, can she?'

Lara looked at Jordan. They were both staying silent but inside they were in almost as much turmoil as the mother and father currently pacing Amy's small room. Neither Lara nor Jordan had the slightest clue how they'd react in similar circumstances or how they'd feel if it was one of their loved ones in that bed. Should Amy be kept alive, albeit artificially and aided by machines, in order to give her baby the best chance of life? Or should the baby be allowed to slip away with her?

Matt looked at his wife, desperate.

'The doctors might be wrong. People have come out of comas before.'

Carey cut across.

'This isn't a coma anymore.'

'Some have even made full recoveries.'

Carey cut across again, more impatiently.

'She's dead, Matt, she's gone.'

Lara could see it in his eyes. He was blocking her out, as he was blocking out everything else even as she continued to rail at him.

'We have to think for her. We have to think what she would have wanted, and I know my daughter, I know the plans she'd made, the dreams she'd had, and they didn't include having a baby at fifteen and if we could ask her right now, she'd tell you exactly the same, she wouldn't have wanted this in the first place and she especially…'

Carey faltered as she contemplated the broken body in the bed before them.

'She especially wouldn't want this.'

Lara looked round. The sole attending doctor was maintaining a silent, watching brief, a nurse doing the same. Rhys, her boyfriend, was out in the hospital gardens. He was just pacing out there, visible from Amy's high window. After being told what had happened with his girlfriend, he'd walked out without saying a single word.

Aaron was sitting at the far end of the room, his ever-present Nintendo in hand, fingers flashing over the keyboard, as seemingly absorbed in his game as ever, but Lara recognised the signs only too acutely. The young boy was in torment, too.

'She doesn't know where she is.'

Carey's voice was low, almost a whisper.

'She doesn't know what's happening to her. She may survive another few days, or it could all be over by tonight, but if that happens, if that's the way this ends that's nature's way.'

Carey faltered again. She must have felt she'd already been torn in two by grief. Now there was something equally agonising to deal with.

'They're not talking about Amy anymore. About a human being, my daughter, our child, Matt.'

Carey gestured across the room towards him.

'Aaron's sister.'

Carey looked back at Matt, pleading with him.

'They're talking about a vessel, a machine.'

Then she fell silent, the battle lines clear and seemingly unresolvable. Carey found the idea of taking Amy's baby to term, or as close as could be managed, grotesque. Matt was clinging onto it, probably as a way of clinging on to a daughter whose loss he was finding equally impossible.

But Lara wasn't looking at Matt and Carey now. She was looking at Aaron, his fingers still moving mechanically across the keyboard of his Nintendo, and now she was starting to wonder: was he just blocking everything out? Or was he doing something else? Then Lara looked across the room at the unaware Amy.

She was starting to sense something here, a connection, over and above that of brother and sister. Maybe that was because she had a similar connection with a sibling herself, a connection that usually manifested itself at key turning points in Lara's life. Sometimes, it was at the start of a potential relationship. Sometimes it was when she was in a personal or even professional crisis of some sort. Georgia would arrive as if summoned out of the ether.

It wasn't a physical manifestation; Georgia certainly never actually appeared in front of her. She was there as more of an invisible witness, sometimes bringing with her an implicit warning to Lara to not let down her guard, to maintain a distance from whatever or whoever threatened to overwhelm her at the time. Sometimes, she was just there for reasons and a purpose Lara didn't understand, but drew comfort from, nonetheless.

Lara looked back at Aaron. The debate that was raging all around that room right now as his mum and dad alternately tore each other apart, before appealing to the doctor and nurse to back each of them up in turn, wasn't even touching him. Lara would have put money on the fact he wouldn't be able to recall a single word that was being said if challenged later. All his attention seemed to be on his screen and on that alone, but all his focus was on Amy, Lara knew it.

Making Lara wonder how deep that connection went. And what they might find if they probed it a little.

Lara turned to Jordan, indicated she wanted a word outside. Once out in the corridor, she nodded back towards the room and the wracked family they'd just left.

'I want to talk to Aaron.'

Then she stopped, as out of the corner of her eye she saw Rhys, still down on the patch of grass below, still pacing back and forth. Lara hesitated for a moment longer as she kept looking down at him. And, as if he could see the struggle now going on inside as to who she should concentrate on first, Jordan cut in.

'Leave Rhys to me. You talk to Aaron.'

Lara hesitated a moment, just catching something in his tone, but there was no time to pursue that now, so she just nodded back.

CHAPTER
FIFTY-FIVE

'How was she the last time you saw her?'

Jordan, now outside with Rhys, was choosing his words carefully. Partly, because this was a difficult and sensitive police investigation. But also, because this was a difficult and even more sensitive personal matter.

Rhys shook his head, impatient. He was still reeling from the latest, crushing, news about Amy.

'I've been over this with all the other officers. She was fine. So was I. We were excited. My dad was away. We were going to spend the night together.'

Jordan persisted.

'There'd been no rows, disagreements, no clashes between the two of you in the last week or so?'

'What about?'

Jordan swerved that one, for now.

'She must have known she was pregnant.

Rhys just nodded.

'But she hadn't told you?'

'Maybe she was going to that night.'

'But she wasn't going to the hotel. She was walking away from Shanklin, not towards it.'

Rhys paused, his shoulders slumping.

'I know.'

'Which suggests she didn't know what to do. It suggests she didn't know whether to tell you or not, so was there anything she'd said in the last week or so that, looking back, might explain that?'

Rhys looked back at him and the expression on his face said it all. He knew – or he thought he knew – exactly what Jordan was trying to say here.

'Was it mine, you mean?'

That was part of it, as Jordan reflected, but there was more to this exchange than that: that potentially difficult and sensitive personal issue, again.

'That's one line of inquiry. And we'll pursue it. But was there anything else that might have upset her?'

Jordan hesitated.

'A row, maybe?'

'I've said all this before, too, we hadn't had a row.'

'If not with you, with someone else then?'

'Who?'

What could Jordan say? With his own daughter?

'A friend maybe, a girlfriend?"

'What about?'

Jordan hesitated. The answer was simple. Could Amy have had a row with Coco about a possible relationship that might have been developing between her and Amy's boyfriend? Jordan really didn't want to open that can of worms, but the longer this was going on the less convinced he was that he'd need to. The expression on the face of the wracked young man before him was already telling him all he needed to know.

Whatever the truth behind the accident, Rhys's love for her seemed totally genuine. His torment right now mirrored that of the white van driver as he re-lived what must have been the worst experience of his life, too.

Looking at Rhys right now, Jordan couldn't see any world in which he'd have given Amy any cause to doubt him.

Meaning that Jordan had no reason to doubt Coco either.

CHAPTER
FIFTY-SIX

'I TOOK A GUESS, NO SUGAR.'

Aaron didn't look up from his Nintendo, so Lara put the coffee down on the table next to him. He hadn't said a word as she suggested they grab a drink and give his parents more time to talk to the doctors about Amy. But he hadn't resisted, either.

Lara studied him. There was never going to be any point trying to hedge around things with this one, she could see that straightaway. So, Lara went straight for the jugular instead.

'Did Amy ever mention the name "Kenwood", to you, Aaron?'

Briefly, for no more than a nano-second, Aaron's fingers fumbled on the keyboard, then resumed their metronome-like progress. Lara leant forward, about to repeat the question. Then Aaron responded.

'No.'

Lara studied him again. Something about that name had registered, she could see it in the young boy's newly troubled eyes. She could see something else, too. He'd accompanied Lara to that coffee shop, believing he was in for more wasted time fielding yet more redundant questions at a time he should be concentrating on one thing and one thing only and that was his game. But she'd ambushed him, shocked him even. But she also knew that she wasn't going to find out why.

Aaron had gone back into some private space now, well away from her, well away from anyone.

To any passing observer Aaron would have seemed to be just a young teen absorbed by his keyboard. But inside, he was screaming.

Why couldn't she just shut up? Why did she have to keep talking like that? Why the hell did she have to get in the way?

Once, when he was a young boy, while on holiday, they'd walked down a cliff path to a beach and for a few moments, unobserved by either Amy or his parents who were all ploughing on ahead, he'd wandered off the path. Distracted by the sunlight, he'd strayed too close to the cliff edge and had then panicked as he saw a yawning abyss suddenly open up below. Equally suddenly, Amy was there, which made no sense because he could still see her, walking ahead of him, her head just visible between Mum and Dad, striding down towards the sand. She was with him at the same time, reaching out her hand, taking his hand in hers and leading him, without saying a single word, back to the path, back to safety.

One hour later, with a picnic spread out before them, and with Dad swimming in the sea and Mum changing behind a rock a few metres away, Amy had looked at him, and had spoken to him directly for the first time since it happened.

'Don't – ever – do that again.'

Aaron nodded back. Nothing else was said. Nothing else needed to be said. Amy knew she'd been there, too. She knew she'd also been walking down that path to the beach with Mum and Dad at the same moment. It didn't matter that it wouldn't have made any sense to anyone else, it made sense to them, and that was all that mattered.

Aaron had reciprocated over the years, of course. He'd never actually steered her to safety like that, but he'd been with her at key times, too, which was why, for the last few days he'd been in torment, believing that the accident had not only robbed him of a sister he hardly recognised anymore, it had robbed him of something else as well.

That is, until a few moments ago. Sitting in this very coffee shop, not next to Amy where he thought it might happen, but a good couple of hundred metres and one floor away, in the company of a stranger asking him a question he didn't understand. Suddenly, Amy had joined him, only for a moment, but she'd been there. At the exact moment that police officer had said that name – Kenwood. He didn't know why, and she didn't say, but that wasn't unusual. Often, they'd both just sit together in silence, even if in actuality she was miles away with some friend at the time and he was at home, up in his room.

He couldn't ask her anything anyway of course, he couldn't risk it, not with that woman sitting opposite. Then he began to calm, a little at least, because Amy had come back, however briefly, and maybe that was all that mattered. Words, actual explanations for what had happened and why, could come later.

CHAPTER
FIFTY-SEVEN

As JORDAN LET himself into his flat a short time later, he stopped as he heard the click of a switch followed by the dim whoosh of running water beginning to sound from the bathroom, meaning Coco had just jumped into the shower.

Jordan paused for a moment longer. Past experience had taught him one thing about his daughter. Once that shower clicked on, he wouldn't see her for at least half an hour, sometimes longer. Previously, that had earned Coco a mild, but chiding, lecture. He wasn't on any sort of meter, but sometimes the condensation count in there could approach Turkish Bath proportions. But now Jordan blessed a teen's obsession with personal hygiene because it was going to give him all the time he needed.

On his drive home, Jordan had given himself a stern talking to. Edie had always said it and maybe she'd been right. Maybe it was his being a cop. Maybe it was something ingrained in him, making him look out at a world through perennially suspicious eyes, doubting everything anyone might say, never taking anything on face value, always looking for the hidden, for something that might be concealed.

Jordan's exchange with Rhys had indeed convinced him there

was nothing concealed here. All the young boy could think about right now was Amy. There was no room in his head, or his heart, for anyone else. Coco was a friend, just one of many other friends he must have, meaning Jordan had done it again; he'd looked out onto the world with those distrusting eyes of his. He'd judged it and found it worthy of investigation, which might be acceptable in his professional life, but which was very much not acceptable when it came to his personal life and his daughter.

Jordan gave a quick, silent shudder as he imagined, and not for the first time, what Coco might have said had she found that bug.

But she wouldn't find it, not with that shower running and her on the other side of a closed and locked bathroom door, and her bag on the floor in front of him. Jordan crossed to his laptop and turned it on, logging onto the bug for one last time before he cut the connection and excised all record of it from his hard drive. Then he crossed to Coco's bag and reached inside, locating and taking out the device in a matter of moments. Then he froze.

Inside Coco's bag was something else. Jordan brought out photo after photo of Rhys, some clearly taken when the young boy was unaware he was being snapped: as he walked out of a shop, as he hopped onto a bus, as he stopped to talk to a friend.

Jordan turned, the bug still in his hand, as the front door suddenly opened behind him and a stranger, a woman, appeared.

A bewildered Jordan just stared at her for a moment. What the hell was a total stranger doing letting herself into his flat like this?

Jordan froze again, as behind her, Edie appeared.

CHAPTER
FIFTY-EIGHT

ONCE AGAIN, Lara stood before the floor to ceiling window, looking out on that ever-changing tapestry on the water below. Behind her, once again, were more case notes from her late mum's files.

Lara needed a few quiet moments after all that had happened back in St Mary's. She needed, if only for a short time, some peace, and she needed more of that. Maybe it was the sight of Carey, Matt, and Aaron, facing the prospect of a lost relationship, but Lara now needed a link back to a relationship she also thought had been lost.

Once again, as she turned back from the window, she elected for the same routine as before. She closed her eyes, then sifted through her mum's old case notes, stopping at random before taking out an entry. Like before, she'd no idea from where this one would feature in her mum's life in care, but it didn't matter. She'd cover them all in time.

Then Lara paused, puzzled for a moment. This entry wasn't strictly speaking a case note at all; it was a record of a visit her mother had made in the company of a social worker.

This was different in another sense, too, because this time, as she started to read, Lara didn't feel herself taken over by the events she was seeing on the page. She didn't experience that empathic absorption into the life her mum had been leading at the time. Instead, she just read about the day her mum had decided she wanted to visit a grave.

Lara knew the grave in question well. Every islander did. It had been part of island folklore for decades. Lara read on for a few more moments.

Then she picked up her car keys.

CHAPTER
FIFTY-NINE

THE GRAVE MARKED the final resting place of a girl in her midteens. There were just three words inscribed on the headstone.

The Unknown Girl.

That's all there was because that's all there could be. No one knew her name. There also wasn't a date of birth or a date of death on the headstone, because that couldn't be accurately recorded either. The islander who found her had spotted her body being washed in from the sea while he was out walking his dog. In the days, weeks and months that followed, no one, be that family or friend, had come forward to identify her. Over the ensuing few decades, no one had ever come forward either.

In the aftermath of the discovery, the local community had come together to buy that headstone, burying her unclaimed body in the nearby clifftop cemetery. They'd adopted her in a sense, and once a year they held a service for her, on the anniversary of the discovery of her body, high above the sea that had washed her ashore in the first place. It was a service that was always covered by the local press and, initially, they'd hoped the publicity might bring someone forward who could cast light on who she was and how she'd died, but that had never happened.

The annual service of commemoration continued though, an enduring and touching act of faith.

It was one such commemoration that the case worker and Lara's mother had attended, at her mother's insistence. The case worker confessed that she herself was puzzled as to why the young girl had insisted on making this trip and had only recorded it in her notes in case any subsequent reason might come to light. Lara's mother herself had stayed silent when pressed.

Lara looked up from the headstone and stared down over the straits below. The case worker may not have understood it, but maybe it was simplicity itself in truth. Maybe one young soul who'd been abandoned had suddenly felt an overpowering compulsion to stand there that day and pay silent tribute to another.

Lara turned to go, but then paused as something about the grave suddenly struck her. She looked around at all the others, just to make sure, then looked back. All the other headstones were pitted, their inscriptions faded over time. But while the grave of the Unknown Girl might have had a lot less in terms of inscription – just a bare record of her existence – the lettering on that headstone was clean and sharp. It had obviously been replaced and quite recently, too. Lara remained there for a moment longer, unsettled without quite knowing why.

Then her mobile pulsed with a new message from Mairead, and Lara returned to her car.

Time to get back to work.

CHAPTER SIXTY

'COULD it have been a warning of some kind?'

It was one hour later, and Lara looked at Mairead as she drove. The first time she'd made this journey, she'd made it alone. That time there'd been two people on the boat she was about to visit, now there was just the one. But, for now anyway, she put that to the back of her mind.

Mairead was talking about a killing, but it wasn't the killing of Edward Mattiss or the killing of the still-unidentified murder victim in the shallow grave in Kenwood. Mairead was talking about a cat.

'It couldn't have posed any sort of threat, so that rules out the intruder angle. It's not as if it was a guard dog. And when a cat gets hurt in an accident, when it gets hit by a car or whatever, they normally go to ground somewhere, they don't usually haul themselves back to the family home to die in the hall.'

Lara cut in.

'What sort of message?'

Mairead shrugged.

'Keep your mouth shut? Don't speak out. If you do, this is what will happen to you too.'

Mairead was doing what Lara always encouraged all members of her unit to do – work around the edges of any investigation, revisit all developments time and again, however tangentially connected they may seem to be, and think outside the box. Airing those often-stray thoughts out loud was something Lara positively insisted on. Whatever was in an officer's mind, just say it, it didn't matter how ridiculous it might sound. The very last thing Lara wanted was for a member of her team to wait for something gold-plated to pop into their heads. Unformed, early thoughts were often the real nuggets, the ones that could be picked up, developed and polished – the ones that might sound crazy at first, in their raw form, but which could just lead somewhere.

'It was a warning to Rhys, you mean?'

'There's not just Rhys living there.'

Lara paused. Mairead was right. There was his father – the high-flying businessman who spent a lot of his time abroad.; the largely absent father who was on his way back to the family home and his son right now.

There was the housekeeper, too, of course, Maisie Gantz, the one other person who would have free access to the house. If that cat had been deliberately killed for some reason, she was another figure an unsuspecting pet might not have shied away from as they'd approached.

Mairead turned off the main road onto a small lane leading down to the river. As she flicked the indicator, she winced, momentarily, the simple movement seeming to give her a sudden jolt. And for a moment – and seemingly out of nowhere – an image of Kieran Walters standing before Chrissie and Harper's graves flashed before Lara's eyes. Along with his strange exhortation to look after someone.

Mairead was concentrating on avoiding a series of potholes on the unmade lane, allowing Lara a few seconds to keep looking at her. It had only been just over a year since Chrissie and Harper's murders. Kieran was probably still suffering the aftershocks. This was a woman he'd planned to marry after all, and a small girl he'd planned to bring up as his own. That stray comment could have been the inconsequential rambling of what could well be a still unhinged mind.

As Lara kept her eyes on her junior officer for a moment longer, two more stray images floated before her eyes. First, that moment a few days ago when Mairead's sleeve had ridden up to reveal that red, angry scar on her arm. And the moment when her back had suddenly seemed to go into some sort of spasm.

Then they pulled on the riverbank, and Lara put that to the back of her mind. That didn't mean she dismissed it completely.

Even from some hundred or so metres away, Andrew Russell looked to be a man in torment, and perhaps it was no wonder. On being notified of the sudden death of his wife that short time before by Mairead, Lara had done some checking. Russell had been married to Jeanette for over thirty years. They'd never had children, and now, with his wife having passed away after a heart attack the previous evening, he was alone in the world,

Jeanette's death was still officially unexplained until the formal post-mortem, allowing Lara the usual right of reasonable access in the event of all sudden deaths of this kind, and it was an access she wanted to exploit for two principal reasons. But as they approached the boat, Lara's heart sank. Russell was up on the deck, surrounded by what looked like family or friends. A large thick-set man tracked their approach and stepped down from the boat to meet them. Barely glancing at their warrant cards, he made it abundantly clear that those same family and friends would very much not appreciate the new widower being disturbed in his time of grief.

Lara could have pushed it. She could have insisted on talking to Russell on the matter that had brought them down here and which had kick-started Mairead's musings on the unfortunate death suffered by Rhys's family pet. Ever since she'd heard of the death of his wife, Lara had been wondering. Russell's wife, Jeanette, had been ill for a long time. In one sense it wasn't surprising that her body had given up what was, by all accounts, an unequal struggle to keep going. But that battle had been lost within hours of Lara interviewing her husband, which could be a complete coincidence. Or it could be another warning: a salutary lesson as to what might happen if Russell opened his mouth.

There was something else too. Lara had visited many bereaved souls during the course of countless investigations. Moments of maximum pressure like that were often times when a mask might slip, when a detail, genuinely forgotten or otherwise, might surface. But as she looked at the milling throng forming a virtual phalanx around Russell, it was only too clear that wasn't going to happen on this investigation, at least not now.

Lara made to turn away, then she paused as something caught her eye. Or rather, as two things caught her eye. First, the press of well-wishers had parted briefly around the slumped figure of Andrew Russell and Lara could see a man leaning close to him, an ecclesiastical collar around his neck, offering words of sympathy and comfort.

Lara kept watching. In a sense, Pastor Simon being with the bereaved widower wasn't all that surprising. If Simon was Russell's pastor, if Russell was a celebrant at his church, it wouldn't be surprising if he he'd called in on a parishioner in his hour of need. But the sight of the two men huddled together still gave Lara pause for thought, even if she couldn't explain why.

Then, behind the two men, she paused again as she stared at the second, slightly jarring, sight that day: an assortment of upmarket cars parked next to the riverbank. In strict contrast to occasionally lazy thinking, river travellers weren't traditionally poor, but the conspicuous consumption on display right now in the shape of Bentleys and Range Rovers still gave Lara reason to wonder, even if, once again, she couldn't really explain why.

Then, at her side, Mairead cut in.

'Lara.'

Lara turned back to see Conran, his face like thunder, advancing along the riverbank towards them.

CHAPTER
SIXTY-ONE

'First, a high-ranking hospital consultant.'

Lara was seated in the passenger seat of Conran's car, a vehicle that wouldn't have disgraced the collection of dream motors still visible further along the riverbank. His elevated status meant he qualified for police help with vehicle financing, and he'd taken immediate advantage of that on arriving at the Major Crime Unit. He hadn't chosen a Bentley, but an Audi A7 with all the bells and whistles had still turned heads.

Conran looked down at a sheaf of papers on his lap, newly extracted from what looked to be a bulging file.

'Now a high-ranking member of the local clergy with links to equally high echelons of the General Synod.'

Lara blinked at that. She'd fallen foul of many personalities in her time. This had to be the first time she'd upset someone with close ties to the Almighty.

Conran looked back at her.

'At the same time, the body count seems to be adding up.'

His face was darkening all the time.

'Amy Waite.'

Lara was about to correct him, but Conran rode on, anticipating and ignoring what she was about to say.

'Not technically dead as yet, admittedly, but given the latest update on her condition I received from the hospital this morning, that's something of a fine distinction.'

Lara subsided, her protest unspoken and destined to remain so.

'Then there's Edward Mattiss, an otherwise fairly unremarkable father and grandfather, but the victim of a killing in, of all places, his garden shed at, on all occasions, his grandson's birthday party.'

Conran picked up another piece of paper from the pile in front of him.

'Then there's the still-unidentified body in an unmarked grave at the site of an old children's home.'

Conran took out from the file and studied yet another report.

'Then the serious injuries suffered by an illegal immigrant implicated in the RTC that's left Amy Waite one power cut away from the grave.'

Lara was tempted to point out that even the straitened resources of St Mary's ran to the provision of a back-up generator, but again, she held her counsel.

'And I accept that this may be totally unrelated, but we now have the wife of one of your latest interviewees suddenly dropping dead, and according to the police log I've just seen, the first thing you've done is hightail it along to conduct a fresh interview with the widower for reasons that are, frankly, beyond me.'

Conran loaded the reports back in the already bulging file.

'Apart from the fact it seems to be connected to an investigation that's coming more and more to resemble some sort of personal crusade.'

Again, Lara held her tongue.

'It isn't any one case in isolation here, DI Arden. Contrary to the impression of most of our happy holidaymakers, there's a dark underbelly on this island, as we all know, and at any one time there's going to be a whole series of crimes. And if we're doing our job properly, we're always going to ruffle feathers.'

Conran leant forward.

'It's the combination. The accumulation of what might be called unfortunate events. And with you at the centre of it all which raises questions. And which, taken together, begs the rather more insistent question as to whether you should remain at, or even near, the centre of anything so far as these cases and this unit is concerned.'

Lara felt her stomach tighten, not because of Conran's dressing-down. She'd endured similar tirades from senior officers before, including Paula, who was still absent from the department of course. So, is this what had happened to her? Had she faced a similar litany of alleged errors, omissions and instances of bad judgement and unfortunate associations? From a body, as she now recalled, chaired by her replacement, Conran, himself.

By her side, Conran's dressing-down continued.

'You're not a copper on the beat anymore. You're a detective inspector. A young one, admittedly, and maybe that's the problem. Maybe your undoubted talents haven't been accompanied by an ability to recognise that, at your level, policing involves a high degree of what we might call politics, too.'

'The art of the possible.'

Conran stared at her as Lara spoke for the first time since she'd seated herself next to him in his upmarket Audi.

'Isn't that what they say politics is all about?'

Lara nodded at him.

'Negotiations, the brokering of deals, the massaging of egos, even?'

Conran's expression began to darken even more, but Lara was already rolling on. He'd had his say. Now, it was her turn.

'Well, it's not what I'm all about, and it's not what my unit's all about. I'm a simple soul in a unit of other simple souls and that's the way I like it, it's the way I operate. We don't negotiate. We don't broker deals. And I don't actually care whose feathers we ruffle along the way, be that high-ranking hospital consultants, the Archangel Gabriel or St Peter and St fucking Paul.'

Lara was tempted once again to leave that perfect interval before the respectful address of 'Sir.'

On this occasion, she decided not to push her luck.

A short time later, Lara was back in the Major Crime Unit pool car, being driven back to the capital by Mairead who was keeping diplomatically silent. Conran had left some few minutes before.

In one respect, it might be said that Lara was due that tirade. But what had impelled her senior officer to make a special trip down to that riverbank to deliver it? He could have waited till she returned to the unit. Indeed, in one sense he'd slightly weakened his hand by coming to her, rather than waiting for her to return to him.

Unless that wasn't the actual reason that he'd made that trip. Unless there was a different reason, perhaps connected to that gathering of mourners and well-wishers on that boat.

Did Conran know Russell? Had he come to offer his own expression of sympathy and support?

While his carpeting of Lara was probably always going to happen sometime, was the timing, and the setting, something of a smokescreen?

CHAPTER
SIXTY-TWO

THE AFTERCARE WORKER had left Edie to get herself settled, promising to call back in half an hour or so to check if she needed anything. She'd also returned the key Coco had given her in case no one was in when they arrived.

Coco, herself, was still upstairs, although the shower, thankfully, wasn't now running. It was twenty-five minutes since she'd turned it on, meaning there was probably another good few minutes before she'd actually make an appearance. Dressing was also something she'd never rush.

Jordan looked at the uncharacteristically quiet Edie sitting on the sofa in front of him. It was also roughly twenty minutes since she'd walked in behind the aftercare worker and caught him removing that bug from their daughter's bag.

Edie would have known what it was straightaway. She'd seen him bring home similar devices when he was engaged on other official investigations in the past. They'd usually earn the largely bored Jordan a lecture on civil rights from his perennially caustic wife, which wouldn't be any expression of a deeply held personal conviction. Edie would just be having a dig. On those occasions, he hadn't believed it was remotely justified. On this occasion, it very definitely would have been.

But had Edie realised what she'd seen? Had she even registered it? She was still on a powerful cocktail of medicating drugs. Jordan had kept up a stream of largely inconsequential small talk, updating Edie on innocuous titbits of school gossip in respect of Coco and her friends – although keeping resolutely off the subject of Rhys. The discovery of all those photos in Coco's bag was still very much playing on his mind.

All the time he searched his still-withdrawn wife's eyes for any clue he'd been rumbled. By the time he heard Coco coming down from upstairs a few moments later, he was no more enlightened than he had been those few moments before.

———

Despite all her father's fond imaginings, Coco had actually only been in the shower for a matter of moments. The rest of the time had been spent doing something much more important.

Taking her mobile out from under a small pile of towels placed over it to protect it from any water or steam, Coco had opened up the display. Sure enough, her message tab revealed four new messages, all from the same number – a number Coco knew well.

The first three were the usual standard fare: an outpouring from a wracked and confused Rhys about Amy, updates on her condition which basically amounted to no update at all. Amy was not going to recover; they all knew that now and that bleak realisation seemed to almost seep through every single one of Rhys's anguished words as they rolled out across her screen. The only issue now was whether her baby would survive or die with her.

Coco sent back her usual comforting text, telling him to contact her at any time, reassuring him that she was there for him, as always – the heartfelt, but still relatively anodyne expressions of comfort and support that any friend might say to another in need. She was careful not to step over any line in case anyone else happened on the online exchange, but it was an unnecessary precaution. Cautious enquiries among the rest of their peer group in school had confirmed what Coco already suspected. Rhys wasn't really in touch with any of them at the moment. Only her, it seemed.

Then the last text made her pause. Suddenly, he'd veered off on what seemed to be a strange tangent. Even the language he was using seemed to have become more fractured, disjointed, almost – although given the strain he was under, maybe it wasn't surprising if he lost it from time to time.

Coco looked towards the door as her dad called again from downstairs, reminding her that Mum was here. Calling back, she told him she'd be down in a minute, then looked back at her phone. Rhys was texting again, and he was almost raving now, telling her that he kept having this strangest feeling that someone was keeping tabs, was watching him. He'd felt it in the hospital on his latest visit, and he'd felt it at home, too. It wasn't just down to that stray figure who'd suddenly appeared in his hall and who could have been just an opportunist intruder looking to take advantage of a house they'd assumed to be empty, this was something else, and last night it had shifted onto a whole new plane. When he'd woken up that morning, he'd had the weirdest conviction that someone had actually been watching him while he was asleep.

Coco answered again, another soothing text, more words of comfort. Then, as she pressed send, a fierce burst of emotion swamped her. Whatever was happening here, whatever the truth behind Rhys's tormented, and probably imagined, outpourings, one thing and one thing only mattered to Coco right now – she was the one he was opening up to.

CHAPTER
SIXTY-THREE

HALF AN HOUR LATER, Lara was back in the Major Crime Unit.

More in hope than expectation, Lara walked out of the main open plan office and down to the end of the corridor, pausing just before she reached the stairway that would take her down to ground level, and through the security doors to the outside. Checking no one was in earshot, she took out her mobile and hit a speed dial button.

She'd tried calling Paula several times over the last couple of days and, on her most recent attempt, had finally hit her answer service. She hadn't left a message. In truth, she didn't know what she would have said. She'd probably have made some feeble excuse about calling to see how she was, a lame subterfuge which the wily Paula would have seen through straightaway. She'd have known immediately that her former junior officer was calling to try and get some inside information on her replacement, as indeed she was. It was something that had begun as mild curiousity. After her latest exchange with Conran, it had become more than that.

This time, Paula picked up on the first ring.

'Paula, it's—'

Paula cut across, flat.

'Hello, Lara.'

Lara paused. Further down the corridor, the door had opened, and Conran himself had appeared from the car park, making for the water cooler just a few metres away. Lara hesitated again, but she didn't need to say anything anyway. Paula – and not for the first time in their eventful and occasionally tumultuous relationship – seemed to be ahead of her. Swiftly, she told Lara she'd text her a postcode before telling her to text back with a time. Then she cut the call. By the time she did so, Conran hadn't even reached the dispenser.

Lara turned away when another door opened, and Mairead appeared.

There was someone down in reception to see her.

The usual protocol with visitors was to escort them into one of the interview rooms on the ground floor. Tea or coffee would then be offered, some degree of small talk would take place, before the visitor embarked on whatever matter had brought them there. None of that happened with Rhys's father, Joseph McGuire.

'Why the fuck are you hassling my son?'

A whiff of an expensive male cologne wafted across the floor of the main reception area as he approached Lara, but this man was no affected dandy like Milton Davalle. His hair was cropped close to his head and salt-and-pepper stubble covered his chin. His well-fitting suit looked as if it had never been within hailing distance of any high street peg and Lara would have bet her mortgage, if she could actually afford one, that the T-shirt he was wearing underneath his suit jacket wasn't adorned with a label from Primark.

'He said you hauled him in, bombarded him with questions. And not just here, but in St Mary's, too.'

A wary Lara just stared at him, giving him his head for a

moment longer as the equally wary duty sergeant watched from the main desk.

'For fuck's sake, hasn't the kid been through enough already?'

Then Lara headed him off. She'd been wrong-footed by Conran down on that riverbank. She'd had to endure that. It wasn't about to happen again.

'No one has hauled Rhys anywhere, no one has bombarded him with questions, and he hasn't been hassled either. He's been questioned in connection with a serious road traffic accident involving his girlfriend, in an attempt to answer a question that must be tormenting him every bit as much as it's concerning us right now.'

Lara nodded at him.

'Namely, what the fuck happened, why the fuck did it happen and who the fuck was responsible.'

Across at the reception desk, the duty sergeant didn't look wary anymore. He looked amused. McGuire didn't. Not remotely.

But he'd shut up, for now at least, and Lara pressed home what might be a temporary advantage.

'Did you know her?'

'Who?'

'Amy?'

'I didn't even know he had a girlfriend.'

Much like Matt and Carey Waite, Lara reflected. So, both Amy and Rhys seemed to be the secretive types. Or both had good reason not to confide in their respective sets of parents.

McGuire stared back at Lara. She tensed, waiting for another outburst. Then, suddenly, he turned and walked away, moving past the still watching duty sergeant, before heading back out to the car park.

Lara watched him go, her mind turning over once more. Joseph McGuire could just be an overprotective father understandably concerned about a son who was going through hell right now, and that was why he didn't want Rhys subject to any more questioning.

Or he could be rather more concerned what those questions might uncover.

CHAPTER
SIXTY-FOUR

LARA WASTED little time in making her meeting with Paula.

Her former senior officer hadn't left for the mainland as Lara might have expected. She wasn't a native islander after all. Paula had elected to spend her period of enforced gardening leave in relatively close proximity to the police unit she'd left. She'd taken a holiday let in the village of Brighstone, a cottage on the picturesque North Street, owned by the National Trust. The setting was genteel, the general atmosphere slow-paced, everything life in the Major Crime Unit was not. Maybe that was why she'd chosen it.

Not that Paula suggested meeting at her actual home, but the postcode she'd texted to Lara was one she'd recognised immediately. It marked the site of a monument in the shape of a Celtic marble cross, commemorating one of the island's most famous visitors, the poet Alfred Lord Tennyson. The surrounding downs were named after him, too. They'd been a favourite walking spot for the great man apparently, and no wonder. The views were spectacular.

Lara and Paula had the downs and the cross to themselves for now, although, given the wide-open vistas on all sides, space wouldn't exactly have been a problem had there been coachloads of day trippers there, which was, again, maybe why Paula had chosen it.

The ostensible purpose for this meeting had been dispensed with quite quickly. Lara had made her phone call wanting background information on Conran, but Paula couldn't tell her much about her new DCI anyway. She distrusted him and believed he was a careerist and not a cop. He'd not actively acted against her in her welfare hearing, but he'd made it crystal clear he wouldn't piss on her if she was on fire. So far as skeletons in his cupboard were concerned, Paula doubted he'd ever taken his nose out of his vellum-bound copy of the latest edition of the Police Statutory Instruments to actually acquire any, which said it all so far as she was concerned. And which, as Lara reflected, might be all there was to say, too.

But there was a second reason why Lara wanted to meet up with her, and it was something she'd had only properly realised on her drive over there.

'It must catch up with you, right?'

Paula looked at her as they continued their walk.

'All those years, being one person, pretending to be another person altogether, it's got to take its toll.'

Paula stayed silent for a moment. She'd risen through the ranks in unusual circumstances, having been part of a specialist unit for almost ten years dedicated to undercover work, although exactly what she'd been doing inside that unit wasn't known and probably never would. Her unit had been disbanded after a couple of its members had gone rogue, like so many undercover cops back then, unable to reconcile what had become two warring parts of the same life. On the one hand, they were cops spying on whatever group they'd infiltrated. At the same time, they were an actual member of that often tight-knit unit, forming friendships, forging alliances. Some officers had done more than that and had begun relationships, even – in the case of one officer who was now revered and despised in equal measure by former colleagues and former friends – starting a family with one of the women he'd been spying on. No one knew the lengths to which Paula had gone in the half-life she'd been living in her missing decade. Again, probably no one ever would.

Lara hesitated again.

'This case. The one we're working on right now. It seems to have some connection to Kenwood.'

Paula stilled at the name, an instinctive reaction.

'We still don't know for absolutely sure.'

Lara paused. That may not be strictly true any longer, but she pressed on, nonetheless.

'But I keep thinking about all the people who used to work there. They've had to reinvent themselves haven't they, build brand new identities, turn their backs, not just on what they did, but even who they were?'

Paula walked on, leading Lara along a nearby path that led down towards the Needles as Lara continued.

'Never letting down their guard.'

Lara looked down towards the three jagged stacks of chalk now before them rising out from the sea. There had been a fourth at one time, but that had collapsed back into the water during a vicious storm some three hundred years before. The chalk spine connected under the sea floor to the mainland, emerging at Dorset's Isle of Purbeck. It was a place Lara returned to time and again when she was searching, in one way or another, for connections.

She looked back at her still-silent companion.

'Can you really do that? Not just for a year, two years, but year on year, for the rest of your life. Can you ever reinvent yourself so completely you actually forget who you used to be?'

Paula stayed silent for a moment as Lara pressed her.

'It has to catch up with you sometime, doesn't it?'

Then she stopped as Paula went off on what seemed at first to be a total tangent.

'Did I ever tell you about the headaches?'

Lara looked at her.

'They were the worst I've ever had. They started about a year after I went undercover. I saw everyone I could, doctors, specialists, police doctors when I could get away safely, other specialists in different hospitals when I couldn't. I even had a couple of scans in case I had a tumour or something.'

Paula stared with unseeing eyes over the distant water.

'It was a junior doctor who cracked it. Not that he ever realised it. But he asked me once what it felt like, and I told him that it was like I was being split in two.'

Paula kept staring out over the water.

'The moment the unit was disbanded, the headaches stopped.'

Then she paused, took a deep, deep breath, and looked back at Lara.

'No, you can't hide away forever and, yes, it has to come out sometime. You might think you can school yourself so completely you actually start to believe the fiction you've created. But it doesn't last. It can't.'

Paula nodded at her.

'Even if your mind doesn't let you down, sooner or later your body will.'

CHAPTER
SIXTY-FIVE

THE CALL HAD COME through from Lara just over an hour earlier. Swiftly, and with his senior officer clearly in her car and on her way somewhere, she'd updated Jordan on the sighting of Pastor Simon on Andrew Russell's boat.

On the one hand, and as Lara had pointed out, it made nonsense of Russell's claim that he knew no one with a Kenwood connection, although, as she also pointed out, it was possible that he was unaware of it. Quite clearly, they couldn't press Russell right now, but they could press the pastor. Then Lara had cut the call. She still hadn't told him where she was going, or why she wasn't about to conduct this interview herself, but Jordan didn't care. He was just glad to get out of his flat right now.

A short time earlier, Coco had come down from her shower. Jordan, Coco and Edie had struggled through the strangest of reunion teas with cakes sourced from a nearby deli. Jordan had kept the fitful conversation going between the three of them, but it wasn't easy. All the time the air was pregnant with the weight of what wasn't being said as well as images dancing before all their eyes of the last time they'd been together, imprisoned in that underwater sluice room.

And all the while, unasked questions hovered, heavy, over

this strangest of family reunions, too. Would Edie really soon be recovered enough to return to their old family home and stay there alone? Would Coco feel impelled, or even choose, to leave Jordan's flat and re-join her? Coco hadn't said anything about her long-term plans after her mother's release from hospital and Jordan hadn't asked.

Added to what might be called all those old concerns was a new one. Or rather, two new ones. First, there were all those photos of Rhys. What the hell were they all about? But there was also the other not-so-little matter of Edie and that bug. Jordan still didn't know if she was so far out of it that nothing was really registering anymore.

Or whether she was just biding her time before she said something.

Pulling up outside the meeting hall a short time later, Jordan's heart sank as he saw the forty-something woman they'd met before parking her car nearby. They'd identified her now as Linda James and had further established she'd been a loyal member of Pastor Simon's church for the past year. Linda saw Jordan immediately and the way her lips set in a disapproving grimace told him that she welcomed the prospect of this second meeting about as much as she had the first. Jordan tried ignoring her, heading for the front door instead, but the human gatekeeper intercepted him before he could make his way inside.

'It's afternoon prayer.'

Jordan just looked at her.

'We set aside an hour at this time for any members of the congregation to join Pastor Simon in a period of silent contemplation and worship.'

Jordan hesitated. He could ignore the protocols and just march straight in but having already skated over the thinnest of ice with Edie, discretion might be best here at least.

'I'll wait a few moments.'

Linda James nodded back. She was still smarting from what was an obvious subterfuge with that fire alarm. She wasn't about to be out-manoeuvred again.

'I'll tell the pastor you're here when he comes out from the communion, and he can decide then when he wants to see you.'

The frosty Linda made for the door. Jordan looked back down the road wondering if there was a decent coffee shop nearby. Something was already telling him he might be in for a long wait.

Then Jordan wheeled round as, from inside the hall, came a piercing scream.

CHAPTER
SIXTY-SIX

IT WASN'T a crime scene so much as an abattoir.

Jordan had dashed inside the meeting hall to find Pastor Kenneth Simon had been crucified. There was no other way to describe it. His naked body was splayed on a large outsize cross. Blood had pooled in a large puddle beneath his legs and wrists meaning the crucifixion had taken place while he'd been alive. Jordan couldn't see what had actually caused his death at first, although it was difficult taking anything in given the hysterical screams emitting from his disciple. For a short time, Jordan wondered if some assailant had simply nailed the pastor to that cross and then let his life bleed out of him onto the floor.

Then he saw the pastor's mouth. Or, rather, the second mouth beneath the one nature had given him, formed by what would later be confirmed as a single violent slash to the throat. There was something else there, too, and for a moment Jordan couldn't work out what it was. He moved closer, ignoring the still-hysterical Linda to see something protruding from the open wound. At the same time, and following his stare, the wild eyes of his helper focused on the strange protuberance as Jordan leant closer, then she screamed even louder as Jordan reeled back, the pair of them realising at the same time just what they were looking at.

It was the pastor's tongue. Whoever had killed him had reached inside his open throat and pulled his tongue through the bloody aperture. Linda's screams began to reach stratospheric levels of volume. Paramedics, alerted by Jordan, arrived moments later although it was already demonstrably too late to save the mutilated Kenneth Simon. There was still a living casualty to treat in the form of Linda James though, who looked as if she was about to expire from shock.

Arriving a short time later from Tennyson Down, Lara was shocked, too, but her police mind was already beginning to whir into action, because this macabre killing, and its manner, wasn't only a murder.

It was a message.

At the same time, Mairead had picked up a call to another incident. Some sort of message seemed to be being sent out here, too.

As she hurried along the riverbank, Mairead could see an extended floral tribute that now dominated the deck of Andrew Russell's boat. The name 'Jeanette' had been picked out in a variety of flowers of contrasting and complementary colours. Mairead had already established that her body was going to be returned from the hospital to the boat, to be taken on her final journey to a crematorium on the mainland the following day.

A dog walker on the opposite bank had seen someone hovering around the boat after Russell himself had left to collect supplies for a wake that was planned for later that evening. The dog walker had lingered for a few moments, keeping watch. When he saw that same someone board the boat as Russell had driven away, he'd alerted the local police to a possible break-in. Uniform would normally have picked it up, but a flag had been placed on anything to do with Andrew Russell, and the call had been re-routed to the Major Crime Unit.

Mairead stopped, staring in disbelief as, on the opposite bank, the dog walker who'd made the three-nines call started shouting in outraged protest, and no wonder. Someone had gone to a lot of trouble to assemble that floral tribute. Right now, whoever was on Andrew Russell's boat, was going to a lot of trouble to trash it.

Mairead stared as the figure on the deck began ripping great handfuls of flowers out of the display before scattering them over the side. Within no more than a second or two the elaborate and lovingly constructed display had been reduced to something that looked like roadkill. Mairead started running towards the figure on the deck who looked, at first glance, to be around Andrew Russell's age. Then the vandal abandoned their seemingly-inexplicable attack and – in a manoeuvre giving Mairead cause to wonder if he – or she – was somewhat younger than she'd first imagined – vaulted over the side of the boat and plunged into the water. The intruder swam strongly downstream for fifty metres or so before hauling themselves out on the opposite bank well away from the dumbfounded and still raving dogwalker and headed into the woods on the far side.

CHAPTER
SIXTY-SEVEN

'HER EYES OPENED.'

It was a few hours later. Lara was back in St Mary's again. Scenes of Crime had now closed down the church hall and Sarah Ryan was already conducting her initial investigation, which was when Lara had taken an excitable phone call from Matt Waite. She'd immediately hurried down to the hospital believing there might have been some development relevant to Amy's accident.

Matt turned, gestured to his son.

'Tell her, Aaron.'

Aaron stayed silent. Across the room, the attending nurse stayed silent, too, her body language telling Lara more eloquently than words alone could have managed all she needed to know.

Matt paced the floor, gesturing down at his unresponsive daughter.

'She blinked for a moment or so, then she opened her eyes, I saw it myself, Aaron was here, he saw it, too.'

Lara looked at the still-unresponsive Aaron, then back at Matt, her heart sinking all the while. There hadn't been any development, just this clear exercise in self-delusion. Matt Waite might be on Cloud Nine right now, convinced his daughter was coming out of a coma from which all medical opinion had assured him, time and again, she would never recover. But quite clearly no one else in that hospital room shared that hopeful conviction.

Not that there were many people in that room right now. There was just Matt, the nurse and Aaron. Of Carey, Amy and Aaron's father and Matt's wife, there was no sign, and Lara knew why. The doctor in charge of Amy's treatment had updated her as she'd arrived. It was another reason her heart was sinking right now.

Matt was still pacing. He hadn't had any response from his son, but he didn't need any. His conviction was absolute, as was his total faith in what he believed he'd just witnessed.

'The doctors are saying it's just a nerve thing, something to do with her reflexes or something, but she looked at me, she actually looked at me and she recognised me, too, only for a moment, but for that moment she knew who I was.'

Lara looked back at Amy. It was one of the cruellest things and Lara had seen it before – a patient in Amy's condition would stir, would make a sound, would even open eyes that had been closed for as long as they'd been in their vegetative state, and relatives and friends would be given momentary hope where in truth none existed.

Carey had pointed that out to her husband, and all too forcibly if that update Lara had received from the hospital doctor was anything to go by. A huge row had ensued. At one point the alarmed nurse had considered calling security, as it briefly threatened actual physical violence on both parts. Thankfully, Carey and Matt had both reined back, and outside intervention hadn't been needed.

It was a classic case of irresistible force meeting immovable object. Matt was convinced their daughter would recover and become a mother to the child she was carrying. Carey was equally convinced that the Amy they'd known and still loved was gone, and that to keep her alive to fulfil some pipe dream fantasy that she might carry their grandchild to term was an intolerable imposition, not only on them but on a young girl who'd suffered enough already. Lacerating grief was behind both arguments, driving Amy's parents into a bitter clash in which neither was right or wrong.

And now it had all had its perhaps inevitable effect. Carey had walked out of the hospital at the same time as making it clear she was walking out on her husband. She was going to stay with friends until Matt came to his senses. It was a shattering development in an equally shattering story.

But it had all seemed to just wash over the myopically focused Matt who now reached into his bag and brought out a folder.

'I've recorded it all here, look.'

Lara stared at a neatly bound diary she hadn't seen before – a record of Amy's time in the hospital, each day filled not only with details of her treatment but snippets from her friends, good wishes, small items of gossip, photos from some gig, snapshots of a day out on a local beach that she'd missed but which she could re-live, by proxy, when she came round. Matt's face as he leafed through it, said it all. He saw hope here. He saw the promise, at least, of better times. All Lara could see was yet another human casualty clinging to wreckage.

Then Lara looked across the room at Aaron as an oblivious Matt continued to show her more entries in a journal that was little more than a monument to private pain. For the first time she could remember, Aaron's eyes weren't fixed on his Nintendo.

Aaron was looking straight at her instead.

CHAPTER
SIXTY-EIGHT

A SHORT TIME LATER, Lara and Aaron were in the coffee shop again. Like last time, there was a latte in front of Lara, but there was now a Fanta in front of her companion. Aaron had actually made a choice this time, rather than let Lara make it for him.

Lara had told Matt she'd bring him something back when they returned to Amy's room, but he hadn't even heard her. He was now as absorbed in his latest diary entry as his son had previously been in his games. That is, until that look a few moments before that Aaron had flashed Lara's way. That steady stare that told her he wanted to say something.

Once again, Lara was sensing a connection, the same connection she shared with Georgia. Theirs had been forged in abandonment and adversity. How the similar bond between Aaron and Amy had been forged she didn't know, but it was there nonetheless, she was becoming more and more sure of it.

'If you know something.'

Aaron looked back at her as Lara pressed him, gently.

'Something that might explain things.'

Aaron kept looking at her.

'Help us understand.'

The young boy reached out, picked up his Fanta, then put it

down without drinking, speaking now for only the second time since Lara had met him.

'About Amy?'

Lara nodded back.

Aaron hesitated once more. For a moment Lara feared he'd retreated to his private space. Then he looked up from his untouched drink.

'She told me not to.'

Lara grew uneasy. Was he under the same delusion as his father? Had he imagined that Amy had somehow been communicating with him, too? But, and as if he could read her mind, he hurried on.

'Not now. Before. She made me promise.'

Suddenly, Georgia was there again. That invisible ghost took up residence on Lara's shoulder once more. All Lara could see was her own sibling, reflected in Aaron's eyes as the young boy struggled. This sounded like this was something he'd been rehearsing for days.

'But if she doesn't come out of this...'

He stopped, abrupt, then looked up at Lara again.

'Then I suppose she'll never know, will she?'

Lara remained silent, letting him try to work this out for himself.

'I keep thinking.'

Aaron looked back at her, desperate.

'That maybe she'll give me permission or something.'

He shook his head.

'I know that sounds stupid, but...'

Then the young, troubled boy stopped again, stared past Lara into the near distance out onto the adjoining corridor. For the rest of their time together, and to Lara's frustration, he didn't say another word.

CHAPTER
SIXTY-NINE

IT WAS ONLY A FLEETING GLIMPSE. For a moment, as she paused out on the corridor, she couldn't be sure if it was her.

Then she saw the young woman lean close to the young boy sitting opposite her across that small table, and for that moment the side of her face was on full view. And Linda James felt her blood start to boil.

A short time earlier, she'd been told she was being discharged. She'd been given some pills to take if she needed them, but they wouldn't erase the sight she'd just seen back in that meeting hall, the image that seemed to be almost engraved on her eyeballs. The macabre murder of a man she'd always thought of as a saint.

She thought she'd never get that image out of her head, would never be able to see anything else. Until a moment ago when she saw that young female police officer again – the one who'd initiated that fire alarm she was now convinced was fake, designed to allow her and her companion time alone in the hall to pry while the rest of them milled, impotently, outside. The fake alarm, she was now equally convinced, that had somehow set in train the chain of events had led to the mutilation and murder of Pastor Simon.

She'd seen the scepticism in the female officer's eyes when she was talking to him. She'd seen it many times before, too. Some had openly challenged the pastor at their regular community outreach meetings, and dark mutterings had sounded about converts being brainwashed, impressionable minds being moulded, but Pastor Simon had always just spoken the simple truth. God's truth. And she was living proof.

The tumour was inoperable, that's what they'd told her. It was just a matter of time. That's when the pastor had come across her, a shaking wreck on the edge of giving way completely, sitting in one of the relatives' rooms in this very hospital, trying to summon up the strength to stand, to put one foot in front of the other, to make for the exit and catch a bus to her one-bedroomed flat she shared with an elderly cat, but no husband anymore. He'd left a year previously, unable to cope with an illness that they both knew was only going to become increasingly debilitating, and which had just been confirmed as a death sentence.

The pastor hadn't talked about that. He'd talked about faith. He'd talked about healing. She didn't understand everything he'd said, at least not at the start. That had taken weeks of study and Bible readings. But he'd given her what the doctors had refused to give her, what her ex-husband was unable to give her, and that was hope. All they'd talked about was a managed decline, but he'd told her to put her trust in the spiritual, in God's force for good and she had. And, while she knew she wasn't cured, she'd lasted a lot longer than the doom-laden predictions she'd heard that day.

She hadn't attended any of the follow-up sessions that had been offered her by the doctors. She hadn't even returned any of her GP's calls in the last few months. She'd focused on her studies instead, on her faith, and on Pastor Simon.

To see him momentarily bowed down like that once that young female officer had finally caught up with him was heartbreaking. To see and hear him being challenged by those who knew nothing of the struggles he wrestled with daily was almost intolerable. Linda swayed in the corridor momentarily, as that image, her last sighting of her beloved pastor, flashed in front of her eyes again.

Then she focused back on the young female officer still talking to the boy in that hospital canteen. The pastor had been doing God's work. He'd been fighting the devil, and that devil came in different forms and assumed many different guises. But whatever form he presented, the lesson was clear, Pastor Simon and the Bible said so.

The devil had to be vanquished.

Evil had to be put to the sword.

CHAPTER
SEVENTY

MATT HAD HARDLY NOTICED that Carey wasn't there, and he didn't know where she'd gone. He hardly even registered the fact that Aaron had gone, too, and he didn't care about that either. All he was focused on right now was his daughter and the child she was carrying.

Because this was a gift so far as he was concerned. Carey couldn't bear the thought of their daughter being kept alive for the sole purpose of bringing forth a child she may not even have wanted anyway. Robbing her of all reason and independent thought, in her eyes at least.

But Matt had always seen himself as the more clear-sighted, better able to see what he'd always described as the bigger picture. And now, as he looked at his daughter, knowing there were two hearts beating inside that one body, his face began to set in that determined expression the family had come to know only too well over the years.

And had come to fear too on occasions, as even Matt himself would have to acknowledge.

Carey had to see this. If she couldn't, he'd have to do what he'd done on more than one occasion in the past, what he'd had to do with Amy and Aaron on occasions, too. He had to make her see sense. He had to bend her to his will.

And, yes, some might say he'd occasionally been a little over-enthusiastic in the punishments he'd meted out over those years, not only to Carey and to his children, but to others as well.

But Matt, both at home and in his former place of work, had always believed in not sparing the rod.

PART FIVE

CHAPTER
SEVENTY-ONE

MAYBE IT WAS that exchange with Aaron. The exchange that promised so much initially but delivered so little. Or maybe it was this ongoing case that seemed to be as far away as ever from any sort of resolution. Or maybe the unsettled Lara had just had enough of people holding back on her.

Jordan was doing that, and so was Mairead. What they were holding back could be none of her business, or it could be a portal into something they could build on in the current investigation, Lara didn't know. But if she kept holding back, too, she never would find out.

'I went to lay some flowers the other day.'

Mairead, at her desk, looked up at Lara, puzzled. The Major Crime Unit office was empty behind her.

'At Harper and Chrissie's grave. I suddenly realised I hadn't thought of them for weeks.'

Lara's face darkened, this still so raw, so painful. Then she paused.

'Kieran was there.'

Mairead stared at her now uncharacteristically awkward senior officer. That silent stare was telling Lara all she needed to know, all she'd suspected indeed since she'd first seen those wounds on Mairead's arms and had witnessed her back going into that sudden spasm, a growing suspicion that had been ballasted by that encounter with Kieran and his last, enigmatic, aside.

'Have you seen him yourself? Since it happened? Since Chrissie and Harper?'

Mairead struggled for a moment, clearly choosing her words ultra carefully.

'Why would I?'

It wasn't a yes and it wasn't a no. For now anyway, Lara let it lie. But now she was even more unsettled. If Mairead was getting involved in the S&M world, then it was something hidden. And much like Jordan's drug-taking all those months before, another ostensibly private matter she'd felt impelled to probe, something hidden in a police officer's life was leverage: a villain's wet dream.

Half an hour later, Lara was with her next target at one of the island's most prominent tourist attractions, Carisbrooke Castle, the place where Charles 1 was confined prior to his execution.

It was one of the regular haunts that Lara often decamped to, particularly the Princess Beatrice Garden in the grounds, named after Queen Victoria's youngest daughter, so Jordan wasn't too surprised when they first pulled up there. A few minutes later and having dodged the donkeys at the sixteenth-century wellhouse, he was feeling as if he'd been ambushed.

'Parkhurst?'

Jordan stared at her.

Lara nodded.

'It was the last time we had one of our chats. Just me and you.'

Jordan remembered it well. That time it had been about

Lara's stepsister, Esther. Something was already telling him this was about something else.

'You got a text. It rattled you; I could see that. I asked you if everything was OK and you made an excuse, told me you had to go and sort out a report for Conran.'

Lara appealed to him, pushing this exchange harder than she'd pushed the one with Mairead. She knew Jordan far better, which was one factor at work here. There was also the possibility that she might one day get to know him rather better, too.

'If this is strictly personal, then tell me to fuck off.'

Lara struggled.

'I know Edie's about to be released from hospital, so if all that was something to do with her, I apologise.'

Jordan cut across.

'She's been released. She's staying in the flat for a few days, then they're going to see if she can go home.'

'So, it was something else?'

Jordan took a quick, deep breath, let a couple of day-trippers walk past, then turned to face her. He wasn't going to get anything past the wily Lara, and he knew it. But right now, he didn't want to. This was something he'd been wanting to get off his chest for too long.

'Coco has been seeing Rhys McGuire.'

Lara stared at him.

'Seeing him as in—'

'I don't know. But she's spending a lot of time with him right now. And given Rhys is a person of interest to us...'

Jordan tailed off, struggling, then looked at her again.

'I don't think anything's happened between them. When I talked to Rhys back in the hospital, he never even mentioned her.'

Jordan paused.

'But then that white van driver said he'd seen a young girl not far from Amy when she was hit.'

Lara reflected. All she'd seen when he said that had been

Esther. Clearly, Jordan had seen someone else. But while Lara hadn't discounted her stepsister, Jordan had clearly now discounted his daughter.

'If there was a girl there, I'm as sure as I can be that it wouldn't have been Coco. But I don't want her to suddenly become a person of interest, too, because of a connection to Rhys, and you found out I hadn't told you.'

Lara didn't reply. She couldn't imagine all that had happened to Amy had anything to do with Coco either. But she also knew that despite her veneer of sophistication there was an element of suggestibility in the young girl – a willingness to be led into areas no girl her age should enter.

And now Lara was even more unsettled.

CHAPTER
SEVENTY-TWO

She watched as Matt, the father, left the room.

One down, just one to go.

She knew it had become a family mantra. She knew that no matter what happened, Amy must never be left alone. She must not wake up to just see the faces of strangers – doctors, nurses and the like – looking back at her.

But that was in the early days after the accident and things had changed. Not with Amy, she remained in the same comatose, locked-in state, nurturing the life inside her, albeit unaware. But Matt and Carey had changed. Whereas, previously, they were almost glued at the hip, now they barely spoke. It had all had its inevitable effect on Carey who'd suffered a minor collapse the previous evening, a combination of exhaustion and the ongoing strain. Right now, she was under doctor's orders to rest in a side ward to Amy's room and not to visit her daughter for at least the next twenty-four hours.

That left Matt and Aaron, and Matt – looking as wired and angry as he always looked these days – had just left for home. Just over thirty minutes later, minutes that had ticked by at an almost funereal pace, she watched as the door to Amy's room opened and Aaron walked out, his ever-present Nintendo in hand, making his way down the stairs to a small collection of benches on a patch of grass directly underneath his sister's first floor window.

She watched him for a moment, she couldn't help herself. He'd always had a strange, detached quality about him. If Amy had ever talked about him, it was with an equally strange quality of amusement and the fiercest of loyalty. She could, and did, criticise him, but if anyone else even tried then Amy's fabled temper, a temper the daughter seemed to have inherited from her father by all accounts, would burn white-hot, scorching everyone in its path.

She hesitated a moment. The staff shouldn't be a problem. Security was an issue, but not usually for someone like her.

There was only one way out to find out though.

Coco took a deep breath, then walked towards the door.

CHAPTER
SEVENTY-THREE

A BEWILDERED KIERAN WALTERS couldn't understand it. He hadn't cut anyone up as he'd been taking his usual route to work, he'd observed the speed limit, his MOT was up to date and his car was taxed. There was no reason for the traffic cop to pull him over that he could see. Having pulled him over, there was also no reason why he should be going through his car in what was fast becoming a near-forensic examination.

His lights were being checked as well as his indicators and the depth he had left on his tyre treads. The officer was even making sure his horn worked. Kieran had tried making a couple of admittedly feeble jokes, wondering if this was part of the force's new policy against 4x4s. After receiving nothing back, he just shut up. All the time the cop kept up the same monotone demands that he turns on this switch, turns off that.

Kieran checked the clock on the dash. He'd left himself plenty of time to get to the ferry to begin his shift, but much more of this and he'd be in serious danger of missing the first sailing. And now the cop had found a faulty bulb and was telling him he was going to issue him with a statutory spot check fine!

'Don't you think...?'

Kieran tried mounting a belated protest, but it froze on his lips as the officer just shot him the sharpest of glances before leaning back on the bonnet and eyeing him, coolly. Then things turned even more bewildering.

'Don't I think, what? That I'm poking around here just that little too much?'

Kieran stared back at him, blank.

'Taking just too much of an interest in something that really isn't any of my concern?'

Kieran kept staring at him. Where the hell was all this coming from?

The traffic cop, still eyeing him grimly, just rolled on.

'Making something my business, when it really isn't any of my business at all?'

Kieran kept staring. While he still didn't know what this was all about, he now knew that this had very little to do with a supposedly routine spot check on an old and anonymous 4x4 being driven to his place of employment by an otherwise anonymous ferry worker.

Then Kieran saw her – parked up, a hundred or so metres down the street. He'd seen the car before without really registering it, but he registered it now as he realised who was at the wheel.

Looking out from behind the windscreen, Mairead held Kieran's stare. She continued to hold his stare before nodding across to the traffic cop. It had taken a while, longer than either of them had expected in fact, but he now seemed to have got the message. As a result, another favour was now due from an officer in the Major Crime Unit, this time to a colleague in the traffic division, but that wasn't a problem, she'd find a way to pay him back.

So long as Kieran had learnt his lesson it was worth it.

CHAPTER
SEVENTY-FOUR

LARA ROUNDED the corner of a cottage that had never resembled any cottage she'd ever seen before, to see a cremation taking place.

Lara hadn't received a reply as she'd knocked on the front door, but she could hear voices from somewhere, so she cut down the path to the rear garden, half-expecting the McGuire's inquisitive neighbour to pop his head up over the adjoining hedge again. She turned the corner and then stopped dead as she saw Rhys and his father bent over a small mound of earth.

Strictly speaking, the cremation had taken place sometime before. The ashes of the McGuire's family pet were now in a box on the ground next to that small mound of earth. Lara watched as Rhys picked it up, placed it lovingly in a shallow hole left by the excavated soil. Then he turned away, upset, and moved back inside the house via the adjacent rear door. Joseph McGuire looked after his son for a moment, quite clearly battling upset himself. Then he paused as he saw Lara.

Lara picked up the second of two spades that were lying close by. Some flowers were lying by them. Without explaining what she was doing there, Lara began to fill in the earth on top of the small casket. McGuire hesitated for a moment, then bent to the same task. Working silently, they replaced the excavated earth, smoothing and patting it down, then he picked up the flowers, a selection of different-coloured roses, and placed them carefully on top. He stood for a moment in silent contemplation, then looked up at her, struggling now, clearly feeling that some bridges needed to be built.

'Back in the station – how I was...'

He tailed off but he didn't really need to say anything. Lara could see the apology in his eyes.

'I've always done it, my wife always said it and she was right, and since she died it's got worse, I know, but I can't seem to help myself.'

He struggled.

'And it doesn't help that I'm away such a lot, too, I suppose.'

McGuire looked down at the small grave at his feet, the small collection of roses.

'If anything happens with Rhys, it's like this massive red flag. I just steam straight in. I don't even think.'

He smiled a smile that was no smile at all, oceans of regret seeming to be swimming behind it as he picked up a glass from a nearby table, a generous dram of whisky inside. He drained it, then looked at her again.

'Rhys isn't mine.'

Lara stared at him.

'We adopted him when he was one. Rhys knows, he's always known, it's no big secret.'

McGuire struggled for a moment.

'Another reason I'm so over-protective, I suppose.'

He looked towards the house.

'It doesn't matter how old they are, does it? To me, he'll always be the small child I used to watch over while he was sleeping.'

McGuire smiled, almost sadly.

'Never tell him this, but I still do from time to time.'

Then, and almost as if he felt he'd just let himself down in some way, McGuire turned away and walked back into the house and the waiting Rhys, leaving the glass behind.

Lara watched him go. She'd called over there to follow up on the possible relationship between Rhys and Coco. But now she might have something else to follow up on.

Lara turned back and looked back down at the small grave. This case was all about ripples. At the centre of those ripples was Kenwood, and Lara was still convinced that whatever was happening here, it all led back there. Rippling out from that were all those other disparate connections, too – Amy Waite, Edward Mattiss, the still-unidentified body in that shallow grave, Andrew Russell, Pastor Kenneth Simon, Rhys and Joseph McGuire.

Now those ripples had spread further. Now there was a birth father, Rhys's birth father to trace as well. Was there any connection to Kenwood there?

Then Lara's phone pulsed again, another message alert, this time from Mairead. The Major Crime Unit had just been contacted by a nurse from a local hospice looking after one of the ex-Kenwood employees Lara had previously traced, John Weston.

There'd been a development.

CHAPTER
SEVENTY-FIVE

COCO HAD REALLY THOUGHT her mum had changed.

Over the previous months, she'd visited Edie in hospital many times, had accompanied her on the occasional walk out in the hospital grounds, and each time she'd had the same impression. Everything that had happened to them in that weird underwater sluice room at the hands of that young woman seemed to have had the same effect on her as it had had on Coco. Suddenly, life wasn't some big game anymore.

There was a time when Coco loved the fact that she could do anything she wanted. But deep down she'd always known that it was an illusion, a teen fantasy of how life should be lived. Dad always said Mum had never grown up, and, for a time, Coco simply didn't listen. But a few months ago, she'd been landed the starkest proof imaginable which had nearly led to her own date with a too-early death.

Edie had faced the same wake-up call at the same time. It seemed to have forced that same sea change in her, which made what had happened those few hours before even more difficult to take.

'You want what?'

Coco stared at the frail figure gripping her hand back in her dad's first floor flat.

'I want you back home, living with me.'

Coco stared at Edie's medication spread out on the table before them.

'Mum, you're still convalescing, you can hardly look after yourself right now, the last thing you need is someone else to worry about as well.'

'I'd worry more about you living with him.'

Coco struggled to stay calm. Within a few hours of her being discharged from hospital it was starting again. The old battle lines were being redrawn. Her dad on one side. Her mum on the other. Coco in the middle, being batted back and forth between them like some demented shuttlecock.

'Things have changed.'

'He hasn't. And it's not right. What he's doing.'

Coco had heard it all before. He'll clip your wings, she used to say it all the time, he tried to do it with her, and he'll do it with Coco, too, and she'd believed it at one time. But that time was gone, and that Coco was gone now, too.

Coco struggled as she tried to work out how to bridge what seemed to be yet another impossible divide, but then she stopped as Edie brought out her phone.

'He thought he'd deleted it.'

Coco looked at her. What was she talking about?

'But he's not as clever as he thought.'

Coco stared at an image on the phone, an impossible image in one sense, a snap of herself and Rhys taken a couple of days ago.

'How the hell?'

Coco stopped, then stared at the image for a moment longer, seeing the beach, the sea behind them, working out exactly when the photo must have been taken.

But how?

And why?

Then she stared back at her mum.

'He's been spying on you.'
Coco kept staring at her.

Now, she was visiting Amy for the first time since her accident. She'd been to the hospital a few times to see if there'd been any news, but she hadn't actually been inside Amy's room. A couple of Amy's other schoolfriends, including Donna, had steeled themselves to do that, but Coco hadn't felt it was her place. She hadn't ever really been the kind of friend to Amy that Donna had been.

But that wasn't the reason for her reluctance, and she knew it. It was guilt that had been keeping her away: guilt over her conflicted feelings towards Amy's boyfriend, a conflict that had been growing ever more acute by the day.

Her mum's bombshell revelation had crystallised all that. Yes, there was dad's betrayal to deal with, and she did feel an initial burst of white-hot anger at that. But she also knew she'd given him plenty of reasons to doubt her over the last year or so. She could never have expected him to simply put all that behind them and start again.

But something else happened then, too. As if she was having some sort of out of body experience, she re-lived her times alone with Rhys: their often-intimate exchanges, their growing closeness. Coco moved into Amy's room, not even seeing the attending nurse who smiled at the sight of another of her young patient's schoolfriends. Coco just looked at the broken figure of Amy lying in the hospital bed before her. All the time she'd been doing that Rhys's actual girlfriend – and the mother of his child – had just been lying there. Now Coco's cheeks burned again, but not with anger this time. Now, all she felt was shame.

Coco leant forward, took Amy's unresponsive hand in hers. She didn't speak, and Amy wouldn't have registered what she was saying anyway. She didn't need to. Coco and her dad would need to have an actual conversation sometime about all he'd been doing, but she needed to have a conversation of her own before that, with Rhys.

In a young life that had been scarred by too many instances of doing the exact opposite, Coco now had to do the right thing for once.

CHAPTER
SEVENTY-SIX

ACCORDING TO MAIREAD, Staff Nurse Carmen Morrison hadn't explained why she wanted to see Lara. For a moment, as she returned her call, Lara wondered if John Weston had finally passed away, but Weston was still hanging on, it seemed. This summons was nothing to do with him either, at least not directly. At which point, Carmen obviously decided she didn't want to elaborate any further on the phone and insisted that if a now puzzled Lara wanted to know more, she'd have to call in person.

'There is another option.'

Lara looked at Mairead. She was driving again while Lara had been working her phone, liaising with Jordan back in Police HQ. For Mairead, who'd clearly put their last exchange firmly behind her, it was blue-sky thinking time again.

'From what you've told me, Weston's not exactly in the land of the living anyway, but Andrew Russell is. He's the only other one who still has some connection to Kenwood, meaning he has to be at special risk.'

Lara looked at her, echoes of Peggy O'Riordan's clear disapproval still fresh.

'So, what are you saying? We take him in? Offer him protection?'

Mairead shook her head.

'We leave him out there.'

Lara kept looking at her.

'But we monitor him, like we've done before. What was it you said, when you suggested the same thing with Tony Stone?'

Instinctively, out it came, the clearest of memories from one of Lara's briefings to the team from a year before, on a different, if potentially still-related, case.

'We track him so closely he won't be able to order a pizza without us knowing what topping he's chosen.'

Not that it had done Tony Stone a lot of good, as Lara now reflected. Within days of their covert surveillance beginning, the unfortunate Mr Stone had been dead.

Mairead nodded.

'If there is some list out there, if that's what this really is all about, then Russell has to be on it. And with the names on that list dwindling one by one, his turn has to be coming round soon.'

'In other words, we use him as bait.'

It wasn't a question, but a statement. Mairead didn't reply. She didn't need to. The idea was out there, and it was a good one.

'Oh – and by the way.'

Mairead reached into her bag, handed Lara a print-out of an email.

'That headstone.'

Lara scanned the print-out, growing puzzled as she did so. She'd mentioned the newly replaced headstone on the grave of the Unknown Girl to Mairead on her return from her visit that day, and her junior officer had found it curious, too. She'd also clearly done some digging but it had only thrown up a fresh curiousity in its wake.

Lara looked back at Mairead, not quite able to understand all she was reading.

'No one knows who paid for it?'

Mairead shook her head.

'A local stonemason was contracted to carry out the work. But when he'd tried to contact whoever had commissioned it to make sure they were happy with it all, he'd hit a dead end.'

Lara looked back at the email again. The stonemason had been paid by bank transfer from an account that had been closed down the minute the funds had been transferred. And he'd subsequently found out that the name and address of the account holder was false. All of which meant that years after the body of the Unknown Girl had been washed up on a nearby beach, someone had gone to a lot of trouble and expense to put a new headstone on her grave, and that same someone had then gone to a similar amount of trouble to make sure no one found out who they were.

Then Lara hesitated. Because, and thinking it through, was it so curious in truth? It could have just been down to a simple well-wisher and there were plenty of those on the island. The grave itself was ample evidence of that. And yes, it might seem strange that they'd gone to such lengths to remain anonymous, but plenty of people acted anonymously when it came to acts of charity.

Then Lara stilled, putting it out of her mind, as they came up to the driveway leading down to the hospice.

One hour earlier, Mairead had ended her call to Carmen, still unsure why she wanted to see her senior officer. Five minutes after arriving at the hospice, Lara was no more enlightened.

The staff nurse met her at the door. She barely glanced at the accompanying Mairead, and when she led the two officers down the corridor it was away from John Weston's room. In fact, she seemed to be leading them away from any of the rooms the hospice reserved for the care of its short- and long-term residents and heading for what looked like a plant room instead.

The nurse Lara was now encountering was also a million

miles removed from the warm and caring soul she'd encountered on her first visit. Then, she'd seemed genuinely thrilled that one of her more problematic charges had found himself a visitor. But now, she seemed troubled, and deeply troubled at that.

As they followed her down a bewildering succession of corridors, the two officers passed a specialist unit catering for residents in the later stages of dementia. Briefly, Lara caught a glimpse of a singer attempting to croon a reaction from the blank, unaware faces in front of him, which seemed appropriate somehow. Blank and unaware was pretty much how Lara was feeling right now, too.

Carmen paused before a small door at the end of another featureless corridor, nodding at Lara, speaking for almost the first time since she'd met her at that front door.

'He didn't want me to call you. Not at first anyway, but he can't keep on like this and neither can I.'

She paused looking even more troubled.

'If the hospital administrator knew what I was doing, if they knew he was here, they'd go mad, but it's not just that.'

Carmen tailed off, struggling for a moment.

'He needs help.'

Two minutes later, the staff nurse, Lara and Mairead were in a small storeroom on the other side of that small door. A forty-something man was lying on a makeshift bed before them.

'They told me to wait. That's all I had to do, just wait. Then someone would drop it off.'

The forty-something man was called Iain Hagan. He'd been a porter at the Hospice for the last five years.

'It got to ten o'clock, then eleven, then midnight. I had to be up by four for the early shift here. I tried calling on the usual number but there was no answer. Around one o'clock I must have fallen asleep.'

Hagan was talking about a payment, payment for information. Still lying on his makeshift bed, he coughed, his voice a croak, every word a painful effort.

'Then I woke up. I heard a click. It sounded close, really close, but I couldn't see anything. I thought maybe I'd left the door unlocked, maybe they'd tried knocking but I hadn't heard, so I grabbed my T-shirt, went out onto the landing, called out, but there was still nothing.'

Hagan paused, a shudder coursing through his whole body.

'Then I got this really weird feeling, like someone was watching me.'

Outside, and from further down the corridor, the faint strain of a sole, reedy, elderly voice joining in with the cabaret crooner floated through the door.

Hagan took a deep breath.

'I've got a mirror in the hall. For a minute I half-expected to see a face behind me, but I didn't. I just saw this.'

Hagan touched his throat, indicating a small mark, little more than a nick, the kind that might be left by a careless shave. But at the very centre of the mark, Lara could still see a single, red dot.

'That was the last thing I remember. After that, everything went black.'

Outside the small storeroom, silence descended again as the reedy, elderly voice tailed off.

'When I came round, I couldn't see a thing, I thought I'd gone blind or something there was this sack on my head, it was tied around my neck, and my hands were tied, too. Then I was hauled to my feet, I thought I was going to be sick, but then I felt the ground getting wetter and I could hear water, getting louder all the time.'

Hagan shuddered once more as he re-lived his ordeal.

'The next thing I knew, I hit it, the water, and it was cold, so cold, and then I was sinking.'

Carmen, still standing by the door, broke in from behind, nodding at Lara.

'This was the night after you came to see John.'

On the bed, Hagan stared up at her.

'I gave them your name, that's all I did. I did what I'd been told to do, if anyone visits Weston, call this number, they'll make it worth my while.'

Lara kept looking down at the porter, still re-living his ordeal in that freezing water. She had a feeling he'd be re-living it for a long time to come.

'I thought I was going to die. I could hear engines starting up, but I was being swept along, and it was like all the lights were going out. Then my foot caught on something, a log or a rock, I don't know and all of a sudden, my head was out of the water and the sack wasn't as tight, maybe the ropes had loosened or something.'

Hagan looked at his visitors, but he wasn't even seeing them now.

'Then I saw her.'

Lara and Mairead looked at him.

'I don't know who she was. I don't even know if she was real, I still don't. One minute, there was just me, in the water, the next minute there was this girl.'

Lara and Mairead looked at each other, the same face, the same name, in front of both of them now.

'I was in this pool, by the bank, I don't know if the water had washed me in there or whether it was something to do with her, but now the ropes around my hands weren't as tight either. I pulled myself up onto the bank and just lay there for a moment. Then I looked round, but she was gone.'

Hagan sank back on the bed, the strain of that retelling sucking the energy out of him, robbing the oxygen from his lungs. Then he looked up at Lara again, coughing painfully once more, his voice now even more of a croak.

'What the fuck is this? Why did one phone call, one fucking phone call, make them want to kill me?'

Lara was hardly hearing him. All she was seeing was that

figure on the bank, that eerie, silent presence who seemed to have saved Hagan's life.

That could indeed have been some strange hallucination on the part of a terrified mind on the cusp of passing over to the other side. But the white van driver had claimed to have seen a similar figure just before Amy's accident.

But if that was Esther, then how could she possibly have known what was going to happen to Hagan that night? And, even if, somehow, she did, why would she have intervened? What side of this increasingly unholy divide did that place her, saint or sinner? Lara had ample good cause never to see her as the former, but if she really did save Hagan's life, then what was that all about?

CHAPTER
SEVENTY-SEVEN

NEARLY EIGHT THOUSAND children on the Isle of Wight live in poverty according to the Office for National Statistics. When she'd first read that, it sounded so extraordinary to Lara that she had to check it again, but there it was, in all too damning black and white. Outsiders often saw the island as prosperous, its residents well-heeled, a typical slice of what used to be called Middle England, and for some it was. For many others, it was far from that.

Lara had arrived back from the hospice to see Jordan already striding out of the door.

'Rhys McGuire's biological father.'

Jordan nodded at her.

'We've found him.'

Now they were heading for Newport South, that biological father's home, often seen as just another holiday spot for most of the tourists arriving from the mainland. But more ONS figures, this time from their chillingly named Indices of Deprivation, placed this particular corner of the capital as one of the most deprived, not only on the island but in the whole of the UK. Lara looked round as they pulled up outside the address Jordan's research had unearthed. Once again, the figures hadn't lied.

By the side of their pool car as they pulled up was a small park with a set of swings and a seesaw. The swings were missing their seats and the see-saw had crashed down on one side and was covered in rust. No child had clearly played there in years. Not that it hadn't been used or visited. Even at a first count, Lara could see syringes, used condoms and numerous smashed beer and spirits bottles. Exiting the car, the two officers moved into the communal dark and windowless hallway of a small collection of maisonettes, on the other side of the cheerless park, where things didn't get any better.

'For fuck's sake.'

Jordan stifled a gag as the stench of urine hit them. There was a lightbulb high above their heads but that had long since blown. A window set into the wall should have offered some dim illumination, but the glass was green and mildewed, having last seen a clean at roughly the last time a child had played on the swings outside.

Lara headed for the stairs, Jordan following. Rhys McGuire's father, Kevin – better known as Kev – Hughes lived on the third floor. Lara didn't know if the complex boasted a working lift but neither she nor Jordan would have risked it anyway.

Coming out onto a narrow walkway, Lara and Jordan stopped outside a door with a hand painted number seventeen on the front. Music pounded from inside. Even from the other side of the thin plywood door, both officers caught the unmistakeable stench of cheap weed. Jordan hammered on the door and a voice yelled back.

'Fuck off.'

Jordan yelled back in turn.

'Police.'

A frantic banging and crashing suddenly sounded from inside as Lara and Jordan waited, grim. In any other circumstances the occupants' desperate attempts to get rid of a probably miniscule stash of illicit substances might have provoked amusement, but not today.

The door opened a few moments later and a teenage girl looked out, wary. Tattoos studded her arms. A new tattoo had just been added to her ankle and the skin was still bleeding. She was holding a baby in one arm, little more than six months or so old. In her other hand she was holding a cigarette.

'What do you want?'

The girl took a deep drag, smoke pooling over the baby's head as she exhaled.

'Kevin Hughes.'

The young girl affected a bewildered frown that would have disgraced the acting efforts of the infant in her arms.

'Who?'

From along the walkway a muffled yell sounded followed by a dull crash as a wasted male, who looked to be in his early fifties, suddenly exited what seemed to be a front bedroom window before haring away. Jordan was about to head after him, but Lara reached out a hand, nodded down the hall where another wasted figure, also seeming to be in his fifties, and a near-double of the first was staring at them, belligerent.

'What the fuck do you want?'

A moment later, Lara and Jordan were in a small rear room. The second scrawny, fifty-something male, now identified as Hughes, was standing by an armchair that had lost most of its stuffing. A sleepy pit bull, almost comatose, probably from passively inhaling the weed that now smelt even stronger now they were inside, was slumped on the floor at his feet.

Lara looked around, comparing the surroundings to Rhys's current home, a world away in Bembridge. Then she looked back at the figure standing in front of them. Lara didn't know the circumstances of Rhys's adoption, but by giving up his son, Hughes had clearly done him one hell of a favour.

'I'd have done the same with her if I'd had the chance.'

It was a few minutes later. Lara had updated Hughes as why they were there, and he was nodding across at the teen girl now sitting across from them, the baby still in her arms, both their heads now drooping from the effects of the swirling clouds of smoke.

'I was in prison when her mum dropped her. When I came out, she just upped and left me with her, the slag.'

Jordan looked back at him. Whether Hughes was talking about the mother or his daughter, he didn't know.

'Not so much as a note to say where she was going, or why.'

He flashed a rabid glance across at the young girl, his yellowing teeth glowing dimly in the darkened room.

'But at least girls can earn their keep I suppose.'

Hughes's daughter stared back, the baby on her lap probably an unintended consequence of the way she'd been doing just that.

Hughes nodded at her.

'Throw us a ciggie.'

'Fuck off.'

Lara tried to get the conversation back to the matter of the moment.

'So, you've had no contact with Rhys?'

'Is that his name?'

Across the room, his daughter's head drooped again, and she dropped her half-smoked cigarette onto the floor. Hughes snatched it up in an instant, taking greedy drags on it.

Jordan took it up, now taking a different tack.

'And have you ever worked at, or had any connection with, an old children's home called Kenwood?'

Hughes paused suddenly, a dim light beginning to gleam in his eyes.

'That's that paedo place isn't it, I read about in the papers.'

Lara and Jordan just looked at him.

'Why are you asking all this anyway?'

Hughes trained a pair of piggy slit eyes on Lara, that dim illumination growing brighter all the while as he dropped the now spent cigarette on the floor.

'Has something happened to him? Because if it has, I should be getting some kind of compo. If them adoption people have put him with a whole bunch of sickos, then I deserve a pay-out.'

He stared, belligerent.

'I trusted them, if they haven't done their job properly, someone should pay.'

Lara leant down to the floor, apparently to extinguish the still glowing cigarette, but placing the spent butt in her pocket as, across the room, the baby was suddenly sick on the floor. Hughes roared at his daughter who made no move to either comfort the infant or to even begin to clear it up.

Lara stood, Jordan following suit. Hughes just kept roaring at his unaware daughter, gesturing all the while at his equally unaware granddaughter who was now being sick again.

Five minutes later, Lara and Jordan stifled gags again as the same stench of urine assailed them from the dark, windowless hallway down on the ground. A couple of kids were hanging around the unattended police pool car, perhaps scenting sport. One look at the large Jordan and the no-nonsense Lara as the two officers approached and they melted away. Lara opened the passenger door, flipping open the glove box. Extracting an evidence bag and a pair of tweezers, she carefully transferred the extinguished cigarette butt now liberally impregnated with Hughes's DNA.

It was a subterfuge that was against all police procedure and protocol. The strong likelihood was that Hughes was also a dead end. The sort of mind that could conceive of, let alone carry out, the murders they'd encountered, seemed far from the venal capabilities of the man they'd just encountered. They'd still run a check to see if his DNA was present on the bodies of any of the victims though, just in case.

Lara had already played the same card with Joseph McGuire. She hadn't lifted a discarded cigarette butt from his property, but when his housekeeper next came to empty his dishwasher, she might be momentarily puzzled to discover one of his whisky tumblers was missing. She'd probably just put it down to a household accident.

Jordan began speaking to comms via the police radio, requesting assistance with the DNA as Lara's mobile rang. Lara took it out, tensing as she recognised the number.

Then Lara listened, growing more chilled all the time, as the administrator in charge of the care home told her that Georgia seemed to have gone missing.

CHAPTER
SEVENTY-EIGHT

AARON STARED at the closed cupboard door in front of him. He hadn't opened it since the night Amy had unexpectedly walked into his room and handed him her iPad along with her bombshell instruction that he hide it for her. And he'd done as she'd asked. He hadn't once taken that iPad out from its hiding place, but the overpowering temptation to do so was growing by the minute.

That brief sense he'd had that Amy was back with him, in that hospital canteen, had gone. She hadn't made any appearance since, which meant he was again in limbo. All the time the potential key to all this was behind that closed door and it wasn't broken, he just knew it wasn't. All he had to do was fire it up, negotiate a password his sister had known would take him only moments to crack, and then he might understand everything: why she was lying in that hospital bed in the state she was in right now and who might be responsible.

But hovering above all that, was his promise. The vow he'd alluded to when he'd talked to that officer, the only one who'd taken the trouble to try to speak to him so far and speak to him properly, too.

There was something else about her as well. He could barely

even remember her name. But he sensed something, some common bond of some kind, although he didn't know why or what form it might take, Maybe that was why he'd wanted her to press him, to urge him to defy Amy's wishes, but she hadn't. Whatever she might have thought he was trying to say, she'd left it to him to elaborate and of course he hadn't, which only made everything worse.

Something else was very much making all this worse, too, as Aaron now heard the doorbell ring.

That had never happened before, either. In a world that had turned on its axis, turning all those inside it upside down at the same time, it was another thing he couldn't get his head around – his dad now rang the front doorbell, for fuck's sake. He didn't do what he'd always done, use his key, open that front door, calling out as he walked inside the house, his house. Now he waited outside for Aaron's mum to haul herself from the front room, to walk down their small hall and grant him entrance.

Aaron tensed as he listened. If that was unusual, what followed was anything but – and sure enough within moments of his dad being let inside, it started. The shouts, the yells, even the screams now as well. Mum's voice, rising in volume all the time, battling with his as they played out the same old battle, as they rehearsed over and over – and ever more violently each time too – the same bitter war.

It wasn't a new war though, even if the cause was new. Rows like the one Aaron was hearing right now had been the soundtrack to his and Amy's early years. The first time his mum had walked downstairs, sporting a single, still-raw, still-angry bruise, they'd accepted her story about walking into the bathroom door. Neither had probed too deeply. The second time it had happened, coinciding with their dad's odd absence from the house for the three or four days it took her bruise to heal, the truth became more difficult to ignore.

It was when it all began, when the two siblings first began to retreat into that private space shared only by themselves, where they could communicate without words.

A lull in hostilities sounded, briefly, downstairs. Aaron glanced towards the closed cupboard door again. Because once again, there it was – the one thing that might stop all this.

Aaron tensed again as he heard a crash from downstairs as his mum or dad slammed a door behind them as they went from the sitting room to the kitchen and something fell to the floor, a picture perhaps or a vase or an ornament of some kind. Another screeched yell sounded, impossible to tell from whom right now, followed by another answering yell in turn.

Then Aaron suddenly had his new idea. He stared at the far wall, without seeing anything for a moment. Then he stood and, unheard and unnoticed by his parents, as always, these days, the young boy walked out of his bedroom, walked down into the hall and, still unheard and unnoticed, slipped outside.

CHAPTER
SEVENTY-NINE

Lara had known exactly where to find Georgia from the moment she'd received that call from the home.

Courtesy of the same sibling instinct, Georgia had also known exactly why Lara had called in on her last visit.

Lara had never mentioned Esther's name once, but Georgia hadn't been fooled. She'd sensed their stepsister in every word Lara hadn't said.

In the old days, the ensuing turmoil might have heralded a fresh plunge into the drugs that used to consume her every waking hour. Now, it had translated into a simple walk in a patch of nearby woods, which might sound like an advance of some sort, but these were no ordinary woods, and this was no ordinary walk, this was Kenwood.

The site of their mother's torture and abuse. The place where she'd first met Finn, the meeting that had led, years later, to the birth of a stepsister.

The place where it all began.

———

'If she is doing all this, if all this is down to her...'

Lara looked at Georgia as she tailed off. They'd now had the conversation they should have had back in the care home that day or so before.

'If she is keeping this going – not like before, not with you, with us – but if she's doing that with all these other people now, too, all those people who used to be here.'

Georgia looked round, struggling again. Through a gap in the trees ahead, Lara could now see the half-size windmill, still intact, but decaying now, like the house in whose grounds it had always stood, some of its remaining sails broken, others missing, a testament to horror like the house behind them: a place of evil that had once claimed their mother and had so nearly claimed Lara, too.

Georgia looked at her.

'Isn't that what we're doing, too?'

Lara just looked back at her, didn't reply.

'I hear the doctors talking sometimes. Haunted, they say. They say I'm haunted by all that's happened, they think I'm just locking it up inside.'

Georgia stared at the windmill, too, for a moment, then looked at her sister.

'But you're doing just the same.'

She shook her head.

'Everyone makes out you're some kind of success story, that you've come out the other side because you get up every morning and you investigate all these different cases, but you're not, are you? Because all the time you're looking at something else and dealing with lots of different people, all you're really doing is trying to turn the clock back and make everything OK again.'

Then, suddenly, Georgia changed tack.

'Sometimes, it's like I see her, you know.'

Lara looked at her.

'Mum?'

Georgia shook her head.

'Esther.'

Lara stilled as her sister started pacing some more, looking tormented.

'I know she was there before. I know she came to the home all those months ago, that she talked to me when I didn't know who she was, but it's not like that, like she's one of the visitors again, it's just something I catch, out of the corner of my eye sometimes.'

Georgia paused.

'Some of the old people will come back from a walk, and I'll look up and it's as if she's there, looking at me, it's like I actually see her, next to them, but then she's gone.'

All Lara could think of was Hagan and that equally strange tale he told of that young woman standing on the riverbank, and the white van driver and the apparition on that coast road.

'And sometimes, at night, I hear the door open. That's not unusual, I know they check on me, the nurses, the care staff, they do it with everyone, and it's good most of the time, comforting I suppose, but…'

Georgia tailed off again before resuming.

'It's only for a moment. And if it is her, she's not doing anything, she's just standing there, looking at me. And it's always before I've really woken up, so I don't know if it's part of some dream I'm coming out of and I can't remember her being in it, but that's weird, too, because I remember my dreams, you know I do, I always have.'

Lara blinked back sudden tears, memories of long, intense conversations from their childhood assailing her as her sister would, indeed, solemnly resurrect all the stories and adventures that had kept her company in her sleep the night before.

'So, did I see her? Was she there? But how, how did she get in, why did no one spot her?'

Georgia chewed her lower lip, her next question perhaps the one that was tormenting her more than all the others.

'What did she want?'

Then she stared out, unseeing into the near distance, but Lara was seeing something now. She was seeing those case notes still waiting for her on her small table back home. She was seeing herself, seated in front of them, just as she had been for the past few nights, fragments of her private investigations floating before her eyes.

Was that the same thing? Was that part of the same refusal to move on, to put all that had happened to them all those years ago behind her? Lara thought she'd been on yet another fact-finding mission – uncovering facts about their mother this time – but had she just been turning round in the same old circle all the time? Far from resurrecting a vital part of their joint past, was she just trapped in it instead?

Then Lara looked up as Georgia cut across again.

'Don't you ever want to do what she did?'

Georgia nodded at her.

'Hit back.'

Georgia looked out into the near distance, but now that stare wasn't unseeing. Now Georgia was seeing something.

But what she was seeing, Lara had no idea.

CHAPTER
EIGHTY

AFTER A RESTLESS NIGHT, and still feeling as if she was getting absolutely nowhere on all fronts, Lara headed into the Major Crime Unit early. As she made for her desk, she cast a quick glance over the duty log – the daily record of all incidents reported in the previous twenty-four hours – and it was as if she'd suddenly been blasted back in time.

Once again, she stared down at a single entry on the log and at an address that now seemed to be screaming up at her.

Once again, she heard the matching, disbelieving scream that was reverberating inside her head.

A year ago, that scream had been provoked by the attack on an ex-squaddie she'd taken under her wing. That ex-squaddie, Rory Evans, ex-Princess of Wales's finest, was still living on the island, although now in desperate circumstances. Perhaps that was no wonder. Rory – or Rollo as Lara knew him – had seen some harrowing sights in his various tours with his old regiment out in Iraq and Afghanistan. The sight of his parents being murdered in his very own flat, yet more victims of Lara's stepsister, probably put any of those other experiences in the shade.

Back in the present day, Lara stepped back from the duty log, her mind racing.

Lara didn't even look up at Amy's window as she parked. Previously, the young accident victim had claimed all interest and concern on her visits, but not this time.

'Physically, we've patched her up as best we can. There's no broken bones thank Goodness – at her age that can be a major worry. But there's still significant bruising along with more superficial cuts and abrasions.'

Lara listened to the nurse, trying to keep a lid on her surging emotions. The mugging of any pensioner would be enough to make most people's blood boil. The fact that this particular pensioner was her old protector, June, was making Lara's blood all but evaporate. She couldn't let that cloud her judgement though, and she knew it. She had to stay calm. She had to glean all available facts. It was the only way of finding out who might have done this.

Those facts were simple, if chilling. June had answered the door in the middle of the day to find a pleasant-faced man standing outside. He had a delivery intended for someone else on the street who wasn't answering their door and he wondered if she could take it in for them. June stepped back to allow her visitor entry to her small hall, and the next thing she knew she'd been bundled onto the floor. A short flurry of punches had followed, leaving the disbelieving June curled up in agony on her hall carpet, at which point her assailant had exited via the rear door, leaving the front door open, which was odd. It meant it was only a matter of time before June was spotted by a passer-by out on the street.

The other odd thing being that when the uniformed police called, they couldn't find anything missing. No drawers seemed to have been opened, all electrical goods remained in place, and June's purse and credit cards –in full view on a small table next to her chair – were untouched as well.

'It doesn't make sense, does it?'

The attending nurse shook her head as Lara bent by June's bed, taking her unresponsive hand in her own. June was under sedation right now and was sleeping.

'Why attack her if he wasn't going to steal anything?'

With Lara still holding her hand, June stirred, but then settled to sleep again.

'Who would do something like that? And why?'

Lara didn't know who, but she was already beginning to suspect why.

This was another message.

Just like Rollo.

CHAPTER
EIGHTY-ONE

HE'D STOOD there for over ten minutes. It was at least as long as Amy had been there according to all the witness statements.

He'd checked and rechecked them all, comparing the different reports there'd been about Amy's accident in the papers, on the local radio stations and in the regional news. He noted the different times the various vehicles had been logged so he knew when she'd first been seen up to that last sighting as that final panicked motorist had called in with the emergency call.

He'd walked the same route, too. He'd doubled back at roughly the same point they knew Amy had doubled back, as if she was having second thoughts about pressing on but had then turned back and continued. He'd heard horns blaring at him much as they must have sounded at Amy, and he'd had several drivers yelling at him from their open windows, too, when he strayed too close to the road. Nothing was working. Aaron still wasn't making any sort of connection.

So now there was only the one path left to take. He'd tried everything else – his abortive IV attempt, the bricks, the wall. Now everything was spiralling out of control. Amy was still locked inside her comatose state. His mum and dad were in pieces. He had to do something more extreme and once he thought about it, he didn't know why he hadn't thought of it before, because it had to be the ultimate connection.

Doing what she'd done.

In the exact same spot, it had happened to her.

Aaron focused on a van approaching at speed, but it was travelling too fast and by the time he'd begun to move off the pavement, the van had already sped past. Then he looked at a car approaching behind, but with its indicator flashing, the car was already beginning to decelerate as it prepared to turn off the main road, so that was no good.

Then Aaron saw the truck. It had just appeared from around the corner and was picking up speed. It wasn't travelling that fast, admittedly, and it wouldn't be by the time it reached him, but the weight of the vehicle meant it wouldn't be able slow all that suddenly, either. So, the impact would still be huge, at least as huge as the one that had condemned Amy to a life that was no life in that hospital bed.

In that moment, the moment of impact, she must feel it as he was feeling it. If that didn't make the connection, then nothing would.

Aaron took a quick, deep breath, focused on the massive iron bull-bars at the front of the truck. He took one step, then two from the pavement. He sensed, rather than heard, a warning blast on the truck's air horn as he took a third step closer.

Then, suddenly, it was as if he was weightless. He no longer seemed to have any control over his limbs, his legs were useless, his arms just hanging loose at his side. He felt as if he was suddenly outside his own body, as if he was rising up into the sky. He didn't see his short life passing before his eyes as he'd read would happen, in all those stories about people passing from one side to the other, but he did see a picture of his mum and his dad, the one they kept in a frame on the hallway table, taken on some holiday somewhere, long before they'd had himself and Amy, smiling out at the camera, a picture perfect white sand beach behind.

Then he saw Amy, and suddenly he knew that this was worth it after all, because it wasn't Amy as she was now in the hospital, but as she was before, sitting on the floor of his bedroom, the pair of them playing a computer game, as if the clock had suddenly been rewound and nothing that had happened these past few weeks had happened at all.

Instinctively, knowing that all he'd just seen had to have taken no more than a second or so, and knowing that if he was still up in the air after being hit by that behemoth of a truck, he had to come crashing down to the ground any second, too, Aaron reached out a hand, and suddenly he felt it. He felt a human hand in his, but it wasn't Amy's, and he couldn't understand it. He also couldn't understand why that picture of her was fading and why he could hear the air horn again, but that was fading now, too, as if the driver had jabbed at it one last time before speeding away.

Aaron opened his eyes and stared into a pair of eyes staring back at him. At the same time, he became aware of the pair of arms encircling his chest, enveloping him in the kind of grip that belied the slight frame of the woman who was still holding him and who'd held him back from stepping into the path of that fast-disappearing truck.

Lara held Aaron's stare for a moment longer, then – and only when she was sure it was safe to do so – she relaxed her grip.

CHAPTER
EIGHTY-TWO

LARA HAD LOST it and she knew it. It was unfair and she knew that, too. Carey and Matt Waite were in no fit state to think of anyone or anything apart from Amy right now, and she knew that as well. But they had another child in equal need in his own way. So, she was flying at them.

Lara didn't know what had been in Aaron's mind as he'd stood by the same stretch of road that was soon to claim his sister's life. But it was obvious what he'd intended to do, and if it hadn't been for Lara passing on her way back from visiting June, he might have managed it, too. To be fair, the shocked expression on both parents faces said it all. As did the totally instinctive way they immediately forgot all about the yawning chasm that separated them right now and had rushed to embrace their still-shaking son. Whether that would prove the first step in a more long-lasting reunion, Lara didn't know, but it was a start at least.

But even as Lara was berating Carey and Matt, even as she was pointing out that they were falling apart just when another child needed them the most, she knew something else was happening here. Maybe it was that exchange with Georgia, but years of her own pent-up frustration and unresolved bitterness were spilling out, too.

Lara's own mother didn't have any choice when it came to abandoning her children. But they did.

A short time later Aaron extricated himself from that unexpected – and not entirely unwelcome – joint embrace and headed up to his bedroom in another strange and conflicted state. In one sense, nothing had been resolved. It hadn't been Amy's spirit that had connected to his and lifted him out of harm's way. But Lara's intervention – and listening to her just now, too – had still resolved something.

Five minutes later, Aaron had done it. He'd taken that fateful step, had finally decided to trust someone other than Amy. Later, a lot later, he'd reflect that maybe it was all part of letting go. The inevitable recognition that all truly was lost so far as his sister was concerned, that her ongoing silence, her continuing refusal to join him as she used to join him wasn't down to a waiting game any longer. He could stay behind that wall he'd built for them from now till the end of time, but she still wouldn't show. Amy was gone. Deep down he knew it.

So, now there was a void, and previously that would have terrified him. In the last hour or so, in what some might have called a late gift from the Gods, he'd been given a way of partly filling the void at least. She wasn't Amy and she never would be, but Lara still reminded him of his sister in some way. There was a strange quality to her that set her apart from all the other adults he knew, including his parents and teachers. They all tried to pretend they had answers, even if it was painfully obvious that they did not. She didn't even pretend to understand the questions and that connected to his previous realisation that she hadn't done what all the other adults would have done back in the hospital that day, either. She must have known he was wrestling with something and that it was connected to Amy. But she'd given him space to decide for himself how much he wanted to tell her.

Look at what had happened just now, too – the way she'd stormed into battle on his behalf. It wasn't just the things she'd said; it was the lid she'd lifted on herself, maybe without even realising it. It all reinforced the overpowering sense that she simply got it. She got him. She understood.

But Lara wasn't only an ultra-rare example of the adult species, at least in his book. She was also a cop and a high-ranking cop at that: a cop who could maybe secure for his sister some belated form of justice.

Aaron crossed to the cupboard and retrieved Amy's iPad from the hiding place where he'd promised her it would remain until she told him otherwise. He opened it up, transferred the few files that were on there onto an external drive and then retrieved the business card that Lara had handed to them all those day ago in the hospital. Then he sent a short message and the content of that external drive to her by way of an attachment.

Next, he lay back on his bed, half-expecting the sky to fall in on him, but nothing happened. No bolts of lightning struck and no cracks of thunder sounded. The world continued much as it had in the moments before he sent the contents of that drive, even though everything had changed, and changed forever.

Aaron remained on his bed, staring up at the ceiling, waiting for whatever was going to happen next.

CHAPTER
EIGHTY-THREE

THE DNA that Lara surreptitiously collected from the dank and filthy flat occupied by Kevin Hughes and his truculent daughter proved to be a waste of time.

It hadn't been present at the crime scene involving Edward Mattiss, and nor was it on the still-unidentified body found in the shallow grave at Kenwood. That still left Pastor Kenneth Simon, but Mairead really didn't hold out much hope of finding any of Hughes's DNA there. That clinical and controlled execution just didn't square with the figure Jordan had described, scrabbling round on a urine- and vomit-soaked floor for spent cigarette butts.

The DNA they'd recovered from the whisky tumbler spirited away by Lara from Joseph McGuire's house told the same tale. His DNA hadn't been present at any of those crime scenes either.

While DNA might have proved a bust, something else had been flagged, though. She'd fed those two names – Kevin Hughes and Joseph McGuire – into a different search engine which had been trawling HOLMES 2, the acronym for the latest version of the Home Office Large Major Enquiry System. If either of those two men had been involved in any brush with the law, major or minor, and whether they were subsequently proved to be innocent or otherwise, it was going to be on record.

Mairead had already found, and discounted, several minor convictions for drug abuse and theft in the case of Hughes. She'd found nothing, so far, in the case of McGuire. Then, suddenly, the software found something else. Mairead read the entry, then quickly forwarded it on to Lara and the rest of the unit.

Mairead had just uncovered yet another link to Kenwood.

CHAPTER
EIGHTY-FOUR

Coco took the deepest of breaths, as she pulled up outside. What she'd come to do was the only thing she could do, but it wasn't going to be easy.

Coco had come to tell Rhys that she couldn't see him anymore. She wasn't going to phrase it as brutally as that, of course. But she also knew that she now had to be something neither of them had been these last few weeks, and that was be honest.

If truth be told, they'd both been aware of the mutual attraction. In the normal course of events that would either have developed into something or faded away to just a few fleeting moments, like so many other young romances. Amy would have become a genuine obstacle or an irrelevance. It happened all the time with so many of their contemporaries, liaisons were formed and relationships foundered. It was all part of the time-honoured merry-go-round.

But Amy's accident, and the discovery of her pregnancy, had changed everything. Suddenly, the stakes had been raised to stratospheric heights. The fall-out from all that might have briefly forged something between herself and Rhys, but she knew now that it couldn't be trusted. Like her previous relationship with the drug-dealing, and now dead, Kris, like the whole of her previous lifestyle indeed, it was an illusion, a bubble that would burst on first exposure to the unremitting reality of outside eyes. As it had when she realised her own father had been watching them all the time.

Coco stepped out from her small run-around VW Beetle which Jordan had found for her on some classified listing somewhere. It might be over fifty years old, but it was still unutterably cool. She crossed to Rhys's front door.

Then she paused, puzzled, because it was already partly open. Hesitating a moment longer, she tapped on the door and it swung open further. She was about to call out for Rhys, but then she saw him. Half-lying, half-kneeling on the hall floor, gasping as he struggled to stand, a large patch of blood visible on his scalp. Coco's mission, everything she'd come to do and say, was instantly forgotten as she dashed to his side.

CHAPTER
EIGHTY-FIVE

LARA STARED at the incoming email alert from Mairead. She read the message, then read it again. She leant back in her chair, stared out over the weekend yachts out on the straits. Then she stood, collected her car keys and put a call through to Jordan as she pulled away from her apartment.

Kevin Hughes's DNA had been recorded at a crime scene some twenty years previously. It was a small-scale case that had never made it past a local magistrate's court given the sums involved. Hughes had stolen some small garden tools and implements and had been caught trying to sell them at a local market. The items in question were returned to their original owners who had been curiously reluctant to press charges at first, but had then had a change of heart after being pressed, presumably by an understandably puzzled police force keen to send a message to this particular repeat offender.

It would probably never have come to light had it not been for the terrier-like attention of Mairead who'd registered the fact that the magistrates court in question was the closest to Kenwood. Sure enough, when she checked the court records, the owners of the small selection of garden tools and implements that Hughes had stolen and then attempted to sell, were the owners of Kenwood themselves.

There was no record of Hughes actually being employed by the home. But he had to have at least a working knowledge of the place to steal those items in the first place. That strange reluctance on the part of the home to prosecute rang alarm bells, too. If Hughes was just a simple thief, why hesitate? They'd taken action against plenty of trespassers who'd intruded on their property in the past. Were they afraid what might have come out if they had pursued him through the courts?

As it happened, Hughes simply accepted his fine, which was also paid with an alacrity that surprised the officers of the court, according to those same records. Hughes had a string of unpaid fines going back years and the clear expectation was that this latest one would simply be added to a lengthening list of arrears, but it wasn't. It was as if someone wanted to put a lid on this particular case as tightly and as quickly as possible.

Suddenly, it happened. Had Lara not been so absorbed by this new development, she might have spotted it before. As it was, the first time it registered, it was already too late.

Had it been tracking her since she left her waterside apartment on her way back to Hughes's flat? Lara had no idea. All she did know was that as she now passed the entrance to the old Kenwood, she suddenly sensed danger. At the same time a sudden roar filled the small cabin of her car. A flash of metal in her rear-view mirror gave way to the grille of an expensive luxury saloon bearing down on her at what seemed like impossible speed. It looked like a Bentley, perhaps one of those she'd seen parked on that riverbank as mourners paid their respects to Andrew Russell.

Or, and this flashed through Lara's mind a millisecond before what she knew had to be an inevitable impact, had she seen, but not particularly registered, a similar luxury vehicle parked in the driveway of Joseph McGuire's house?

Lara wrenched her steering wheel to the side, seeking the

sanctuary of a nearby layby, but the huge saloon behind struck the offside rear of her car sending it spinning. Lara felt the world turning upside down as, much like the white van on the banks of the Medina those days before, her tyres scrabbled for grip, a battle lost before it had even started. She felt herself rolling, again and again, the roof smashing down on the unforgiving tarmac before the car bounced back on its wheels only to career down onto its roof again.

Then there was nothing.

CHAPTER
EIGHTY-SIX

AARON HAD BEEN PACING his small bedroom for what felt like days but had been only hours, staring at his mobile all the while, willing it to ring.

But nothing had happened. There'd been no call. No contact.

So, he grabbed his coat, headed outside and boarded a bus. The ride over to the police station seemed to take forever. His subsequent silent vigil outside seemed to last even longer. Every moment with no contact was torture, and Aaron had no idea why Lara was putting him through it.

She had to have received and downloaded the contents of Amy's iPad by now. He hadn't penned any accompanying message, but she'd have seen his name and email address. The minute she saw the accompanying attachment she would realise what it was.

But he'd heard nothing. It had been delivered; he knew that much. It had been viewed, he knew that too. The trace he'd put on the message had told him that much. What he wasn't being told – and what was tormenting him more and more every moment this continued – was what Lara was doing about it.

Then the door to what he'd identified as Lara's home unit – the Major Crime Unit – opened, and Aaron tensed, but it was another woman who now came out. He recognised her immediately. She was on Lara's team and had been to his house with her once, but she wasn't Lara. Aaron didn't know what to do. He'd never been good with people he didn't know. It had taken him a long time to feel he could trust even one stranger. He couldn't just turn to a new one instead.

However, he wasn't going to have much choice, because now the woman he recognised, but didn't know, was looking across the road towards him. She paused, and he could see from the look on her face that she recognised him in turn. Then she began to walk across. Aaron, instinctively, turned away, started heading back down the road, but suddenly the woman was at his side.

And partly because he was growing increasingly desperate, Aaron began to tell her just why he was there.

CHAPTER
EIGHTY-SEVEN

A SHORT TIME EARLIER, Coco had been begging Rhys to get help.

The wound to his scalp was still bleeding, but it wasn't just that. He was acting strangely, too, beginning sentences, but not finishing them, his tongue running in a hundred different directions at once, almost as if his brain was short-circuiting, just like it had that time with his texts.

It wasn't just the disconnected sentences and phrases that didn't make any sense, she couldn't get anything coherent out of him regarding what had happened. All he kept saying was that the intruder had been there again, had been in the house when he'd walked in. Then he kept repeating, over and over again that he knew who it was, but when Coco kept pressing, that was all he'd say.

She wasn't destined to get anything else either, as suddenly he started snatching up money, keys and his phone. He wouldn't even tell her where he was going, just hissed back at her as she tried to reach out a restraining hand that Amy was in danger, that he had to keep her safe, then he was running out of the house as if his life depended on it. Maybe it did. Coco didn't know. She didn't know anything anymore.

She just stood there for a moment. Briefly, and with a sudden start, she wondered if she should get the hell out of there, too. Was that intruder still in the house? Could they still be around? But the house felt empty. She couldn't explain why, but it did.

And, of course, she still hadn't done what she'd come to do, and Rhys could return home just as quickly as he'd exited, given the unpredictable state he was in right now.

Irresolute, she moved through the house, heading into one room after another. But then she stopped as she saw the door to Rhys's ground floor bedroom open before her. Coco had only been in the house a couple of times before but had never been inside. It was his private retreat, as he'd always made clear. Even his dad was never allowed to venture in, and the housekeeper didn't even have a key.

Suddenly, her heart lurched again. Had Rhys's intruder been in there all the time? Had her instincts let her down, was that intruder now waiting to strike for a second time? Coco stood for a moment, ears straining to catch any sound, any movement from inside, however small. But all was as still and quiet as the grave. Then a sudden movement to her left caused her to yell out loud, but it was just the sun coming out from behind a cloud, peeking in through a nearby window.

Cursing herself for letting herself get spooked, and suddenly angry at herself, too, Coco turned for the front door. Then she stopped as, through that partly open door to Rhys's room, she spotted something.

CHAPTER
EIGHTY-EIGHT

LARA CAME ROUND, slowly. For a moment she had no idea where she was, but then she suddenly realised.

Twelve months previously, Lara had been outside that same strange windmill, looking up at the blades. She'd climbed up behind one of them, waited for the wind to die down and the sails to stop moving, then she'd braced herself and jammed her foot down on one of the blades in particular, concentrating on the point at which it was attached to the motor by a couple of bolts, before she'd broken it off and used it as a tool to lever first one plank, then another out of place.

For a moment back then, as she'd peered inside, she could see nothing, just blackness, but then, slowly, her eyes began to adjust to the gloom. Then Lara had retched as the smell hit her, and that wasn't due to just the urine and faeces she could see littering the floor. It was the stench of evil that seemed to permeate the very pores of the building.

She was sensing that same evil now as a door opened in front of her. A year ago, it had been Lara opening that door, looking in on a terrified young woman who believed she must be another persecutor come to glory in her captivity. But now it was Lara who was the captive, and her very own persecutor and captor was looking straight at her.

Lara stared for a moment, unable to take in what she was seeing. Lara had seen many instances of men and women almost physically twisted out of shape as powerful impulses claimed them. She'd seen hate, fear and frustration wreak transforming effects on otherwise unremarkable souls, making them unrecognisable. She'd witnessed almost superhuman strength displayed by the most mild-mannered of individuals, seen the smallest, slightest women fighting like lionesses to protect a child from attack, had stared in disbelief at formerly totally anonymous beings suddenly donning the mantle of superheroes as they charged into burning buildings to rescue loved ones from blazing infernos.

But there was always some tenuous grip on a previous reality; the human being beneath the apparition was still there. What Lara was seeing right now was something else.

She was looking at someone she recognised immediately, at the same time as never having seen them before in her life.

CHAPTER
EIGHTY-NINE

WHILE LARA WAS COMING ROUND, Mairead, Aaron and Jordan were speeding to Aaron's house.

A quick check on Lara's work computer had explained her inexplicable lack of response to Aaron's email and its accompanying attachment. She'd never received either.

A similarly quick check on Aaron's email account established what all three already now strongly suspected. A person or persons as yet unknown had somehow intercepted it. How they'd penetrated the Major Crime Unit firewall was something to be pursued later. All that mattered now was what was on that attachment. What had made it of such interest to that person or persons unknown? The quickest way of establishing that was to return to the source, Amy's iPad.

It wasn't just what had happened to Amy, there was Lara now, too. Despite several attempts, Jordan and Mairead had both drawn a blank each time they'd tried to contact her. Lara, equally inexplicably, seemed to have disappeared.

Mairead, Jordan and Aaron pulled up outside the Waite family home less than fifteen minutes after leaving Police HQ. The house was empty; Matt and Carey were in the hospital with Amy. Less than one minute later, Amy's iPad was open on the kitchen table after having been brought down from his bedroom by her brother. With Mairead watching, Jordan scrolled through the contents until one file in particular appeared on the screen: a file marked by a single name.

Jordan looked up at Mairead. It was a name they knew well. Aaron stood and turned away, moving across to the other side of the room where he picked up his own laptop. Jordan and Mairead remained in front of Amy's iPad. The file was now open and page after page was unfurling out onto the screen, all written by Amy in the days leading up to her fateful accident.

The two officers scrolled through it all, first in disbelief, then in mounting panic. Jordan's mobile rang, and he snatched it out of his pocket. Was it Lara? Jordan hesitated a moment as he saw Coco's name and number on the display, tempted briefly to divert it to his message service, but some instinct stayed his hand. Jordan listened, growing ever more chilled, as a near-hysterical Coco told him what she'd just found in Rhys's bedroom as, by his side, Mairead, reached the final entry on the iPad, the last entry Amy had posted just before she'd set out on that coast road that night.

Mairead turned to Jordan as he finished his call, but he was already heading for the door. She exited, too, following, but out of the corner of her eye she just caught sight of Aaron, still in front of his laptop, now engaged in some strange ritual which seemed to involve some sort of metronome-like count.

Aaron didn't realise that his mother knew, but she did. Carey had already told Mairead and Lara about Aaron's strange trades with the fates, and while she had no idea who he was trying to keep safe by this latest ritual, Mairead decided not to disturb him.

Just in case.

CHAPTER
NINETY

'RHYS HAD NO CHOICE.'

Lara stared as the figure in front of her bent his head up towards the sky, just visible through a gap in one of the rotting planks.

'Why couldn't you see that? You of all people?'

Lara kept staring. It was his voice, and it wasn't. It was him and it was a different creature altogether. The voice she was hearing was older. More weary, careworn somehow, incongruous, and chillingly so, in the circumstances. But she'd definitely caught an echo of identical inflexions from somewhere before, and suddenly she had it.

It was McGuire. She was listening to Joseph, his adopted father. But it wasn't the father standing before her. Rhys couldn't physically change shape to that extent, but he was aping almost exactly all of his father's cadences. And it wasn't simple mimicry, either. To all intents and purposes, the young man had become his parent and guardian. He seemed to have slipped into his very skin.

Then, suddenly, it was like a switch had been flicked. The older, Joseph began to fade as Rhys's shoulders hunched, his eyes narrowed, and a calculating quality beginning to replace what had been, up to then, a genuine-sounding appeal. At the same time, Rhys's hand suddenly ascribed an arc, as if reaching out for a cigarette that wasn't even there, and suddenly Lara could see it again. Joseph McGuire had been replaced by Kevin Hughes, the adopted parent replaced by the birth father. Lara could see it only too clearly in the young man's simple mannerisms, in the set of his face. She could almost see that flat again.

Fascinated and almost repelled at the same time, Lara kept watching as another transformation then took place as Rhys's voice softened, as his shoulders straightened, and as his tone took on a mellower hue.

'I tried talking to him, tried making him see there had to be another way.'

Lara kept staring.

Who was he now?

Who had Rhys become this time?

'But he just said he had to, that he couldn't do anything else, because the poison's inside.'

Lara strained against the bonds restraining her as Rhys, or the incarnation he'd now become, suddenly seemed to battle upset.

'But this is a baby. How can a baby be part of anything like that?'

Lara stilled as she realised. He was Amy. He'd suddenly become the mother of his unborn child.

'It's in the blood. It's all he kept saying. It's in there and there's nothing we can do about it. And yes, it's a sacrifice, but it would spare so many sacrifices in so many others further down the line.'

Lara stilled further as the reason behind Amy's panicked flight along that coast road towards the ferry that night suddenly began to become only too clear.

Lara kept staring at him. Dimly, she struggled to recall something she'd once read, a medical report dealing with a disorder involving multiple personalities, although now, she also dimly recalled, it was called something else. Was that what she was witnessing? Had that stray report she'd once scanned suddenly assumed human form right here, in front of her eyes?

Swiftly, more images flashed in front of her eyes too, of Rhys in the police station where they'd first met, of Rhys in the hospital. There'd seemed to be no hint there of any of this then, but had there been and had they just not spotted it?

But all that had to be dealt with later, she couldn't even think about that now. Lara had to focus on something much more pressing, like how the hell could she get out of this? Then, as she kept staring at him, the germ of an idea began to form, and it was Rhys himself who was unwittingly providing it. If he could slough skins, if he could assume a new skin that was not his own, then so could she.

Lara leant forward slowly, carefully, taking care not to make any sudden movements, then she whispered, soft, entreating, reaching out to him in what seemed to be his latest incarnation's hour of need.

'Come here.'

The creature that was Rhys, for now anyway, responded immediately, almost instinctively, to the soft invitation. He moved closer. As Lara did so she felt him changing once more, mutating into someone else, but she didn't have time to probe this latest incarnation and he didn't have to time to fully inhabit it, either.

Lara craned her head back as if inviting him to lean closer, then she launched her head forward, as hard as she could. The top of her head collided with the bridge of the young boy's nose, smashing it with the sharpest of cracks. Briefly, fireworks exploded in front of her eyes, blurring her vision as Rhys howled an animal scream.

Lara lashed out with her legs at the same time, but the young boy was strong or perhaps he was just more than usually motivated. He lashed out in turn, chopping his hands down at her legs as they scrambled for a grip around his torso. Lara tried hanging on, but another savage chop nearly fractured her knee, forcing her to relinquish her grip.

For a moment the now gasping Rhys just looked at her. For that moment she feared she was about to be added to a lengthening list of victims, but then he stilled, calmness beginning to descend as he took in Lara's wrists, still secured by the rope that secured her in turn to the wall of her makeshift prison. Then he nodded at her, as if to say that she'd keep, that despite this last-minute instance of trickery, she could be left till later. For now, he had other priorities.

As he turned and exited, Lara felt the ropes give slightly as she flexed her wrists again. Her exertions hadn't done anything to impede Rhys, at least to any significant degree.

But it had loosened one of the ropes he'd tied at least.

CHAPTER
NINETY-ONE

JORDAN AND MAIREAD arrived at the hospital less than ten minutes after leaving Aaron. All the way over there, Coco's hysterical phone call had been reverberating inside Jordan's head.

Coco had walked into Rhys's bedroom to find scribbled sketches out on a small desk next to his bed, more scribbled sketches on the bed itself. Where there weren't manic-looking sketches or scribbles, there were photos. There was something else, too, because then, on a large piece of card, she'd found a family tree, or what she took to be a family tree at first. When she realised what it really was, her blood froze.

It looked like a many-headed hydra, but with a building, not a distant ancestor at the head. She recognised the building instantly from everything her dad had told her about the place. It was Kenwood. The branches that stretched down from it listed different names and faces. Some of those names and faces had black marks scored through them. Problems, Coco would realise later, that had been eliminated. And a couple of the names she vaguely recognised, being names she'd heard Jordan talk about, too.

Then she saw a name she recognised only too well. For

reasons she couldn't begin to understand, Amy's name was there, but what connection did she have or could possibly have to Kenwood? That made no sense. Then Coco saw another photo next to Amy's face, and she stopped dead as she realised she was looking at a scan photo. And slowly, sickeningly, she began to understand why Rhys's pregnant girlfriend might be taking centre stage in this twisted tableau, as well as the danger she and her unborn baby might be in right now, which was when Coco had made her panicked call.

A few miles away, Jordan pulled up and dashed inside the main reception area, leaving Mairead at the hospital entrance to oversee the security operation that was already being put in place. Jordan headed inside to supervise the similar ring of steel that was being placed around Amy's room, and Amy herself. Carey and Matt Waite were there, but they were soon bundled outside. They had no idea what was going on and Jordan didn't enlighten them. There was plenty of time for that, once Rhys McGuire had been apprehended and in custody. That, and Amy's safety, was the only priority right now. For now, only medical staff and authorised police officers were to be allowed anywhere near her.

The problem was that Amy's journal had only dealt with Rhys's often-incoherent vendetta against their baby. Inhuman and inexplicable as it had seemed to her, that had driven everything else from her mind. His deranged explanation that he was somehow infected with evil, courtesy of his birth father's connection with a place of pure evil, was all she'd heard. As well as the implications of all that for his similarly infected baby.

The strange personality shifts he also seemed to undergo barely received a mention. The way he could assume another identity so wholeheartedly that he almost became a different person entirely was hardly referred to either. Lara knew that now of course, but she was in no position to enlighten her fellow officers.

So, when a white-coated student doctor joined a small group of other, newly-arrived, student doctors on a corridor adjoining Amy's room just a short time later, none among the security detail gave him so much as a second glance.

CHAPTER
NINETY-TWO

It had taken fully half an hour, but finally Lara had slipped one of her wrists from the ropes that secured her. After that it was a matter of another moment or so to slip the rope from her other wrist and dash outside.

Rhys was long gone of course, courtesy of his father's commandeered Bentley. And she knew where he'd be, too. He'd taken Lara's mobile as a precaution, but she was gambling on the fact he wouldn't have had time to find and retrieve her work mobile, secreted in her smashed car. Lara burst through the trees ahead and her heart soared as she saw sunlight glint off metal in the field ahead.

Then she paused as she smelt it – acrid and choking. A second later she stood before the burnt-out wreck of her former pride and joy. The world had just lost yet another example of a fast-dwindling breed, the first incarnation of the Alec Issigonis masterpiece, given further classic status by the equally legendary figure of John Cooper.

Lara kept looking at her charred car for a moment, then she started to run again. She could get to the main road in a few moments and use her warrant card to flag down a passing motorist.

The torching of her car had secured Rhys a few minutes at the most. But as Lara raced for the nearby road in the distance, she was only too aware that it was a window of time that might make all the difference in the world right now.

CHAPTER
NINETY-THREE

BACK IN ST MARY'S, that ring of steel was now in place.

Mairead was covering all the hospital entrances. Jordan was the gatekeeper inside. There was no way in which that security detail could be breached, the officers had taken everything into account, had planned for every eventuality. Apart from one.

Amy's baby.

Jordan had been aware of the increased activity around her bed for some time, but he'd been busy checking and double-checking the increased security precautions as well as liaising with officers currently flooding different parts of the site. If he'd paused to think about it, he'd probably thought it was all part of the routine checks on this most unusual of patients in her extraordinary condition.

But it wasn't.

'We need to move her.'

Jordan stared at the female doctor and lead paediatrician in front of him.

'Now.'

Jordan kept staring. Move her? What the hell was she talking about?

'We need to get her down to theatre.'

Jordan looked across at Amy, comprehension beginning to dawn.

'Her baby's on its way, we can't wait.'

The doctor nodded at him, grim, neither of them even seeing the young-looking student doctor along the corridor who'd now slipped in behind. All eyes were on the lead paediatrician and her firm and unequivocal insistence.

'We need to get her baby out now.'

CHAPTER
NINETY-FOUR

COCO DASHED up from the hospital reception towards Amy's room. Alerted by her call, Jordan met her at the top of the stairs as, behind, preparations were now being put in place to transfer Amy herself to theatre.

Swiftly, Coco hissed more details to her father on the macabre tableau she'd stumbled across in Rhys's bedroom.

Behind Jordan and Coco, the doors opened, and the team of white-coated doctors emerged from Amy's room, with Amy herself being pushed along by them on a trolley. Coco barely gave them a second glance, she was too busy checking out the adjoining rooms and corridors, searching for her dangerously deranged friend. But Lara, now dashing up from the reception area, too, now had that same team of white-coated doctors in full sight.

Swiftly again, Lara provided her own update on the different personalities, not just the one, they now had to find. But they weren't different personalities of course, they were all Rhys. But Lara had no idea which of those manifold, multiple identities he'd be assuming right now.

All the time and by Jordan's side, images assailed Coco, including those texts she'd received from Rhys when someone else seemed to have taken over his phone. Then there was his torment as he'd reported that intruder. So, was that another fiction of his tortured imaginings: a paranoia he had no way of controlling made real?

Lara and Jordan wheeled round as a sudden commotion broke out behind them. Matt Waite was berating the white-coated doctors, insisting they were panicking unnecessarily, that Amy wasn't even close to her full term yet. Carey and Aaron appeared behind him, both just looking on, helpless for a moment, as nurses tried to steer the ever more distraught Matt away.

Everyone on that corridor knew what was really happening here. The child inside her was the key to what little remained of Amy's life. Her baby was the only reason she was still alive. Once she'd given birth, her reason for being was at an end. From the look on his face right now, so was Matt's.

Carey stepped forward, put a hand on her husband's arm and Matt turned to her. For a moment their eyes connected as the doctors wheeled Amy on towards the lift, and Matt stilled. Nothing was said. Nothing needed to be said. All those years before, in this exact same hospital, Amy had announced her entrance to the world. Now the birth of their first grandchild meant her death.

Lara turned away, blinking back sudden tears. Jordan did the same. Coco couldn't even look at the trolley that was now waiting outside the lift. At the other end of the corridor, Matt lay his head on his wife's shoulder.

Then Lara stilled as the lift doors opened in front of the small throng of student doctors. Her vision cleared as quickly as it had been obscured by her previous tears. Her heart began to pound. It had been less than an hour since she'd last laid eyes on him, but it was like looking at a stranger again. And, for a moment, as Rhys looked back at her, almost involuntarily, aware of Lara's steady stare, two worlds collided – Rhys's fantasy world and the real world – illusion crashing up against reality. Then Lara moved forward.

'Stop this, Rhys, now.'

Coco and Jordan wheeled round, stared at him, too.

'For Amy's sake. For your baby's sake. Stop this.'

Rhys hesitated, put up his hands, a surrender gesture. Then, and as Lara began to relax, he suddenly turned and hared away.

Lara gave chase, Jordan close behind. They couldn't let him get away and Lara knew it. He was capable of hiding out in that hospital for days, if need be, assuming different identities almost by the hour, just waiting for the one chance he would surely be granted at some point, to strike.

The two officers hurtled behind Rhys as he dodged incoming patients and porters, clattering into trolleys, scattering files and records, running blindly, first down one corridor, then another, and Lara had the strangest sensation as it continued. It was almost as if he wasn't just trying to get away. It was almost as if by running, and as hard and as fast as he could, he'd somehow escape the demons that had now claimed him for too long.

Suddenly, Rhys burst from the side of the hospital via a breached fire alarm door. Sirens instantly sounded, but he took as little notice of them as he was currently taking of Lara and Jordan, still in close pursuit, and their yelled entreaties imploring him to stop.

Upstairs, and with Amy now in theatre on the other side of the door behind them, a totally bewildered Carey, Matt and Aaron watched from a window as the crazed pursuit unfolded below, staring down at Rhys as he zig-zagged his way across the hospital grounds, making all the while for the roads that surrounded the complex.

Down at ground level, Lara was getting closer. She was getting a second wind, just as Rhys was beginning to flag. He had youth on his side, but something was happening to the young man now. Maybe the strain of holding all those competing voices and personalities inside that one head was finally taking its toll. Maybe Rhys – if Rhys even knew who he was anymore – was simply closing down.

Then some last spurt of resolve seemed to claim him. Somewhere, deep down, his doomed, crazed mission resurrected itself. Taking the pursuing Lara and Jordan by surprise, he suddenly veered to his right heading back to the hospital, as an ambulance accelerated away from A&E, the crew having just received an emergency call.

High above, Mairead heard the crash at the exact same moment she heard a baby's cry from the operating theatre next door. Carey and Matt Waite turned, instinctively, towards the sound. Aaron remained where he was at the end of the corridor, a boy transfixed.

From the operating theatre, the baby's cries grew louder, and Carey and Matt turned to each other as they heard their grandchild announce her presence to the world, the single most bittersweet sound imaginable for them right now, because as one life began, they both knew that one would now end. On the other side of that door, Amy's fate, already ordained, was now inevitable.

Outside the hospital, Jordan reached out to his daughter as she appeared behind him, Coco standing helpless and weeping as the paramedics struggled from their stricken ambulance. Lara scanned all exit roads, but she already knew she wouldn't see Rhys. The diversion involving the swerving and now destroyed ambulance had given him all the cover he needed and now he was gone.

Meanwhile, Jordan did what Carey and Matt Waite could now not do. He just held his daughter while he could.

CHAPTER
NINETY-FIVE

Less than an hour later, Lara had put three more rings of steel in place, a trio of other protection measures.

John Weston's room in the hospice was placed under twenty-four-hour police guard. However much it may have stuck in the collective craw of the unit – and in the craw of Peggy O'Riordan in particular – there was a known killer hell-bent on a clear vendetta still out there. Weston demanded, if not deserved, protection.

A similar precautionary measure was put in place for Andrew Russell who was intercepted as he manoeuvred his boat away from its latest mooring, all ready to set off into the Solent for a destination unknown. He didn't enlighten his police interceptors as to that destination either. No one in the Major Crime Unit knew whether his connection to Kenwood was innocent, as he'd always claimed, or otherwise, but Russell himself was placed under the nautical equivalent of house arrest. He protested that confinement loudly, vehemently rejecting the visiting officer's justification that it was for his own good and demanding to know how long it was to last. Lara only wished she knew.

Finally, uniformed officers from the local force visited and swiftly took Rhys's birth father, Kevin Hughes, into a similar protective custody, although he was more resigned to all that was happening and much less vocal with protests about his confinement, but perhaps that wasn't all that surprising. Spells interned at His Majesty's pleasure seemed to be something of an occupational hazard for him.

They were all necessary and sensible measures, cleared and agreed with Conran who had no hesitation in approving each and every one.

Little did the two officers know it, but all their precautions were already being rendered redundant.

CHAPTER
NINETY-SIX

THE OLD SEASIDE boarding house looked just as ramshackle and run-down as it did before. As before, too, it presented itself as unremarkable to the point of anonymity.

The manager hadn't been replaced yet after the previous one had vanished. No one knew why or where he'd gone, and no one cared too much either. If anyone did reflect on his sudden disappearance it wouldn't have been for long, As ever, too, it was that kind of place with that kind of staff and, largely, that kind of clientele. But it meant there was one less pair of eyes to keep watch on the small building at the rear of the main boarding house, which suited Rhys just fine.

The young man broke in via the special, smaller, door let into the side wall. Moving inside, he took a moment as he stared up at the specially supported beam in the ceiling, well aware of its purpose and function. There was no rope hanging from it now, so that beam looked unremarkable and anonymous, but it was far from that, as Rhys knew. It had borne witness to its own horrors in its time, less than its sister establishment over at Kenwood, admittedly, but these walls could still tell plenty of tales. Rhys looked round for a moment longer, then looked down at the jerry can he'd brought along with him.

Everything had changed now, and he knew it. He really believed he'd have had more time, because he'd never expected Aaron to break his promise to Amy like that. But the moment he saw that email he'd intercepted, along with its accompanying attachment, he realised that Amy's brother had broken ranks. In that moment, he'd known that the end game was well and truly upon him.

Rhys looked round again. Perhaps it was fitting that it was here that it should play out. Even though this place would never be the testament to evil embodied in Kenwood itself, it was close enough in its own way.

Rhys sprayed the petrol around the meeting room, soaking as much of the floor and walls as he could. Then he stood underneath the specially supported beam, just under the point where the rope would normally be suspended. He extracted a single match from a box, hesitating as he did so, but only for a moment.

Then he ignited it.

PART SIX

PART SIX

CHAPTER
NINETY-SEVEN

THE NEXT MORNING a full debrief was taking place in the Major Crime Unit. Conran was in attendance along with the rest of the team. There was only one item on the agenda.

Across the room, Jordan was reflecting on his own unofficial debrief on this to Coco the previous evening. She'd looked pretty much like all the other officers in that room looked right now, Lara included: floundering, and more than a little lost.

'It's an extreme case, but not un-heard of according to everything the psychotherapists have been telling us.'

Lara paused.

'Inevitably, a lot of this is now guesswork, but they believe the key to all this lies with Rhys McGuire's birth father.'

She paused again.

'His connection with Kenwood.'

She could see a thousand questions on the lips of every attending officer right now. At any moment, she expected the whole place to erupt into a babble of interrogating voices. Apart from one. By her side, Conran kept his eyes cast down to the floor.

Lara continued, concentrating on the officers who were actually engaging with her right now. There'd be time enough to investigate the one who wasn't and try to work out why.

'We don't know how or when he found out about that. He knew Hughes existed of course, he always has, but the Kenwood connection took us enough time to find, so how he found out is another mystery. But when he did, and if the hospital is right, it seems to have blasted his world apart.'

For a moment, Lara faltered, memories of the different transformations that saw Rhys mutate almost into a different being before her eyes still haunting her. It used to be called multiple personality disorder. Now it had been accorded the acronym DID, standing for dissociative identity disorder, but it was essentially the same thing. In Rhys's case, it had all seemed to somehow fuse with a conviction that the evil present in that old home was a living entity, reaching down through the generations. An infection for which there was only one cure: cut it out at its root.

Lara continued.

'But Rhys kept functioning. And his way of doing that – and yes, this is the first time I've personally come across anything like this, too – was to create other personas, so he could live with all he was discovering, each one different from the other. He'd actually have looked different, sounded different, if you'd come across him at different times in different situations.'

Mairead cut in.

'But it wasn't deliberate? He wasn't trying to fool anyone?'

Lara shook her head.

'For the time he inhabited a different character, he was that character. The others simply didn't exist.'

Lara paused, still feeling more than a little helpless.

'When we first met, he'd even wiped all knowledge of Amy's pregnancy, even though he must have already known about it.'

Jordan took it up.

'And when he came out of each one, he wouldn't even remember who he'd just been?'

Lara nodded.

'He'd even have been able to watch himself assuming those different identities, according to the therapists, without ever making the connection he was actually watching himself.'

Jordan pressed her again.

'And he wouldn't remember what he'd just done?'

Lara hesitated, then shook her head, which was when Conran spoke, for the first time, since the briefing began.

'Even the killings?'

Lara fell silent at that. Across the room everyone else fell silent, too, the same thought in all their minds right now, if their expressions were anything to go by.

The diagnosis from the hospital wasn't in question. That hadn't just been supported by the evidence of Lara's own eyes, there was all those manic scribblings and diary entries found back in his bedroom, too. But she could still see her own misgivings reflected in the eyes of all the other officers in that room. Images of the crucified Pastor Simon were dancing before them. Lara and Mairead were also seeing the terrified Iain Hagan, who'd escaped his own grisly death by a whisker. There was a common thread there that no one in that room could easily square with the otherwise totally normal teenager, distraught at the accident that had befallen his girlfriend, and as confused as everyone else, as to why and how it could have happened.

They'd only seen the one version of that young boy though, as Lara reflected. They hadn't been there, with her, in the grounds of Kenwood. In the time-honoured phrase, they'd only seen the face he'd prepared to meet the faces he'd meet.

Now, no one would see any other. DNA recovered from that crumbling – and now destroyed – seaside boarding house the previous evening had been confirmed as belonging to him. Little else had been left behind in the inferno that had consumed it, but they'd manage to recover that at least. It meant that the full story of whatever macabre imperatives had driven his twisted actions would now never be known, but maybe they would never have been anyway. If everything those psychotherapists were saying was right, even had he survived, Rhys could have been as much of a stranger to himself as a blank bewilderment to everyone else.

Inside the office, Jordan was the first to break the new silence.

'The killings weren't all down to Rhys though, were they?'

Lara nodded, relieved to get back to something she could try to understand at least.

CHAPTER
NINETY-EIGHT

'I THOUGHT IT WAS OVER. I thought he was…'

The old lady struggled for a moment.

'…cured, I suppose.'

It was one hour later, and Lara was looking at the bent head of the elderly Charlotte Mattiss as she twisted a collection of rosary beads in her hands.

'I really thought it was behind him. Behind us. That all those…'

She struggled once more.

'…dark days were gone.'

Then she stopped, staring out over the immaculate lawn that fringed her upmarket home, the lawn that led down to her late husband's garden shed, before looking back at Lara.

'But I could see it in his eyes. The moment he saw that boy. It was starting all over again.'

She stopped again, ever more tormented, then hissed back at the waiting, watching Lara and Jordan.

'And this wasn't like the children from before. This was our grandchild's friend.'

She looked down, helpless, at the beads in her hands again, but this time those hands remained still.

More updates from the hospital had now been received. After giving the family time to say goodbye, Amy's life support had been turned off, the last act in the tragedy that had begun with that accident out on the coast road between Shanklin and Sandown. All of which meant that Rhys and Amy's baby – a girl, also now called Amy – had lost both her parents without ever knowing them, but at least Carey and Matt had reunited to provide for their granddaughter's care. Matt had moved home and was now living with Carey and Aaron again and the house was being prepared for the small baby's arrival. It was one note of hope at least in what had become yet another living example of Kenwood's savage legacy.

But not everything that had happened in the last few weeks was down to Rhys. Lara had spent part of the previous evening with Jordan, going back over the different killings in preparation for that morning's debrief. And the more she looked at them, and the more the two officers had talked it over, the more convinced Lara was that her first instincts had been right.

All the other killings had been precise, methodical. The killing of Edward Matiss was anything but. Meaning there were indeed two killers at work here and the second of them was even more unlikely, at first glance anyway, than the first.

'I just snapped.'

Edward Mattiss's widow looked up at her again.

'I knew instantly what he was thinking. I'd seen that expression on his face before. And I knew what I had to do, what I promised myself I would do if I ever saw it again.'

She started twisting the beads with her frail fingers once more.

'I picked up the spade. I can't remember if he even turned round, but it didn't matter anyway. Within a moment or so, less maybe, he was gone.'

Lara kept looking at her, stilling a sudden flare of pity for the broken old lady before them, reminding herself that she'd known for years. She'd known about her late husband. She'd known his history, and she'd known about Kenwood. She'd lived with him, slept with him, had borne his children, all the time knowing the creature that lurked inside.

And, yes, she'd finally acted against him, had finally snapped that fine summer's day, when a child's birthday party was taking place on the other side of that shed door, but all Lara could see were all the other souls that had been sacrificed in the years when she'd looked the other way.

Lara cautioned Charlotte Mattiss, then nodded at the two uniformed officers who were accompanying herself and Jordan that morning. Then she watched as the old woman was taken into custody for some belated justice to be exacted for those sacrificed souls at least.

CHAPTER
NINETY-NINE

NIGHT WAS FALLING as Lara returned home, having received another update from the hospital about Amy's baby, who was doing well by all accounts. There was every chance she would be going home in the next few days. One part of the Rhys and Amy story could then be put to bed at least.

Perhaps it was time to put something else to one side, too. Partly prompted by Georgia and their last exchange at Kenwood, Lara spent the rest of the evening in front of her floor to ceiling window overlooking the Solent, working her way through the remaining files kept on her late mother by the various social workers who'd overseen her care all those years. Because it was the end of something else now as well. The final act in Lara's private investigation.

She couldn't pretend she'd resurrected a lost relationship in the way she'd hoped. She still felt at a considerable distance from a mother she barely remembered. She'd journeyed with her to some limited extent, at least, through a life she'd known nothing about before. But maybe in the end, Georgia had been right. Maybe this was less to do with any sort of fact-finding exercise and more to do with Lara simply not wanting to let go.

But first, and working as methodically as ever, she completed her journey so far as she could, tracking her late mother from her teens to late twenties. She'd already charted her path through various short-term care homes, but now she accompanied her through various other rites of passage, including two court appearances for minor offences: the first for soft drug abuse, the second for shoplifting.

Then she kept company with her as she started and abandoned various short-term jobs, all the way up to her short-lived and early marriage to Lara's long-lost father, at which point official interest in her seemed to have ended as there were no updates after that.

Aside from one, and as Lara made to close the file for the last time, she spotted it. It was a follow-up hospital appointment a year or so after that marriage which sent an initially puzzled Lara back to another, earlier, case file and an entry she'd skimmed over the first time.

It was just a stray note, recording her mother's admission to hospital suffering from exposure some years before, and a recommendation that she be seen once a year for the next few years for precautionary check-ups. She hadn't bothered with any of the follow-up appointments initially, so maybe Lara's dad had talked her into finally going along before he'd walked out on her, and on them.

The initial admission had been put down to just another teenage girl spending too much time out in the open at the wrong time of year, but something about the date of that admission rang a bell, and, after a little more digging, Lara realised why. It was the day after the storm. The day after her mother and her – still unnamed – friend had been heading for the ferry before the weather fates had intervened leading to them seeking shelter in the house Lara herself visited overlooking the ferry terminal.

She stared out over the water for a moment, those bells ringing louder now all the while, then she crossed to her laptop, checked when the Unknown Girl was washed ashore on the island's north coast. Lara stared at the date. It was one day after her mother's hospital admission. One day after she'd been brought in, suffering from exposure, another young girl had been found drowned just a mile or so away.

Lara felt her pulse quicken.

So, was that the mysterious 'J'?

Jade?

Lara kept staring out over the water.

CHAPTER
ONE HUNDRED

As evening continued to settle over the island, Mairead was concluding some unfinished business of her own.

After the morning briefing had concluded, she'd checked her iPad, and had then travelled across the island. A short time later she was outside the latest meeting of the local S&M club.

The image of the tortured Rhys that had been presented to the Major Crime Unit by Lara had affected them all in different ways, but it had hit home with Mairead in one very particular way. Because underneath it all was one thing and one thing only of course, and that was unresolved guilt and of perhaps the most corrosive kind. All that had happened at Kenwood wasn't Rhys's fault, but that didn't seem to have stopped the young man taking on a burden that was not, and should never have been, his to carry. And the more she thought about that, and the more she pondered unwanted and undeserved burdens, the more all she'd come to do had crystallised.

Mairead tensed as a familiar-looking Jeep swung around the corner ahead. It wasn't the one she'd seen in a local harbour car park all those months before: Kieran Walters's Jeep that had transported his late girlfriend to her death. Given all that had happened in that vehicle, it had been scrapped as quickly as it had been returned to him. But he'd gone for the same model as a replacement, probably in memory of the times he'd taken Chrissie's small daughter, Harper, out for rides and she'd looked down on all the other cars on the road from her elevated vantage point, feeling – as the young girl had proudly proclaimed to anyone who cared to listen – like a princess.

As it stopped, just a short distance away, Mairead exited her police pool car. Kieran Walters looked out at her from the driver's seat, instantly wary. Then he kept looking at her, evermore wary, as Mairead reached into her pocket and handed him some cash, exactly equivalent to the fine he'd had to pay courtesy of that spot-check on his way to work those few days before.

Then she said just one word.

'Sorry.'

Mairead had said that exact same word many times in the last few weeks. But this time, it didn't feel like it did before. This time it felt like a goodbye to all that.

Kieran, a man not unused to uncharacteristic behaviour in times of deep personal crisis himself, kept staring at her for a moment, then nodded back. Then Mairead turned and walked away.

CHAPTER
ONE HUNDRED ONE

LATER THAT SAME DAY, Lara was back in St Mary's, but this visit was nothing to do with the Waites this time. This was to escort her old friend and protector home for a period of convalescence after her attack, although June was much less concerned about her injuries, it seemed, than her bag.

When Lara loomed in the doorway, June was already checking and double-checking the bag's numerous pockets, making sure that her miniature umbrella was in place in one of the pockets along with her blood pressure pills, that her statins were in another pocket, and that a keepsake from her time on the railways, as well as a much-prized photo of Lara and Georgia as small children, was in another of the pockets, too. Lara seated herself on the bed as June's hands roamed ceaselessly, tears pricking her eyes as she watched her unofficial guardian clearly desperate to assure herself that she was still in control of something, even if it was just an outsize handbag.

But while she waited, Lara put some of her recent investigations to good use as she updated June on all she'd discovered about her late mother. All the while, June's fingers maintained their ceaseless checking, but she was clearly listening at the same time.

Lara ran through the homes her mother had been in after Kenwood, the disappointment of that failed foster placing, the friendship she seemed to have formed with 'J' who could have been Jade, as well as Lara finding the actual house where they'd taken shelter on the night of what seemed to have been some great storm, which was when June cut in.

'I remember that night.'

As Lara looked at her, June began supplying her own memories of fallen trees and shattered roof tiles and smashed windows, even stopping the checking of her bag for a moment. For a few moments, the sharper, more focused June she'd always known was back before Lara's eyes.

Then the old lady hesitated.

'I'm so pleased you're doing this, you know.'

Lara looked at her again, June seeming to be unsure now if she should say what she next wanted to say. But she said it anyway.

'For years, it's just been work, work, work, it's all you've ever talked about. But you need to do this from time to time, too. Step aside, take time out, take time to look, not just what's in front, but what's around you as well.'

Then June stopped, her brow creasing.

'I don't suppose that makes a lot of sense, does it?'

But it did. Lara couldn't have put into words exactly what June was trying to say, either. But she understood it perfectly, nonetheless.

The nurse came in to give June the small selection of pills she was to take home with her, and the next few moments were spent deliberating exactly in which pocket in her bag they should be placed. And while all that was going on, and perhaps emboldened by all June had just said, Lara told her about more of her attempts to step aside, to take time out, to try and see not just what was in front of her, but what was all around her, too.

Lara told June all about her mother's visit to the grave of the Unknown Girl, a local landmark that June knew as well as anyone on the island. She also told her of her new suspicion that the girl might even be Jade, even though that didn't really make too much sense now Lara had thought about it a little more.

If that was true, then why would her mother have kept quiet about her identity? Why not allow her the dignity of a name on her headstone at least? Why condemn her to a final resting place marked not even by a simple record of who she was?

June shrugged, helpless, that as much of a mystery to her, too.

'I don't know.'

The nurse had left by now and Lara stood, picking up another bag that June was taking home with her, containing a change of clothes.

'But...'

Lara looked at her as June stared into the near distance, her bag on her lap, not moving for a moment, the contents of those various pockets forgotten for a moment now, too.

Then June looked up at her.

'I did hear a rumour. At the time.'

CHAPTER
ONE HUNDRED TWO

THE LAST DAY or so had been an eventful time for Jordan as well.

There'd been those three rings of steel to maintain around Weston, Russell and Hughes for one thing, although no one expected that to last much longer. That inferno in the seaside boarding house had seen to that.

The security operation hadn't made a lot of difference to the unaware John Weston, but Andrew Russell was still loudly protesting his continuing incarceration in a safe house in Freshwater. Given the fact he'd probably been most at risk following Rhys's escape from the hospital, Kevin Hughes was still in his holding cell in Albany, although he still didn't seem to be finding the ordeal too onerous. A nice warm billet and three hot meals a day were slipping down very nicely, according to all accounts.

So far as more personal matters were concerned, Edie was now back in hospital. That one brief moment of lucidity with Coco aside – doubtless sparked by the tantalising prospect of scoring a victory over her ex – she'd lapsed back into the same near-catatonic state she'd inhabited for the previous months, just staring, unseeing, at a far wall. And, on her next follow-up visit, the aftercare support officer had arranged for her return to St

Mary's almost immediately. There was clearly still a long road ahead for her.

And, so far as Coco was concerned, she'd volunteered for extra duties in the animal rescue centre. Right now, her days were mainly spent trying to settle a very excitable Yorkshire terrier who seemed to go from manic high maintenance to a state of depressive withdrawal, sometimes within just a couple of wags of his tail. But it was therapy again for her, of a sort anyway, and Jordan knew it. His still-troubled daughter losing herself in displacement activity while trying to get to grips with the conundrum that had been the even more troubled Rhys McGuire.

Perhaps, as Jordan reflected, as his senior officer who'd joined him just a few moments before, was doing right now, too.

'If that's right. If "J" – Jade—'

Jordan cut in.

'If "J" was Jade.'

Lara acknowledged that with a nod but pressed on regardless.

'If she was pregnant, it definitely explains the secrecy.'

Amy Waite floated before Lara's eyes. That pregnant young girl had been fleeing the island in panic, trying to escape a threat she believed to be posed by Rhys. So, and if the rumours she'd just heard from June in St Mary's were true, had Jade been fleeing in a similar panic? Aided by Lara's late mother, had she also been trying to escape another threat?

Jordan could already see the answer to his next question in Lara's eyes.

'And if that's right, you think this could be down to Kenwood again?'

Lara nodded.

'If one of those abusers was responsible for her pregnancy, then her giving birth would have effectively signed their arrest warrant.'

Jordan fell silent for a moment. Given the age of Lara's

mother at the time and, thereby, the probable age of her companion, a paternity test on the infant would indeed have provided evidence of abuse. Killing her – and thereby killing her unknown child as well – would have removed that threat at one fell swoop. If that was true, then no wonder the two girls were running that night.

'But if that's right...'

Jordan tailed off. Because it still left that huge and unanswered question. Why hadn't Lara's mother ever told the world who she was?

Lara took it up. She'd had more time to work that out.

'Because those tentacles spread everywhere back then. And identifying Jade would have alerted the father.'

Lara hunched closer over the desk, warming to this all the while.

'We know they had connections all over the island at that time. So, they could easily have had connections in the hospital, too. A word in the right ear, and they could have buried a dog in her place and simply incinerated her remains.'

Lara fell silent, Jordan turning all that over now, too. But if she remained a mystery, if no one knew who she was, it meant she could be laid to rest, undisturbed and undefiled. And maybe, in years to come, her remains could be exhumed, and tests carried out at last.

Lara had already set in place an application for that exhumation. In the meantime, Mairead had been tasked with sourcing all the old police files on the case of the Unknown Girl. Within the next day or so they'd be ready to be passed on to Doctor Sarah Ryan. If that girl had been pregnant, it was eminently possible that whoever had fathered that unborn baby was now dead himself, but it was also possible he was among the dwindling list of Kenwood survivors. In which case, some belated justice might be secured at last.

Across the desk, Jordan paused again.

'But...'

Lara nodded as he stopped. She knew what he was going to say. Some last twist might be found in this particular part of this tale. But it would be very much the last act in the story, and this investigation, if it was. Just like she'd done with her own mother, it was time to put that to one side, get on with other stories, other investigations.

But that wasn't what Jordan was about to say. For once, Lara's much-fabled intuition when it came to her junior officer had let her down.

'You're not going to be here to check it out anyway, are you?'

Lara looked back at him.

'Hasn't Conran worked out you're owed about six years leave?'

Lara stifled a smile. It was an exaggeration, but not by much. And Conran had indeed not only pointed out the amount of her excessive outstanding leave but had made it only too clear that she had to take it. And, for once, she hadn't protested.

The bizarre thing being Conran's tone. Her senior officer had lifted his head from the record on his desk in front of him of all her missed holidays and leave days not taken, and in strict contrast to all of their previous exchanges, he sounded almost mild.

'It ends here, Lara.'

With something of a jolt, she'd realised it was the first time he'd actually done that. It was the first time he'd ever called her by her first name and not her more usual title of DI Arden.

'You need to take a break.'

And now Lara was wondering if, and despite all initial impressions to the contrary, there was a human being in there after all.

Lara smiled back at Jordan as their eyes connected, a connection that lasted just that little longer than strictly necessary, something Lara realised with another slight jolt, that had been happening with increasing frequency lately. Then she turned and headed out to the corridor.

But as she passed the water cooler by the door to the stairs, Lara was stopped by a puzzled Mairead.

'That exhumation you asked for.'

Lara stared at her, equally puzzled. It had to be far too early for any decision to have been made on that, surely.

But that wasn't why Mairead had stopped her.

CHAPTER
ONE HUNDRED THREE

'I'D no idea he'd done that.'

Lara looked at him, sitting across from her in the kitchen of the McGuire family home. Joseph McGuire's neatly trimmed salt-and-pepper stubble was now bushy and unkempt, and his former spare frame seemed to have collapsed in on itself. He looked, now, much like Matt and Carey Waite had looked for the past few weeks: adrift and bewildered.

The hospital specialists who had updated Lara and the Major Crime Unit had attempted to explain Rhys's condition to him, too, but Lara could see only too clearly that he couldn't, and perhaps wouldn't ever, properly understand. Perhaps some part of him didn't ever want to.

McGuire shook his head, another mystery piling on top of too many already.

'I've no idea why he'd even think about it in the first place.'

Lara just stared at him, more than a little rocked, and for not the first time when it came to anything to do with Rhys McGuire. They still didn't know whether the body in there was indeed Jade, and wouldn't until permission for the exhumation came through. But courtesy of a CCTV camera that covered the grave-yard, and an initially puzzling visitor, Mairead had managed to solve the mystery of the grave's new headstone at least. The benefactor, apparently, was Joseph McGuire.

That had puzzled Lara mightily. From the little she'd seen of him, she hadn't formed the impression of an overly generous or empathic man, despite his obvious wealth, but McGuire had cleared that up within moments of Lara's calling.

Rhys had paid for that new headstone it seemed. He'd accessed his father's bank account to raid the cash required some months before. He'd admitted the theft quickly enough and had told his father what he'd done with the money. But, no matter how hard the bewildered Joseph had pushed, Rhys had remained obdurately silent as to why.

Lara stared out over the garden where she'd seen Rhys help his father bury the family pet. Did Rhys know about the possible connection between that grave and Kenwood? But how could he? Lara herself had discovered a possible link – and it was still not any sort of definite link – only a short time before.

Lara looked back at his now-silent father again. But there was no way of finding out now anyway of course. And so, and after a few more moments, Lara stood and made for the door, leaving McGuire where he would now be for a long time to come, locked in his own private hell.

CHAPTER
ONE HUNDRED FOUR

IT WAS the strangest of feelings.

The next day, her packed bag on the ground at her feet, Lara was in Ryde waiting for a ferry to the mainland, taking her place among a crowd of holidaymakers, about to head off for a holiday of her own. Aside from visiting a classic car dealer in Devon who specialised in classic Minis and collecting a Cooper he'd sourced for her to replace the one Rhys McGuire had torched, she had no plans for at least the next month. All she had to do was collect her car, and then drive, in no particular direction, and with no particular destination, in mind. Lara just had to empty her head in other words. Think of nothing – and especially not think about work; and she couldn't remember a time in at least the last five years when that prospect had suddenly opened up in front of her. No wonder everything felt unutterably strange.

Ahead, the ferry hove into view. As it docked a few moments later, Lara stood back to allow the other foot passengers to file past her, taking a moment to breathe in the salt spray as a gust of wind whipped all around. Then she moved to take her own place on board, opting immediately for a bench seat on one of the outside decks from which she could watch her home island disappear in the distance and think of nothing, apart from getting behind the wheel of a decades-old car which she could hopefully come to love as much as she'd loved her old one.

Briefly, as she stood on the deck, she gazed over the same stretch of water that had returned the Unknown Girl back to the shore, and Rhys was back before her eyes once again. She'd spent most of the previous evening puzzling over his seemingly inexplicable gesture with that headstone, but what was the point of digging too deeply into what was probably just another loose end anyway? What, indeed, had really been the point of tasking McGuire on it, in truth? That single act of mystifying charity somewhat paled into insignificance when set alongside all the other acts initiated lately by his damaged son.

Lara turned away, putting all that out of her mind now, too. Then she paused as she saw a familiar-looking figure rushing to get on board before the gates closed.

The figure in question was a girl in her teens, struggling along with a large bag in hand, while pushing a buggy that hosted a bawling baby. Already, other travellers were moving away, as unobtrusively as they could, as she yelled at the infant, only provoking more protesting cries from the baby in turn. For a moment longer, a curious Lara eyed her, as the teen girl reached into her bag, bringing out an outsize packet of crisps, stuffing some into the baby's hands. Then she straightened up, the infant placated momentarily at least, and Lara suddenly placed her.

She was the young mum Lara had last seen in the fetid flat she'd shared with Rhys's birth father, Kevin Hughes. Lara kept looking at her as she fed her baby some more crisps and then some more again.

Five minutes later, Lara and Beth Hughes were sitting side by side on the bench seat on the deck. Lara had now established her name and the name of her baby – which was Keren and not Karen, Beth was very particular about that. And Beth was telling

Lara why she was on the ferry and all about her plans, which seemed to involve putting as much distance between herself and her old home as she could.

'A couple of girls I know are working there.'

Beth looked out over the spray towards Portsmouth, looming ahead of them in the distance. Then she looked back at Lara, immediately defensive.

'It's legit. The woman who runs it, she's got qualifications and everything.'

Lara stayed silent. Beth was heading for work in a massage parlour on the mainland which was very much her business and not Lara's. That work certainly wouldn't be legit in even the loosest sense of the word, but that wasn't Lara's business either. Something did intrigue her though.

'And your dad?'

Lara hesitated. What would be his reaction to being suddenly deprived of his meal ticket when he was finally released from protective custody? It had been only too obvious, in their only previous meeting, just how much the venal Kevin Hughes counted on the money his daughter brought in.

Beth flushed, Lara's meaning only too clear.

'This ain't nothing to do with him. And anyway...'

The young girl shot a quick sideways glance at her, aggressive now as well as defensive.

'He ain't around no more, is he?'

Which was true enough, but Hughes's incarceration wasn't destined to last too much longer.

'So, does he know where you're going?'

'No reason he should.'

Lara persisted.

'But could he find out? Have you told anyone else?'

Something passed across the young mother's face, something Lara couldn't quite place as her baby stirred in the buggy at her feet. And now Beth was getting more aggressive and defensive by the minute.

'Why are you so interested anyway?'

'Because he might be coming home any day now.'

Lara faltered as once again there it was, that same something flashing across the young girl's face – the same something Lara still couldn't place.

'So, you might want to make sure you've covered your tracks.'

Beth cut across, a sudden flare of frustration and temper that seemed to come out of nowhere.

'This is all down to you anyway. You and your lot. You ain't ever going to let it go, and you ain't ever going to let him go neither. Don't matter what we do, you're always going to come knocking on our door.'

Lara tried to keep her tone mild, her voice non-judgemental.

'Believe it or not, that was for his own protection.'

Beth just snorted in disbelief and Lara eyed the refreshment outlet, wondering if she had time for a coffee before they docked. Maybe it was time to cut this unexpected reunion short. By her side, Beth stood, picking up her large bag. She seemed to have come to the same conclusion.

'Yeah well, you ain't as clever as you think.'

Then she broke off as, perhaps disturbed by her mum's sudden movement, Keren suddenly started wailing again. Beth let fire with another flurry of curses and tore open another outsize packet of crisps.

'And we ain't as stupid as you think neither.'

And there it was once more, as she turned back to her baby. That same something flashing across her face again.

And this time Lara did place it.

CHAPTER
ONE HUNDRED FIVE

A GRINNING Jordan picked up the phone, recognising instantly the mobile number that had just flashed up on the display. He exaggerated, ever so slightly, his greeting and Lara's name so everyone would know who was calling.

Across the room, Mairead, standing by the moka pot, checked a list of timings on the wall, as did every other officer in the unit that day. A sweep had been initiated that very morning. Every officer had inserted their own predictions as to when Lara would make her first contact from what was supposed to be her much-postponed holiday. Estimates had varied from a couple of days to a week. No one imagined she'd be back in touch in less than two hours and from a ferry that couldn't even have docked yet.

Jordan, still grinning, scanned the wall as wind noise buffeted his ears from the other side of the line, noting with some gratification that while he may have been wildly inaccurate in his own estimate – he'd opted for two days – his was still the closest guess.

Then Lara's voice sounded in his ear, uncharacteristically hesitant, tentative even; and Jordan's knowing smile begin to fade.

'Kevin Hughes.'

Jordan sifted some papers on his desk, checking all the while.

'His release has been scheduled for tomorrow morning.'

But that wasn't why Lara was calling.

'Who actually picked him up?'

'I don't understand.'

Lara persisted.

'It was uniform, yes?'

Jordan nodded.

'They collected him from his flat, delivered him straight down to Albany.'

'And had any of them had any dealings with him before?'

Jordan stilled as an image began to form in front of his eyes.

'Had any of them actually seen him before?'

Once again, Jordan saw again the shadowy figure dropping from that front bedroom window as Hughes's daughter had opened the door, the figure they themselves had taken for Hughes before they'd seen the man himself standing next to his pit bull in that rear room along the hall.

It was the same image that was dancing before Lara's eyes now, too.

'Was he even fingerprinted?'

Across the room, Mairead stared as she registered the tension beginning to creep across Jordan's shoulders, always a tell-tale sign that something was wrong.

Jordan shook his head.

'There'd be no reason, you know that, he wasn't being arrested, he was just being taken in for his own protection.'

For a moment, neither Lara nor Jordan said anything else. Neither needed to. Then Jordan snatched up his car keys and made for the door.

CHAPTER
ONE HUNDRED SIX

FOR ONCE, Aaron didn't count the steps on the way down from the maternity ward. He also didn't count the steps from the front entrance to the waiting ambulance either. He also hadn't completed any circuits of his bedroom the previous night.

Partly, that was because none of that had worked. None of the rituals he'd put in place had kept his sister safe, and she was gone now, and he couldn't bring her back. But there was another reason as well and that reason was currently being carried by his mum a few steps ahead.

Amy, the baby, was coming home. And over the last few days the conviction had been growing in her big brother that, from now on, he'd just have to look after her in more traditional ways. From now on he'd just have to help care for her, feed her, play with her, and love her. Forget all those former deals with devils that hadn't made any difference anyway.

Carey handed Matt a small case packed with nappies and formula, and Aaron smiled as his anxious mum checked for the umpteenth time that Amy wasn't too hot or too cold. For the next few moments, as his dad fussed over her too and Aaron duly helped as well, they only had eyes for their new small bundle of joy right now. So, no one took much notice of the ambulance driver who'd been deputed to take them home.

Carey settled herself with Amy in the rear of the ambulance next to Matt and Aaron, reaching out for some bottled water that the considerate ambulance driver had placed there, before handing bottles to Aaron and Matt as well.

CHAPTER
ONE HUNDRED SEVEN

COURTESY of a hastily scrambled police helicopter, Lara returned to the island in a fraction of the time it had taken her to make her outward trip, three developments giving her return journey almost literal wings.

First, there'd been Jordan's panicked dash to Albany and his confirmation that whoever those uniformed officers had picked up it wasn't Kevin Hughes. That wasn't totally those uniformed officers' fault. There was a strong physical resemblance between the man in that holding cell and the man they'd gone to take into custody, so perhaps it was indeed the friend or family member Lara and Jordan had seen attempting his panicked escape that day. But there was little reason to suspect any sort of subterfuge at work anyway. Who, after all, would agree to be taken into custody, albeit of the protective kind, for no good reason?

Hughes must have believed, much like his daughter, that this latest arrest was the first of what was going to be many, now the island police had him in their sights, so he'd engineered a simple substitution. It was clever enough, in its way. His stand-in would be released speedily enough once the switch was discovered, and it would allow Hughes to do what his daughter and grandchild were doing right now: get off the island and make a fresh start somewhere else.

But in fleeing the frying pan, had the doubtless-exultant Hughes plunged straight into a literal and ferocious fire? Was it his remains that had been discovered in that destroyed meeting room at the rear of that ramshackle boarding house? Did he flee those police officers only to be intercepted by his son?

Given the very close family connection, Sarah Ryan had already confirmed that it was eminently possible that the DNA identified in the meeting room as belonging to Rhys, could have been from his father. Meaning, if Rhys had intercepted him, then Rhys could still be very much alive. And very much a clear and present threat.

Then there was the follow-up phone call between Lara and Jordan as her helicopter began its descent to land at the rear of the Police HQ.

'Amy's baby.'

Lara stilled.

'The paediatrician has already signed off on the discharge.'

Jordan hesitated, his tone already making Lara grow cold.

'They left the hospital an hour or so ago.'

Lara stared out through the window of the rapidly descending helicopter, looking towards St Mary's itself, just visible on the horizon.

CHAPTER
ONE HUNDRED EIGHT

IT HAD BEEN SUCH a long and gruelling time.

From the moment that knock had sounded on their front door that night and Matt had opened it to find two police officers outside, Carey had been in a tunnel. It was as if life had just stopped. At times, she'd wanted her own life to simply stop, too. To not wake up – even on those rare occasions when she could finally sleep – without that suffocating weight pressing down on her.

But in the last day or so – and courtesy of the small infant sleeping in her arms right now – she had glimpsed some distant prospect of recovery at least, had embraced at least a semblance of hope. And she didn't, now, even entertain the thought of not going on. This new baby made that notion unthinkable.

But it had taken its toll. How else could you explain the massive waves of tiredness that were now washing over her, and which seemed to be washing over Matt and Aaron, too, if the way their heads were drooping, and their eyes were beginning to close, were anything to go by.

Carey looked out of the window, telling herself not to be stupid. It was only a short ride home, she simply had to stay awake. But the sights outside the window seemed to be passing by without her even seeing them.

For some reason, all she could see in front of her was a now-empty water bottle.

CHAPTER
ONE HUNDRED NINE

TRYING to keep her raging emotions under control, Lara watched the increasingly panicked emergency response crew as they checked, double-checked and then checked again.

Back in the Major Crime Unit, Mairead had already put out an all-points notice to the ferry companies who were now on the highest of alerts for a young man travelling with a new-born baby.

The police helicopter had been retained and was currently flying across the island to conduct an aerial search while drones were also being sent up.

CCTV covering all exit routes from St Mary's was being trawled, but so far there was nothing: no clues, no leads, no connections.

In the first-floor office, Lara kept looking at the response crew. The ambulance that was transporting the Waite family had been fitted with the latest Judt tracking system, along with keyboard integration to monitor the start point of any journey, and the time at which an ambulance reached an incident location. It meant the emergency response team could accurately monitor the location of all their emergency vehicles, helping to save precious time in an emergency by directing the closest vehicle to any incident.

All of which sounded eminently reassuring in theory, and all of which had just been rendered completely useless in practice. Because as the response crew kept checking co-ordinates and scanning monitors, the same result returned each time. The system monitoring the ambulance transporting the Waites wasn't working, or it had been disabled inside the vehicle in some way.

Either way, the vehicle and its occupants – including a few-days-old baby – had disappeared.

Lara turned and stared out of the window at cars and ambulances approaching and passing below. All everyone was thinking about was Rhys. But, and strangely, it wasn't Rhys she was seeing right now.

For some reason, all she could now see was Iain Hagan, lying on that makeshift bed in the hospice, telling her and Mairead about that strange apparition on the riverbank. Once again, she heard him telling them that he didn't know who she was, or even if she was real. All he knew was that one minute, there was just him, in the water, the next minute there was this girl and then she was gone.

Then Hagan faded to be replaced by the white van driver, who was still resolutely refusing to offer up his real name and identity, in case his family could be identified and revenge taken on them by the traffickers who'd facilitated his passage across from France. And Lara was seeing again was that other girl he also believed he'd seen close to Amy, before he'd hit her.

Then Lara felt a huge surge of anger erupt inside. She'd done this all through this investigation. She'd continually mistaken illusion for reality, had been chasing shadows over substance, and she was doing it again. Just at the moment she should be focused on one thing, and one thing only, and that was the deeply deranged and dangerous Rhys McGuire, all she was thinking about was Esther again.

Then she stilled as another recent exchange suddenly flashed across her mind.

'It's just something I catch, out of the corner of my eye sometimes.'

Lara remained where she was by the window as more of her last exchange with Georgia returned to her.

'It's as if she's there. I actually see her, but then she's gone.'

Lara kept staring out of the window.

'Don't you ever want to do what she did?'

But now, Lara felt herself holding her breath. Because maybe something else was happening here. Maybe this wasn't just Lara chasing yet more shadows. Maybe this was all down to connections again: the connection she'd sensed between Aaron and his sister, and the connection she'd always known was there between herself and her own sister. Maybe, somewhere in all this, her mind was leading her somewhere without her even realising it.

And, as if by way of confirmation, more of Georgia's words now echoed inside.

'Don't you ever want to just hit back?'

And, suddenly, Lara had it.

She knew where Rhys might be.

CHAPTER
ONE HUNDRED TEN

RHYS CARRIED the sleeping baby from the back of the ambulance, after removing her from the unprotesting arms of her now-comatose grandmother, with her equally comatose grandfather and the young uncle similarly helpless at her side.

He laid the slumbering infant down on a blanket on the ground, the wind from the sea far below whipping all around them, but the child was warm enough. Rhys had checked, but she was fine.

It was the strangest feeling, one he hardly understood himself. All his life he'd felt as if he was being borne along by whatever had been the strongest current buffeting him at the time. Maybe that was why he'd never felt there was anything at his centre, nothing to hold onto. No one he could actually call himself.

Rhys looked at the grave in front of him, the new headstone sparkling in the sun. Maybe that was why, from the moment he'd seen that simple inscription that year or so before, something in those few simple words on that headstone had just resonated deep inside. And standing in front of it, as sometimes he had for hours, it was as if there were two unknown souls there, and not just one.

Rhys looked back at the small baby again. All that had changed now, though. For the first time in his life, Rhys finally had a reason to keep going where, so often before, he'd felt like there was nothing to do but give up. He felt as if he had a goal now, a mission. It wasn't like his previous mission, which now felt as if it belonged to some other person completely. Previously, that person had seen this baby as part of the problem, but the minute Rhys had seen her, as in seen her properly, in the flesh, he knew straightaway she wasn't any sort of problem. It had been like the brightest of lights suddenly breaking through the darkness. The infant Amy wasn't the problem, she was the solution.

So, now they just had to rest here for a short time, make sure he'd got everything for the next part of the journey he'd planned, and then they'd be on their way.

Then Rhys tensed as he sensed someone else coming into the graveyard. And then he wheeled round as a voice sounded behind him.

'Hello, Rhys.'

CHAPTER
ONE HUNDRED ELEVEN

RHYS STARED at Lara in disbelief. Far below, the sea crashed down on the beach. But up on that clifftop, all sound, all movement indeed, suddenly seemed to cease.

Rhys stared at her for a moment. Lara didn't speak. She just let her eyes roam behind him, over the sea. She was looking out over the exact same stretch of water again that had washed in the Unknown Girl. They were standing in the cemetery that had played host to her body ever since. If Lara was right about her identity, and her late mother's reason for keeping that a secret, this was the place she'd chosen to do what she hadn't been able to do for so long in her short life. What Georgia had also dreamt of doing, indeed, just a short time before. It was the place where, in the only way she could, her late mother had hit back.

In front of her, and still silent for now, Rhys hesitated a moment longer. Then he looked down at the sleeping baby at his feet, and took a deep, deep breath.

'I got it wrong before.'

Lara stared at him, disbelief momentarily occluding her vision.

Got it wrong?

'I know that now.'

Lara kept staring at him.

Murder.

Abduction.

Imprisonment.

Got it wrong?

What planet was he living on!?

Rhys looked down at the baby, wrapped in her blanket, still sleeping peacefully on the grass.

'I was in a fog, I couldn't see any way forward, even any way back, I was just...'

Rhys paused, helpless, suddenly looking a lot younger than even his modest number of years, then his face set, determined, as the remnants of what had been an old resolve suddenly coursed through him again.

'But you know what happened to them. Those kids, you probably haven't found most of them, and you never will, they'll just rot, wherever they were buried.'

Lara didn't reply. He was right.

Rhys nodded at her.

'So, tell me they don't deserve everything that's happened to them.'

Lara cut across.

'And does she?'

Rhys followed Lara's nod towards the still-sleeping Amy and for a moment, just a moment, his features softened as Lara pressed on.

'That's what it's all been about hasn't it? Legacy? All that bad seed, travelling down through the generations?'

Lara broke off.

'We've read Amy's journal, Rhys, we know what you said to her, what spooked her so much she was running away.'

Lara moved closer to him.

'It's set in stone, that's what you said, that's what you told her, no possibility of change, no prospect of any sort of redemption, it's fixed in the stars, the fates, no matter what happens to her, no matter the life she may want to lead, it doesn't matter that she may never hear the name Kenwood, she'll still return to it, and she'll become one of the creatures that used to haunt it, she has to, because it's pre-ordained.'

Rhys cut across.

'I don't think that anymore.'

Lara studied him. This incarnation of Rhys may not. But what about the next one?

'I've changed, that's all changed.'

He looked at her, desperate.

'But she still can't stay there, not with him.'

Lara paused. not understanding what he was talking about for a moment. Was another transformation taking place? Was Rhys already beginning to inhabit some different persona once again?

'It's like a...'

The young boy struggled

'...a cancer, it'll twist a body inside out, make it unrecognisable, but it's effect, not cause, that's what I got wrong, you have to go back to the root cause, the prime mover and one of them is there, in that house, her house.'

Rhys gestured down at the unaware baby and Lara kept staring at him as comprehension began to dawn.

Matt?

Was she talking about Matt?

Rhys rolled on, evermore insistent.

'Nothing will happen this year, or next year, maybe not for years to come. But it'll happen in time, it has to, I was right about that at least.'

Suddenly, Lara was back with Charlotte Mattiss, seeing the old lady twisting those rosary beads in her fingers again, his widow reliving the moment she watched a doting grandfather turn back into a monster.

Lara filed that away. Matt Waite would be investigated. But removing Amy from his custody to Rhys's care, even if all he was now alleging was true, was never going to be an option. Given all he'd done, no matter what he was saying now, Rhys was every bit as much a monster as those he believed he'd been setting out to slay.

Distant, faint but distinct nonetheless, a siren sounded. It could be any emergency vehicle, responding to any of a hundred different shouts that came into the emergency response team daily on the island, sometimes by the hour. Or it could be Jordan, acting on the message she'd left before she set off to pursue this clifftop hunch. She couldn't even tell if it was approaching or heading away.

Rhys didn't even seem to hear it. He just looked down at Amy again. Lara, almost instinctively, followed his look, and so she missed it. She missed the first tell-tale sign of the change, but that wasn't down to any sort of subterfuge on Rhys's part. Despite his genuinely best efforts it was starting to happen again. He was starting to lose focus. The darkness that the baby had kept at bay was creeping back.

And, suddenly, out it came, almost literally out of nowhere. One moment, Lara and Rhys were just standing there on that clifftop, over the still-sleeping Amy. The next, there was a flash of something metallic, sunlight sparking from it as Rhys lashed out. If it hadn't been for that, Lara might not have seen the weapon at all. Where Rhys had been concealing it up to then, she had no idea.

Lara flung up her hand just before the knife connected with her neck, and it clattered to the ground as a now-unbalanced Rhys let it slip from his grip. For a moment he just stared at her, wildly. Then he turned, hared for a distant path that led down to the beach. Lara stared after him, then down at Amy, torn. From the beach, he'd have a choice of at least four different exit points. If he could put enough distance between himself and Lara in the next few moments, she'd be wheeling round impotently down on the sand, trying to make the impossible choice of which path to take to follow him.

Lara hesitated a moment longer, looking back at Amy again, but she'd be safe enough for now. She was far from the age she could even roll over, let alone crawl to a place of danger such as nearer to that cliff edge. So, Lara took off after Rhys, knowing he could not, must not, be allowed to get away again. Once he disappeared, and for a second time, they'd be back in no man's land again, waiting once more for a strike that could come from a direction and at a time no one would be able to predict.

But it was already looking like a pursuit lost almost before it had been engaged, because Rhys was already out of sight. Lara ran as fast as she could, but as she reached the top of the path and looked down, he wasn't even in sight. From her high vantage point, Lara scanned the beach, frantic, the wind buffeting into her as she stood at that most exposed of spots. It was impossible – a human being simply could not run that fast – but no matter how many times Lara scanned those sands, Rhys was nowhere to be seen.

Then Lara turned, and only just in time, to see Rhys, not below her as his decoy run had suggested, but behind her, and just feet away, ready to pounce.

Lara flung herself to one side as Rhys launched himself down onto her. Scrabbling for grip, she latched onto a large clump of grass growing out of the cliff edge, but her momentum carried her over, hands tearing at the grass all the while. If it gave way, she'd fall, but it held, albeit protesting all the while, its roots scrabbling for grip as she was. But as the world swam back into focus, Lara could see it was only a temporary reprieve. Her leap to safety, her bid to escape, had only taken her over a jagged slash in the cliff face.

Lara clung to the cliff face, the wind roaring into her even stronger now as Rhys leapt across the small ravine. Within another second they'd be face to face on that cliff edge and from there Lara knew that only one of them would be returning to safety.

As he landed, just inches from her, the young man swayed,

momentarily unbalanced again, and it was all the opportunity Lara needed. Rhys had his youthful build and stamina on his side, but Lara had a boxer's reach. She lashed out, making sure to smash her pursuer back towards the cliff face and not towards its edge and Rhys crashed down, blood pouring from his mouth, winded. He wouldn't stay that way for long, and Lara knew it.

Lara scrambled up the cliff and then ran on, criss-crossing a series of smaller, but no less treacherous, small ravines, in turn, zigzagging back towards Amy. She heard a yell of what sounded like almost pure fury explode from behind and she knew that Rhys was up again and resuming his pursuit.

Then she heard the siren again, and this time there was no doubt about it. It was definitely closer at hand. Lara had just been handed a small, but potentially crucial advantage and she pressed on, heading for Amy. Rhys hadn't seemed to want to hurt the small infant, but with the personality shifts she'd witnessed before, and was still witnessing now, Lara couldn't be anywhere near sure that would endure.

Ahead, Lara could see Amy beginning to stir, perhaps disturbed by the police siren that was now sounding louder again. Lara wheeled back as she sensed rather than saw Rhys racing up behind her. If she could incapacitate him once more, for even a few more moments, then with reinforcements getting closer all the time, she'd have him.

Suddenly, Rhys flung himself through the air again, crashing down into her once more, sending Lara somersaulting in turn towards the cliff edge again. Dimly, she heard herself mounting a feeble protest, but she was spinning now, over and over, too fast to stop herself, too fast to even begin to grip the clumps of grass and small bushes she was crushing beneath her as her momentum carried her on.

With one last desperate lunge she flung out an arm, feeling her shoulder blade almost wrench out of its socket as she wrapped it round a tree root protruding from the very edge of the cliff face. Then her legs swung over the side.

Lara hung on to the root as it bent against her weight. She jammed her legs into a crevice in the cliff face, momentarily relieving the pressure, but she couldn't hold herself there for long and she knew it.

She wasn't going to get the chance anyway, because Rhys now appeared above her.

For a moment, as Lara stared up at him, all sound attenuated again, even the wind from the sea seemed to hush as if it too was holding its breath.

All there was in the world was Lara and a sheer drop to her death below.

CHAPTER
ONE HUNDRED TWELVE

A FEW HUNDRED METRES AWAY, Jordan pulled up on the clifftop, but, as he dashed from the police pool car, time suddenly seemed to stand still for him, too.

From his vantage point, he could see Lara clinging onto her precarious perch just those couple of hundred metres or so ahead, but just at the moment he should be springing into immediate action, his body suddenly ambushed him. All of a sudden, he felt as if his whole being had turned into a lead weight. Every movement he tried to make felt as if he was trying to drag himself through quicksand.

For a moment Jordan just stood there, Lara still in his sights. And it was the moment Jordan knew, the moment he finally understood just what she meant to him, what all those snatched looks, lingering just that fraction too long, had all been about. How else to explain his sudden, near-terrified, immobility as he was faced with the prospect of losing her?

Then, albeit struggling all the while, Jordan recovered his wits, regained control of his body and began to run.

CHAPTER
ONE HUNDRED THIRTEEN

Rhys was lost again.

He'd found himself for Amy.

But now he was lost again

Yet this wasn't exactly like before, because something had changed. For weeks – ever since he'd found out about Kenwood – he'd just had his vendetta in mind, no one else counted, nothing else mattered. Through the different incarnations that he knew had occasionally claimed him, that had remained constant and now it was back again, dominating his thoughts, directing his actions, but with one difference.

Now, looking down at Lara, knowing what he had to do, he couldn't do it. Rhys closed his eyes, willing himself on because it should be simple. She was an obstacle, and obstacles had to be removed, and if he did that quickly, then despite those fast-approaching police sirens he'd heard, there'd still be time to complete what he had to do.

So, why was he standing there, hesitating, looking down into a pair of eyes looking back up at him?

Suddenly, he wheeled round as for the second time in what felt like as many minutes, he again sensed someone approaching, fast, from behind.

And then, instinctively again, he lashed out once more.

Less than a couple of metres away, and still clinging onto that cliff face, Lara also sensed it rather than saw it. She was aware of a presence momentarily above her and then to her side and then she was aware of nothing. Dimly, she heard more emergency sirens again, and they were close, very close this time. Then she looked up, to see Rhys still above her, but staring down beyond her.

Lara had no idea what had happened for a moment. Then an ice-cold chill started to claim her as an appalled-looking Rhys just kept looking down towards the beach. Twisting her head around, Lara stared down, too, just in time to see an incoming wave claim Jordan's broken body before starting to suck it back out to sea.

With a strength she didn't know she possessed, Lara clawed her way back up the cliff edge, which was when she saw Rhys, now already over fifty metres away. Briefly, Lara paused as they locked eyes, then he hissed across at her from the other side of what was always going to be an unbridgeable divide.

'I'd have kept her safe.'

Rhys nodded across at the still-sleeping Amy before hissing back at Lara again.

'This is your fault.'

Lara looked down to the beach.

'This is on your hands.'

Then Rhys was gone.

Lara kept looking down towards the beach.

But Jordan was gone now, too.

ACKNOWLEDGMENTS

With grateful thanks to the inspirational Adrian Hobart and Rebecca Collins and also to the uber-talented Jayne Mapp.

Aaron's almost telepathic connection to his sister, Amy, derives from my long-standing fascination with the relationship between twins and close siblings. This interest began shortly after I moved to my present home in Wales in the late 1970s. Twin sisters, Jennifer and June Gibbons, lived close by and were soon to achieve national notoriety as the so-called Silent Twins since they only communicated with each other. It inspired the question – what if something caused that bond to be broken? How would the other twin cope? And what would they do to try and reconnect? Although I've read and consulted countless articles and books on the subject since, I want to acknowledge the twins who ignited my original interest and the work of the journalist and author, Marjorie Wallace, who first wrote about Jennifer and June and brought their story to wider attention.

My interest in Amy's condition as a brain-dead mother who was nevertheless able to give birth, was inspired by a series of pioneering medical studies. I'd like to acknowledge two in particular, the first, from 2010, from BMC Medicine – the medical journal published by BioMed Central – and the second, a study from 2014 from the Department of Obstetrics in Kumamoto University Hospital. There are many other studies of similar real-life cases. I found the ethical issues here compelling and have tried to reflect and debate those to some extent in this novel.

Rob Gittins

ABOUT THE AUTHOR

Rob Gittins is a screenwriter and novelist. Rob's written for almost all the top-rated UK network TV dramas from the last thirty years, including *Casualty*, *EastEnders*, *The Bill*, *Heartbeat* and *Vera*, as well as over thirty original radio plays for BBC Radio 4.

He's previously had six novels published by Y Lolfa to high critical acclaim. This is Rob's fourth novel for Hobeck and is the second in his series set on the idyllic, if occasionally sinister and disturbing, Isle of Wight. Rob's other Hobeck novels, both stand-alone psychological thrillers, are *The Devil's Bridge Affair* and *Can I Trust You?*

Visit Rob's website at: www.robgittins.com

CRIME AND THRILLERS BY ROB GITTINS

The Devil's Bridge Affair

Can I Trust You?

Gimme Shelter

Secret Shelter

Shelter Me

Investigating Mr Wakefield

All available from Amazon and bookshops.

PRAISE FOR ROB GITTINS

'Rob Gittins is a highly acclaimed dramatist whose work has been enjoyed by millions in TV and radio dramas.'
Nicholas Rhea – author of the Constable series, adapted for TV as *Heartbeat*

'Visceral, strongly visual and beautifully structured... powerful, quirky characters.'
Andrew Taylor – Winner, Crime Writers' Association Cartier Diamond Dagger

'Gittins introduces the reader to a dangerous and troubled part of society, and his murky, damaged and at times violent characters are as vividly (and disturbingly) portrayed as those of Elmore Leonard.'
Susanna Gregory – crime author

'Unflinching... as vicious and full of twists as a tiger in a trap.'
Russell James – crime author

'The definitive interpretation of 'page turnability' ... characters that step effortlessly off the page and into the memory.'

Katherine John – crime author

'TV writer Rob Gittins .. hits hard from the start.'
Iain McDowall – crime author

'Visceral realism doesn't come much better than this. Brilliant.'
Sally Spedding – crime author

'Noir at its most shocking.'
Rebecca Tope – crime author

'Terrifying and suspenseful, non-stop jeopardy. Just be glad you're only reading it and not in it.'
Tony Garnett – TV Drama Producer, *Kes, Cathy Come Home, This Life*

'Gittins is an experienced and successful scriptwriter for screen and radio ... startling and original.'
Crime Fiction Lover

'Well-plotted and superbly written.'
Linda Wilson, *Crime Review*

'Full of intrigue and narrative twists ... powerfully written and uncompromising in its style.'
Dufour Editions

'Corrosive psychological consequences which match those in the best Nicci French thrillers.'
Morning Star

'If there's one thing you can be sure of when it comes to Rob Gittins's literary output, it is that he's not afraid of a scintillating pace ... this has all the hallmarks of a cult classic and I couldn't recommend it highly enough.'

Jack Clothier, Gwales

'Well-drawn characters and sophisticated storytelling.'
Publishers Weekly

'Unputdownable … this deserves every one of the five stars. I would have given it more if I could have.'
Review on Amazon.com

"Uncomfortable, taut, brutal, it will hold you gripped right to the end. A wonderful piece of writing.'
Cambria

'Fast action, convincing dialogue, meticulously plotted throughout. Every twist ratchets up the sense of danger and disorientation.'
Caroline Clark, Gwales

'Thrilling … bloodthirsty.'
Buzz

'Gripping and exciting, fast-paced. There is something a bit different about Gittins's writing that I haven't come across before.'
Nudge

HOBECK BOOKS - THE HOME OF GREAT STORIES

We hope you've enjoyed reading this novel by Rob Gittins. To keep up to date on Rob's writing please do look out for him on Twitter or check out his website: **www.robgittins.com**.

Hobeck Books offers a number of short stories and novellas, free for subscribers in the compilation *Crime Bites*.

- *Echo Rock* by Robert Daws
- *Old Dogs, Old Tricks* by AB Morgan

- *The Silence of the Rabbit* by Wendy Turbin
- *Never Mind the Baubles: An Anthology of Twisted Winter Tales* by the Hobeck Team (including many of the Hobeck authors and Hobeck's two publishers)
- *The Clarice Cliff Vase* by Linda Huber
- *Here She Lies* by Kerena Swan
- *The Macnab Principle* by R.D. Nixon
- *Fatal Beginnings* by Brian Price
- *A Defining Moment* by Lin Le Versha
- *Saviour* by Jennie Ensor
- *You Can't Trust Anyone These Days* by Maureen Myant

Also please visit the Hobeck Books website for details of our other superb authors and their books, and if you would like to get in touch, we would love to hear from you.

Hobeck Books also presents a weekly podcast, the Hobcast, where founders Adrian Hobart and Rebecca Collins discuss all things book related, key issues from each week, including the ups and downs of running a creative business. Each episode includes an interview with one of the people who make Hobeck possible: the editors, the authors, the cover designers. These are the people who help Hobeck bring great stories to life. Without them, Hobeck wouldn't exist. The Hobcast can be listened to from all the usual platforms but it can also be found on the Hobeck website: **www.hobeck.net/hobcast**.